SANTORINI
SUNSETS

also by anita hughes

SANTORINI SUNSETS

ANITA HUGHES

St. Martin's Griffin ⪫ New York

SANTORINI SUNSETS. Copyright © 2016 by Anita Hughes. All rights reserved. Printed in the United States of America. For information, address St. Martin's Press, 175 Fifth Avenue, New York, N.Y. 10010.

www.stmartins.com

Designed by Steven Seighman

The Library of Congress Cataloging-in-Publication Data is available upon request.

ISBN 978-1-250-09412-4 (trade paperback)
ISBN 978-1-250-09413-1 (e-book)

Our books may be purchased in bulk for promotional, educational, or business use. Please contact your local bookseller or the Macmillan Corporate and Premium Sales Department at 1-800-221-7945, extension 5442, or by e-mail at Macmillan SpecialMarkets@macmillan.com.

First Edition: August 2016

10 9 8 7 6 5 4 3 2

To my mother

SANTORINI
SUNSETS

Chapter One

BRIGIT WALKED DOWN the circular staircase and glanced around the living room of the villa. Every surface—the antique grand piano, the mahogany coffee table, even the pastel-colored love seats—was covered with wedding presents. There were silver boxes from Harrods and robin's egg blue squares from Tiffany's and parcels wrapped in Bloomingdale's plain brown paper. She walked to the Regency desk and picked up a pair of silver candlesticks tied with a gold ribbon. She examined the ivory card and smiled at the note from the prince and princess of Spain wishing them well but regretting they couldn't make it.

She thought about the thank-you cards she'd be writing for the next few months and desperately needed a cup of coffee. She entered the kitchen and glanced at the platters of sliced melon and fresh figs and prosciutto and was glad they had decided to get married in Santorini.

They had only been there for two days but already she adored everything about the villa perched above the town of Fira. She loved the square with its quaint boutiques and cramped cafés and twinkling lights stretched across the cobblestones. She loved the steep walking paths that were flanked by beds of white daisies and purple hyacinths.

When she woke up in the four-poster bed, wishing Blake was beside her instead of staying at a nearby villa, the ocean was the first thing she saw out the window. She loved running to the balcony and gazing down at the white sails and green fishing boats. She loved standing in the garden and seeing the white villas clinging to the cliffs and the glittering blue water far below.

She poured coffee into an enamel mug and thought of all the places they could have held the wedding. The easiest thing would have been to get married at the Plaza or the Carlyle in New York. It had a large ballroom with crystal chandeliers and thick marble columns. But she would have had to wear a satin gown by Escada or Versace with a full skirt and a twelve-foot train. The silver stilettos would have pinched her toes and the diamond tiara would have given her a headache.

Blake's friends Leonardo DiCaprio and Tobey Maguire and Ben Affleck would have been uncomfortable in tuxedos and starched white shirts. She imagined shaking hands with five hundred guests and repeating that she was so pleased the Vanderbilts or the Rockefellers could attend.

Blake had suggested they get married at the Beverly Hills Hotel or the Chateau Marmont or even in his own home in the Hollywood Hills. Brigit had somehow thought that would have felt unreal—like their own wedding was part of a movie. She pictured Blake's house with its tall glass windows and low leather sofas and still couldn't believe she'd be living part time in California.

There were things she liked about Los Angeles—the wide stretch of Pacific Coast Highway, the pink and purple sunset, the smell of coconut suntan lotion—but she couldn't get used to men and women strolling down the street in shorts and flip-flops, and how everyone ate salads in brown takeout boxes and that she couldn't step outside without wearing sunglasses.

She had sat at the round kitchen table in her parents' Park Avenue town house and told her mother they wouldn't be getting married at the house in East Hampton. Her mother's mouth turned down at the edges and her brow furrowed and she suddenly needed a gin and tonic.

Brigit wanted to explain she loved everything about Summerhill: the green lawn that rolled down to the Long Island Sound, the wide rooms with their worn oak floors and plump sofas and the kitchen with the murals she and Daisy had painted as children. But she couldn't possibly get married there; it held too many memories.

Her mother smoothed her glossy blond hair and wrapped her arms around her and said no matter where they got married it would be perfect. They were so glad Brigit had found Blake and knew they would be happy. Blake entered her parents' paneled library and said he didn't mind if they got married in a rowboat on the Hudson and her mother laughed and replied that that was a terrible idea, they'd have to fish a dozen reporters out of the river.

Brigit stirred her coffee and pictured Blake's wavy dark hair and green eyes. He had tan cheeks and a cleft on his chin. They'd met at a fund-raiser for the Save the Children foundation at the St. Regis. He'd stood at the podium in a black tuxedo and she thought his smile could light up the ballroom.

Brigit's parents were leading New York philanthropists and she grew up attending galas for libraries and schools and hospitals. She took a semester off from Dartmouth to dig wells in Africa and last year she took a three-month sabbatical from the law firm to travel through India. Everywhere she went she saw children with stomachs as big as their eyes and blue lips and skin like paper. She hunched in her tent at night, trying not to cry and vowing she would change things.

Now she sat listening to Blake and a tingle ran down her spine. She had just given notice and was going to join her father running the Palmer Foundation. She would miss the law firm on the fifty-fourth floor of the Empire State Building with its glass conference room and views of Central Park. She would miss the thrill of winning a settlement for her client and beating a large corporation.

She gazed at the women in Chanel evening gowns and men in Armani silk tuxedos and was excited about everything they would accomplish. She already had files full of goals for the foundation: to stock school libraries in low-income areas with her favorite books, *Little Women* and *The Jungle Book* and *Anne of Green Gables*. She wanted all children to grow up loving to read and knowing the world was full of wonderful places.

"Good evening, if you don't know me, I'm Blake Crawford." Blake's voice came over the loudspeaker. "I've acted in a few little films like the remake of *The Hunt for Red October*." Blake paused as the room erupted in polite laughter. He rustled his notes and blinked into the lights. "Five years ago I was shooting *The Silk Road* in Nepal with Steven Spielberg and Katie Holmes. When I wasn't admiring Miss Holmes's wonderful delivery or Steven's superb directing, I visited villages where children had never had a glass of milk or visited a doctor. Families lived in a single room and didn't have drinking water. After I returned to Hollywood I vowed every time someone watched one of my movies, part of the ticket price would go to needy children in Nepal and Pakistan and China. I know you think people in the movie industry only care about the weekend box office and the price of popcorn, but I am committed to helping end worldwide poverty and starvation." Everyone clapped and Blake bowed and gathered his notes. "Now if you'll excuse me, I'm going to enjoy some of that Veuve Clicquot champagne and stuffed Cornish game hens."

Blake crossed the room and pulled out the chair next to Brigit. He wiped his brow and waited for the waiter to fill his champagne glass.

"Your publicist writes a wonderful speech," Brigit said, eating a forkful of braised duck with grilled asparagus.

"Do you think because I'm an actor I can only read from a tele-prompter?" Blake turned to her.

"We all know how it works." Brigit shrugged, smoothing her hair behind her ears. She wore a silver Dior ball gown and gold sling backs. Her hair was held back with a gold clip and she wore diamond teardrop earrings. "The foundation hires you to champion their cause and in return you get free publicity for your next movie."

"Just because I recite lines for a living doesn't mean I don't have my own opinions," Blake bristled. "I'm sure you're more aware of poverty in your parents' Park Avenue town house with its maids' kitchen that is as big as most apartments."

"I'm sorry." Brigit looked at Blake and noticed the yellow flecks in his eyes and the lines in his forehead. "Sometimes I speak without thinking, it's a bad habit."

"That probably comes from years of people listening to whatever you say." Blake's shoulders relaxed and his face broke into a smile. "I've read all about you: Brigit Palmer, attended Spence School in Manhattan, followed by Dartmouth and Columbia Law School. Recently gave up her partner-track position at Bingham and Stoll to head the Palmer Foundation."

"Where did you read that?" Brigit flushed.

"It's on the back of the program." Blake picked up a gold sheet of paper. "I'll tell you what, why don't we start from the beginning." He put down his champagne glass and held out his hand. "I'm Blake Crawford, it's a pleasure to meet you."

The next day Brigit arrived at her office to find two tickets to *The Book of Mormon* with the note: "You may not be a big fan of movies, but can I convince you to see a Broadway show and have dinner at the Four Seasons?"

Brigit pictured Blake's dark wavy hair and bright green eyes and wide shoulders. She glanced from the note to the bouquet of a dozen yellow roses and couldn't think of a reason to say no.

Blake started spending weekends in New York and they ran in Central Park and ate dinner at Eleven Madison Park and Per

Se. They drove to Vermont to see the leaves change and flew to Palm Beach to watch the polo matches.

At first she was hesitant about dating an actor, she wasn't used to being followed by cameras or having her photo in magazines. She had lived her whole life inside a doorman building on the Upper East Side and behind the gates of the house in East Hampton. But Blake was charming and witty and really seemed to care about getting rid of poverty and educating children. She gradually let down the wall she had built around her heart and allowed herself to fall in love.

Brigit put the cup in the sink and rubbed her lips. She wished Blake had decided to stay in the villa with Brigit and her family instead of taking his own villa with his groomsmen. She missed waking up beside him with their legs tangled together and his arm draped over her waist. In four days they were getting married and then they would have three weeks of a glorious honeymoon in Paris and Aix-en-Provence. They could make love all night and eat breakfast in bed and do whatever they want.

She opened the french doors and walked into the garden. She stood at the fence and gazed at the green cliffs and clusters of white houses. Stone churches had blue domed roofs and stained-glass windows. She leaned over the fence and gazed at the black sand beach and chipped fishing boats and clear blue water. She inhaled the scent of hibiscus and anemone and thought she was the luckiest girl in the world.

The wedding was in four days and tonight her parents were hosting a small dinner for their closest friends. Her mother insisted Brigit relax but she wanted to be sure the champagne was chilled and the waiters served the strawberries and fresh whipped cream she'd bought at the market. She turned to go inside and heard footsteps coming up the path. Two men were dressed in shorts and T-shirts and she wondered if the caterers had arrived early.

She looked more closely and saw one man wore a hat and carried a nylon backpack. He wore leather thongs and a black leather watch. The man took off his hat and Brigit's eyes flew open. She put her hand to her chest and ducked behind a rosebush.

She watched them walk toward the villa and thought she must be seeing things. It couldn't possibly be Nathaniel; she hadn't seen him since he'd walked out of their Upper East Side apartment two years ago. She pictured his curly blond hair and blue eyes and her heart turned over. What was her first husband doing in Santorini?

She held her breath as they opened the gate and approached the wooden blue front door. She crouched behind the bushes and suddenly heard footsteps on the gravel. She looked up and saw Nathaniel fold his arms across his chest. His hair was cut short and the stubble on his chin was gone but he had the same long eyelashes and wide white smile.

"You never were good at hide-and-go-seek," he announced, parting the rosebush. "Even when we were children, you would stand in the middle of the tennis court and count to ten and invite everyone to find you." His face broke into a smile. "Hello Brigit, how are you?"

"How dare you come here." Brigit stood up and smoothed her

hair. She adjusted her floral dress and tightened her white leather belt. "I'm getting married in four days, and if you ruin it I'll never forgive you. If you're on vacation, you can pack your bags and go to Avignon or Tuscany."

"That's a fine greeting for someone who four years ago vowed to stay with me in sickness or in health, for richer or poorer, 'til death do us part." Nathaniel slipped his hands into his pockets.

"You were the one who walked out." Brigit walked to the stone fence. "Now what on earth are you doing here?"

"That's a long story and I'm very hot and thirsty." Nathaniel hesitated. "You are the one who filed the divorce papers."

"I waited three months," Brigit replied. "You didn't call or write or send a postcard."

"I was busy." Nathaniel leaned on the fence beside her.

"Lying on the sofa watching the Yankees game and drinking cans of lemonade?" Brigit's cheeks turned pink. "Wearing the same T-shirt four days in a row and eating the marshmallows out of the cereal box. Being too drunk at night to find the bedroom."

"Being indolent is very time consuming." Nathaniel furrowed his brow. His shoulders sagged and his eyes flickered. "I only drank at the end, when it was hopeless."

"You made it hopeless." Brigit twisted her watch. "You threw away a book contract and a whole career, and wasted your time doing the *New York Times* crossword puzzle."

"Doing the *New York Times* crossword puzzle is never a waste of time," Nathaniel protested. "I was looking for inspiration, after you sucked every original word and thought from my body."

"I was trying to help you, I couldn't watch you avoid your

computer as if it caused cholera," Brigit replied. "If you had just sat at your desk, the words would have come to you."

"Writing a novel isn't like proofing a legal brief," Nathaniel corrected. "And I wrote a damn fine book of short stories which is more than eighty percent of writers in America ever accomplish. I can't help it if the critic at *New York Times Book Review* said: 'If Nathaniel Cabot thinks he is equipped to write about social reform in America, then I'm going to publish a book of Southern recipes. Cabot should write what he knows: growing up with a silver spoon in his mouth and deciding whether to attend Harvard or Princeton,'" Nathaniel rubbed his brow. "If he had done his research he would have discovered I got rejected at Harvard and wait listed at Princeton. Anyway, I never would have gone anywhere besides Dartmouth because I couldn't breathe without you."

"I still don't know why you're here. I haven't seen you in two years and now you show up at my wedding!" Brigit exclaimed, glancing at his tan arms and legs. "You look like you've been doing a pretty good job of breathing. Let me guess, you've been running around Europe as a tour guide or a gigolo."

"I'm glad you think my performance in the bedroom was worth money but I don't think I'd be suited to romance wealthy women. I'm sure I'd say something to offend them." Nathaniel smiled. "My parents cut me off because they thought I was wasting my life, so I've been freelancing for newspapers and magazines. I moved to London and it suits me. It's easier to be depressed when the sky is gray and you have to eat sausage rolls and meat pies."

"I don't have time to discuss your emotional well-being, I have to get ready for a party." Brigit blinked back sudden tears. "Please leave or I'll tell Blake to remove you and your friend."

"That would be tricky." Nathaniel's face broke into a smile. "It's your fiancé who invited us."

"What are you talking about?" Brigit demanded. "Blake would never invite my ex-husband to our wedding."

"You're getting that peaked look you used to get when you skipped breakfast." Nathaniel frowned. "Let's go inside and feed you some scrambled eggs and bacon, then I'll tell you how Robbie and I arrived in Santorini." Nathaniel stopped and looked at the man with dark hair and large brown eyes. "The terrible thing about living alone is I've completely forgotten my manners. Robbie, this is the soon-to-be head of one of New York's most prominent charity foundations, Brigit Palmer."

"How did you know about my new position?" Brigit asked.

"I keep track." Nathaniel entered the villa and put his hat on a mahogany end table. He glanced at the mosaic ceilings and plaster walls and thick burgundy curtains. He saw the crystal chandeliers and oak floors and worn Oriental carpets. He walked to the bar and filled a shot glass with vodka. He handed it to Brigit and whistled.

"You couldn't have picked a more authentic setting for a Greek wedding." He examined a painting in a gilt frame. "Any minute I expect a singing waiter to appear from the kitchen with a platter of grilled eggplant and hummus and a bottle of ouzo. Then the director will yell 'cut' and the bride and groom will leave on a bicycle with cans rattling behind them."

"That was a scene from *Mamma Mia!,* we saw it at the Roxy in the East Village," Brigit murmured. "Blake had nothing to do with picking the villa. My mother and I found it in the back of *Town & Country.*"

"I'm glad to hear Sydney is still reading *Town & Country*." Nathaniel admired a marble bust. "She might want to add *HELLO!* to her subscription list."

"My mother would never read *HELLO!*" Brigit replied. "It's as bad as *People*."

"She might," Nathaniel mused. "If her daughter was on the cover."

"What are you talking about?" Brigit gasped, fiddling with her gold necklace.

"I got a call from Winston Powell, the editor-in-chief last week," Nathaniel continued. "He read my piece on Carla Bruni's marriage to Nicholas Sazorky in *Paris Match*."

"How can you write for those magazines?" Brigit interrupted. "They have no respect for people's privacy, they'll print anything that sells copies."

"You've never bought a sweater for warmth rather than if it matched your Burberry jacket." Nathaniel raised his eyebrow. "Your standards drop quickly when your flat doesn't have central heating and the space heater sounds like it has a death rattle."

"You could have stayed in the apartment," Brigit said quietly. "Your parents bought it for us."

"As a wedding present," Nathaniel replied. "I thought you had to get something out of the marriage, since you sent back the engagement ring."

Brigit pictured the pear-shaped sapphire surrounded by diamonds and flinched. "It was your grandmother's, I could hardly keep it."

"Then we're even." Nathaniel sighed. "You got a one bedroom at Eighty-Second and Lexington and I escaped a drillmaster who made sure our toothbrushes were lined up and the books on the bookshelf were alphabetized and we never ran out of toilet paper."

"I still can't imagine you writing for *HELLO!*" Brigit shuddered. "They'd ask you to write an exposé of your own mother."

"Winston asked if I wanted to write about the wedding of the year: Hollywood movie star and perpetual bachelor, Blake Crawford weds New York society ice queen Brigit Palmer."

"He said I was an ice queen?" Brigit's lips trembled.

"I might have thrown that in but it makes a great pull quote." Nathaniel shrugged. "The cover and a four-page spread including photos. And full access to the bride's family and the wedding party."

Brigit put her drink on the sideboard and walked to the Regency desk. She sifted through the boxes wrapped in silver tissue paper and found her phone.

"I'm going to call Blake, he'll call Winston and threaten to sue unless this is stopped." She punched in the numbers.

Nathaniel crossed the room and took the phone from her hand. He walked to his backpack and took out a sheet of paper.

"You might want to look this over first." He handed her the paper. "Blake is the one who gave Winston the exclusive."

Brigit's heart raced and she felt slightly dizzy. She sat on the yellow silk sofa and scanned the contract. She looked up at Nathaniel and her blue eyes were huge.

"Why would Blake do that? We both agreed to keep the wedding private, that's why we chose Santorini—so it would just be our families and closest friends."

"He is donating the two-million-dollar fee to charity," Nathaniel said grudgingly. "It's on the last line."

Brigit glanced at the bottom of the contract and the air left her lungs. She thought about Blake's passion for helping the underprivileged and felt her shoulders relax.

"Well, that's wonderful! I knew there had to be a reason." She smoothed her hair. "I wonder why he didn't ask me first."

"It's not a good idea to keep secrets this early in the relationship." Nathaniel nodded. "Who knows what he'll agree to next."

"We don't have any secrets." Brigit put the contract on the mahogany end table. "I've been so busy this week seeing to the caterers and florists, he probably told me and I forgot."

"The girl with the photographic memory who got a perfect score on her SAT?" Nathaniel asked. "Maybe you haven't been eating correctly and it's affected your thinking. You do look thinner." He studied her shoulder-length blond hair and high cheekbones and slender neck. "You're missing that wonderful cleavage. Let's go into the kitchen and fix a sandwich. I'm starving, our expense account doesn't stretch past a wedge of feta cheese and a bowl of bean soup."

"How dare you!" Brigit crossed her arms. "My breasts are my own business."

They entered the kitchen and saw a young woman standing next to the fridge. Her auburn hair was pulled into a ponytail and she wore a knee-length turquoise dress. She wore lace-up espadrilles and a silver charm bracelet.

"Nathaniel, what on earth are you doing here?" Daisy turned around. "You are the last person I expected to see in Santorini." She turned to Brigit. "Surely, his name wasn't on the guest list."

"Of course, he's not invited," Brigit snapped. "I found him in the garden."

"Well, you better leave," Daisy said to Nathaniel. "This is a family affair, and you gave up membership when you walked out on Brigit two years ago."

"I'm supposed to be here, Brigit will explain." Nathaniel paused. "Daisy, you're all grown up. And you're so glamorous, don't tell me you've gone Hollywood like your sister."

"I'm twenty-six." Daisy put a loaf of bread on the tile counter next to an heirloom tomato. She searched in the cupboard and found a jar of mustard and a bottle of olive oil. "I was grown up the last time you saw me, it's only been a couple of years."

"I can't help it if I still remember the little girl who always got stuck in trees." Nathaniel turned to Robbie. "Robbie, this is Daisy Palmer, the other most beautiful girl in New York and a terrific pastry chef. I stood in line at Cafe Lalo on many Sundays to get her delicious coconut custard cream pie."

"I quit." Daisy spread mayonnaise on whole wheat bread. "I'm not a pastry chef anymore."

"The Upper West Side must be in mourning." Nathaniel took a green apple from a ceramic fruit bowl and rubbed it on his shirt. "What are you doing these days?"

"I'm designing clothing." Daisy layered the bread with prosciutto and lettuce and red onions. "I have my own line of dresses called Daisies, I hope to get them into Bergdorf's."

"Nathaniel is writing a story on the wedding for *HELLO!*" Brigit opened the fridge and took out a bottle of milk. "Don't tell him anything you don't want to appear in the pages of a gossip magazine."

"Is there anything to tell?" Nathaniel picked up half the sandwich and took a large bite.

"I thought about becoming a nun but I don't like scratchy fabric against my skin." Daisy took her plate and walked to the round kitchen table. "Now, I really think you should leave. The last thing Brigit needs is to be feeding her ex-husband a sandwich four days before her wedding."

"But I'm being paid to gather background material." Nathaniel wiped his mouth with a napkin. "*HELLO!*'s readers love to get a glimpse behind the scenes."

"I'm afraid Nathaniel does have to be here." Brigit turned to Robbie and smiled. "Daisy and Nathaniel still squabble like children. Daisy has never forgiven Nathaniel for ruining an Easter egg hunt. All the other children were collecting eggs but Daisy said she was going to wait for the Easter Bunny to bring them. Nathaniel announced the Easter Bunny wasn't real and Daisy burst out crying." She glanced at her watch. "I have to go, I told the florist I'd approve the table arrangements for tonight's dinner."

"There's a dinner tonight?" Nathaniel sat up straight.

"Grilled octopus followed by moussaka and honey baklava for dessert," Brigit said.

"God, that sounds delicious." Nathaniel wiped his mouth with a napkin. "What time are cocktails?"

Brigit walked to the door. As she turned around her blue eyes sparkled. "My mother already did the place settings and you're not invited."

Brigit ran down the steep path to Fira. She rubbed her lips with pink lip gloss and slipped on her oval sunglasses. She didn't really have an appointment with the florist but suddenly she couldn't breathe. Even with his blond curls cut short, Nathaniel made her stomach churn and her blood boil.

She entered a café and ordered a cone of strawberry ice cream. She strolled past boutique windows filled with wide straw hats and soft leather sandals and began to feel better. She was in one of the most beautiful spots in the world, about to marry the man she loved. She pictured Blake's wavy dark hair and green eyes and felt her shoulders relax. Having his photo taken was part of his job and she would have to get used to it.

She glanced at couples holding hands and remembered the first time Blake whispered, "I love you." He had surprised her with two first-class tickets to Athens. They stayed at the Hotel Grande Bretagne and visited the National Garden and Temple of Zeus. They climbed to the top of the Acropolis and ate a picnic in the Theater of Dionysus. They strolled through outdoor markets and sampled cucumber tzatziki and Kalamata olives and ripe feta cheese.

On their last night they sat at an outdoor café on the Plaza Syntagma. Brigit ate lamb medallions and smoked eggplant and felt a warmth spread through her chest. Everything was perfect: their hotel suite with its Carrara marble bathroom and balcony overlooking the Parthenon, the driver who drove them around in a sleek black car and showed them every part of the city, the way Blake held her hand when they crossed the street and was eager to explore the Old Parliament House and the Temple of Hephaestus.

"You're Blake Crawford, the actor." A young boy approached their table. He had dark curly hair and large brown eyes and olive skin. He wore a gray T-shirt and frayed blue jeans.

"How did you know?" Blake asked, putting down his wineglass.

He wore a white linen shirt and blue blazer. His dark hair was smoothed back and he wore a black leather watch.

"My brother works in a cinema, he lets me take out the trash and watch the movies," the boy replied. "I learned English by watching *Mission: Impossible* and *Spider-Man*." He gazed at the platter of sautéed scallops and calamari and capers and his eyes widened. "My name is Matthias. Could I have your autograph?"

"It would be my pleasure." Blake took a pen out of his blazer pocket and scribbled on a napkin.

The boy folded it carefully and put it in his pocket. He was about to walk away when he turned around. "Could I please have autographs for my three brothers and sister and parents?"

Blake laughed and scribbled on a stack of napkins. "Tell your parents they raised a polite son, and try to watch some of the great directors: Francis Ford Coppola and Martin Scorsese and David Fincher."

They shared baked pears with chestnut puree and crumbled spices for dessert and talked about Blake's next movie and Brigit's upcoming trip to Ecuador. Brigit gazed at Blake's green eyes and wide mouth and felt a chill run down her spine. It had been so long since she'd talked with someone who made her feel excited and alive. He shared her drive to accomplish great things: provide doctors to remote parts of Peru and start small farms in Central America.

"I want to teach children in Honduras how to milk goats and grow barley." Brigit scooped up pistachio nuts and hazelnut ice cream. "I want villages to become self-sufficient with a bank and a post office and a grocery store. I don't want to just build schools and libraries in Fiji and Bhutan, I want to create whole universities."

"I've never understood actors who keep buying mansions and Porsches and sailboats." Blake sipped a glass of port. "I love owning Tom Ford suits and Bruno Magli shoes but I couldn't slip them on in the morning if I didn't know I was doing something to put shoes on the feet of children in Bangladesh and Pakistan."

Blake paid the check and they strolled through the Plaza Syntagma. They saw tourists carrying silver cameras and children licking lime ice cream cones. They saw a young boy surrounded by men and women. He handed them scraps of paper and they reached in their pockets for euros and dollar bills. Brigit looked closely and saw it was the boy who'd asked Blake for his autograph.

"Matthias." Blake strode across the square. "Are you selling my autograph?"

The boy looked guiltily at Blake and stuffed the money into his pocket. "I'm saving to buy a video camera, I'm going to shoot a movie and come to America."

Blake frowned and rubbed his chin. Suddenly he took off his watch and handed it to Matthias. "The back is engraved with my initials, make sure you get a good price for it." His face broke into a smile. "And if you make it to Hollywood, look me up, the movie business needs fresh talent."

They entered the tall glass doors of the Hotel Grande Bretagne and crossed the black-and-white marble floor. Brigit glanced at the gold inlaid ceilings and ivory columns and felt her cheeks flush and her heart race. She inhaled Blake's Ralph Lauren cologne and couldn't wait to slip off her sandals and unzip her dress and lie down in the king-sized four-poster bed.

"Blake, tell us about your new girlfriend." A man wearing black jeans and a black T-shirt approached them. He was followed by a man with reddish hair carrying a black camera. "Is she an actress or a model? She looks like a young Grace Kelly."

"You know me better than that." Blake stopped and slipped his hands into his pockets. "I'm not going to betray my date's privacy by telling you anything that's going to end up in the newspapers."

"Give us a hint," the man persisted. "Is she the girl who's finally going to drag Blake Crawford to the altar?"

"Does she look like the kind of woman who has to drag a man anywhere?" Blake's green eyes sparkled. "I'm lucky she let me buy her a cup of coffee. If you gentlemen don't leave us alone, I'm going to end up sleeping in the doghouse."

"Rumor has it that she's from an old New York family who has no interest in Hollywood," the man persisted. "How is she going to feel about you globe-trotting around the world and being photographed with beautiful actresses?"

"Have you ever felt so lucky that you want to knock on every piece of wood you pass and throw rice over your shoulder?" Blake mused. "I've felt like that three times in my life, when I dropped out of Ohio State and took a Greyhound bus to Los Angeles, when I was a waiter at Nobu and spilled potato leek soup on Brian Grazer, and when I was seated next to Miss Palmer at a charity dinner and discovered we both liked French champagne and tiramisu." He pressed the button on the elevator. "Now if you'll excuse us, we're going upstairs and do something boring like play canasta and watch an old Sean Connery movie."

"Did you really spill potato leek soup on one of the most important producers in Hollywood?" The man raised his eyebrow.

"See how lucky I am, if it had been tomato soup it would have stained." Blake stepped into the elevator. "And my acting career would have been over."

Brigit entered the suite and put her evening bag on the glass end table. She gazed at the polished wood floor and plush gold sofas and shivered. Suddenly she didn't want to be here with Blake, eating petit fours on a silver tray and watching the lights flicker on the Acropolis. She didn't want to be grilled by reporters and listen to gossip about Blake's old girlfriends.

"I'm sorry about our friends at the elevator." Blake slipped off his blazer. "I hope they didn't spoil our evening."

"They seem to know a lot about you." Brigit walked to the balcony. She glanced at the stone columns of the Parliament Building and the dim outline of Mount Lycabettus. She listened to the sound of horns honking and tires screeching and wished she were home in her Upper East Side apartment.

"I'm thirty-four and don't get thrown out of bars or start fights at Hollywood parties. I don't show up at the airport with a two-day stubble or a new earring." Blake stood beside her. "They have to think of something to write about."

"When my mother was young she was featured in a story about debutantes in *Vanity Fair*." Brigit rested her elbows on the railing. "She was furious when she read it because they made the debutante season sound like a marriage market. She said it was much more than that: it was about history and philanthropy and finding one's purpose." Brigit turned to Blake and smiled. "Of course they were right, that's how my mother met my father."

"Reporters are like monkeys at the zoo, you have to feed them some stories so they don't grow hungry and rattle the cages, but there's so much they don't know about me: I'm afraid of snakes and love margarita pizza and I'm sucker for a beautiful blond attorney who keeps a copy of *The Snows of Kilimanjaro* on her bedside table." He pulled her close and kissed her softly on the lips.

Brigit felt his mouth on hers and her shoulders relaxed. She kissed him back, tasting wine and chocolate and hazelnuts. She pressed herself against his chest and felt a moistness between her legs.

"And they don't know that I've never told a woman 'I love you.'" He pulled away and touched her chin. "Until now."

Brigit sucked in her breath. She fleetingly pictured Nathaniel with his curly blond hair and blue eyes and felt an odd flickering in her chest.

"We've only known each other a few months but you're like no one I've ever met." Blake tucked her hair behind her ears. "You're more beautiful than any model on the cover of a magazine but you run out of the house without a stick of makeup. You have a whole closet of designer clothes but you walk down Fifth Avenue in jeans and sneakers. And you're so passionate about what you do you're like a shooting star."

Brigit felt his hand on the small of her back and the image of Nathaniel disappeared. She unbuttoned his shirt and ran her palms over his skin. Kissing him was the best feeling in the world. His arms were strong and he made her feel safe and happy.

Blake took her hand and led her into the bedroom and watched her unzip her dress and slip off her gold sandals. She stepped out of her lace panties and felt a surge of something hot and wet. Her heart raced and she walked over to Blake and unbuckled his belt. She took a deep breath and ran her hand down his thigh.

Blake leaned forward and kissed her on the mouth. God, she was beautiful! Like a Greek goddess. He rubbed the sweet spot between her legs and suddenly inserted a finger deep inside her. He pressed her breasts against his chest and watched her eyes flicker and her shoulders tighten.

Brigit tensed her muscles and the familiar warmth rushed inside her. His fingers moved faster and she strained her body to reach them. She felt the liquid filling her up and carrying her to the edge. She bit her lip and let her body rise and gasp and shudder.

He waited until her breathing subsided and then drew her onto the ivory bedspread. He kissed her neck and her breasts and ran his hands over her stomach. He buried his head between her legs and thought he had never tasted such sweet wetness.

Brigit wrapped her arms around his back and pulled him on top of her. Her breathing quickened and then she felt the long, slow pleasure. She grabbed his shoulders, urging him to go faster. He picked up speed and she felt a sudden surge of happiness. Then they came together in one long, endless thrust.

Brigit tucked herself against his chest and listened to his even breathing. She glanced around the room at the crystal chandelier and silver wallpaper and marble busts. Blake had whispered "I love you" and she realized she hadn't answered. She closed her eyes and pulled the Egyptian cotton sheets over her shoulders.

Brigit climbed back up the steep path to the villa from the main square of Fira. Her head throbbed when she thought about Blake allowing *HELLO!* magazine to cover the wedding and Nathaniel showing up in Santorini. But then she felt the warm sun on her shoulders and stopped and gazed at the view. She saw the deep blue Aegean Sea and black stone of the caldera. She saw the pale blue sky and high white clouds and silver cruise ships.

She pictured tonight's dinner of spinach salad and baked eggplant and grilled swordfish. There would be platters of lamb skewers marinated in olive oil. She imagined Blake's favorite double chocolate cake and vanilla custard and colored macaroons.

She thought of their friends who were arriving tomorrow from New York and Los Angeles and London. Blake had planned so many activities: visiting the ancient ruins at Akrotiri and having dinner on the beach in Kamari and hiking to Oia Castle and watching the sky turn pink and purple and orange over the ocean. She pictured the rehearsal dinner at the *taverna* on Amoudi Bay and the wedding ceremony in the Church of Panagia Episkopi.

She walked faster up the path and decided she wasn't going to let Nathaniel spoil her wedding weekend. She was going to pretend he was a piece of antique furniture or an Oriental rug and ignore him. She pictured Blake in a white tuxedo and felt light and warm and happy. She imagined her father raising his crystal champagne glass in a toast and announcing: "I'm so pleased to announce the new Mr. and Mrs. Blake Crawford."

She remembered the day she'd signed her divorce papers and flinched. She'd hurried down Lexington Avenue with the papers crushed against her chest and vowed never to change her name again. She adjusted her sunglasses and thought that was before she met Blake. Now she couldn't wait to become Brigit Crawford. She pictured Nathaniel's face when the priest declared them man and wife and put her hand over her mouth.

Chapter Two

DAISY FLICKED THROUGH THE DRESSES in her closet and thought again she should have come up with any excuse—she couldn't get anyone to pet sit Edgar, her French bulldog, she had a first meeting with a buyer at Bergdorf's, she had been invited on a last-minute weekend trip to Cape Cod—to avoid coming to the wedding in Santorini.

She held up an orange linen dress and sank onto the white cotton bedspread. Of course she would never miss her sister's wedding; she just wished they had done something simple like have a small ceremony at city hall followed by lunch at Tavern on the Green. Something that would have been over in four or five hours so Daisy could gamely try to catch the bouquet and throw rice at the bride and groom and then go home to her own apartment to watch *Gilmore Girls* on Netflix and fiddle with her design sketches.

She gazed at her long auburn hair and brown eyes in the mirror and thought of all the events she had attended in Brigit's honor: prize day at Spence School when Brigit received the Hamilton

Prize for Math and the Woods Prize for English and the Ellen Hope award for being voted Future Business Leader of America.

She thought of Brigit graduating from Dartmouth with honors and in the top tenth of her class from Columbia Law School. She remembered the dinner party at her parents' town house to celebrate her being hired by one of Manhattan's top law firms. She thought of Brigit and Nathaniel's wedding on the lawn at Summerhill and cringed. Brigit had worn a silk Vera Wang gown and satin pumps and Daisy had never seen anyone so radiant.

Daisy wasn't jealous of Brigit; she hadn't applied to Dartmouth because she couldn't stand the thought of spending winters wrapped in scarfs and sweaters and seeing nothing but fields covered in snow. And she could have easily gone to law school after Swarthmore, but the thought of spending another three years lurking in a university library and existing on black coffee made her stomach turn. But she admired everything about her: the way her hair was always perfectly brushed and her cheeks glowed and she wore only the faintest trace of lipstick. The way her clothes seemed to be made just for her and she wore just the right amount of jewelry. Mostly she admired that she always smiled so that people flocked around her like moths to a flame.

Daisy stepped into the orange dress and thought about the only time she had seen Brigit in pain—when Nathaniel walked out of the apartment. She remembered finding Brigit huddled under a checkered Burberry blanket. She wore a navy Theory dress and beige Gucci pumps and was clutching her red leather briefcase.

"Go to bed." Daisy stroked Brigit's hair. "I'll call the law firm and tell them you came down with a fever."

"I can't miss work because Nathaniel is acting like a child," Brigit insisted. Her eyes were watery and her cheeks were pale and she couldn't stop shivering. "I knew I shouldn't have married him, do you remember when we were children and he hated losing at Monopoly? If I won, he'd gather all his money and toss it on the board like confetti. And he was always stubborn, if he couldn't be the shoe he wouldn't even play."

"He'll come back," Daisy soothed. "He's like a fish in the Sahara desert without you."

"Of course he'll come back." Brigit stood up and smoothed her hair. She scooped up an empty soda can and a half-eaten bag of potato chips and a stack of old *New Yorkers*. "And he'll find a clean apartment and a Whole Foods chicken in the oven and fresh flowers from the flower market. I'm not going to let him turn our lives into a scene from his Dartmouth fraternity house. We'll have a delicious dinner and a bottle of Penfolds cabernet and talk like two sensible adults." She looked at Daisy and her blue eyes filled with tears. "I'm a lawyer, I know there are two sides to every story. I want to help him write his novel, I just can't stand him wasting his talent lying on the sofa and playing Pac-Man on his iPhone."

Daisy remembered the week after Nathaniel left when Daisy slept in the alcove that served as a guest room. Brigit shuffled around in a yellow bathrobe and white slippers. Her hair was flat and her skin was papery and her cheekbones were narrow. She remembered her curling up in her Pottery Barn bed with an old teddy bear and a bottle of NyQuil.

Daisy brushed her auburn hair into a ponytail and tied it with an orange ribbon. She added gold hoop earrings and a gold necklace and thought about when Brigit had introduced her to Blake. She remembered seeing his smooth cheeks and impossibly white smile and thinking only Brigit would recover from a broken marriage by dating one of the most eligible bachelors in Hollywood.

She remembered Brigit describing dinners at Le Bernardin of warm artichoke panache and poached skate and roasted figs with vanilla ice cream for dessert. She pictured her displaying gifts of a Philip Treacy hat or a Tory Burch scarf or a first-edition copy of *The Sun Also Rises*. She remembered the morning Brigit insisted Daisy meet her for brunch at Sarabeth's on Madison Avenue and Ninety-Second Street.

"God, these eggs are delicious." Daisy ate Popeye eggs and a berry corn muffin and sipped a glass of banana and pomegranate juice. She wore a fisherman's sweater and green leggings and beige suede loafers. Her hair was wound into a ponytail and tied with a green ribbon.

She glanced at Brigit in a floral Alice + Olivia dress and thought she'd never looked so lovely. Her smooth blond hair was held back with a gold clip and her eyes were coated with thick mascara. She wore a shimmering blush and her lips were painted with coral lipstick. "I should quit Cafe Lalo and work here. I love their menu:

Popeye eggs and Goldie Lox and vegetable frittata with scallions and peppers."

"You love being a pastry chef." Brigit sprinkled pink Hawaiian sea salt on green-and-white eggs. "You've never been happier."

"I'm tired of waking up at four a.m. and always having my hands covered with a layer of powdered sugar." Daisy smoothed her napkin. "I might work in a flower shop or paint houses."

"You're terrified of ladders." Brigit giggled. "Whenever the gardener left the ladder out at Summerhill you walked around the whole lawn to avoid it."

"It would be so satisfying to finish work and see a room painted magenta or sunflower yellow or turquoise." Daisy spread butter on a pumpkin muffin. "Maybe I'll become a dress designer; my art professor at Swarthmore thought I was talented and I always loved making clothes for my American Girl doll."

"You could design my bridesmaid dresses," Brigit said slowly. "I picture knee-length dresses with a gathered waist and a full skirt. And some wonderful light fabric, a green chiffon or a pale blue Italian silk."

"You're getting married?" Daisy gasped. She picked up her glass of pomegranate juice and took a long sip.

"Blake proposed in Crete." Brigit flushed. She tucked her hair behind her ears and fiddled with her gold necklace. "He packed a picnic of stuffed grape leaves and ricotta cheese tapas and ripe peaches and we spent all day exploring the palace of Knossos and the Psychro Caves and the pink sand beaches of Elafonissi. We hiked to a tiny church in Plaka at sunset and watched the glorious sunset.

"We entered the church and Blake took my hand and said he felt like Odysseus when he finally found his way home. He never thought he would get married because he couldn't imagine spending his life with one person, but now he couldn't survive a day without me. Then he dropped to his knee and pulled out a black velvet box." Brigit stopped and smiled. "To be honest I was afraid it might be over the top with a ten-carat diamond and a jeweled band." She held out her hand and displayed a yellow oval diamond flanked by two small rubies. "But he designed it himself with Neil Lane and it's lovely. I can't imagine anything I'd like better."

"But you only met last fall." Daisy frowned. "Isn't it a little sudden?"

"We won't get married until the summer," Brigit mused. "We'll have the wedding in Mykonos or Sardinia where we don't have to worry about photographers bursting into the church." She stopped and suddenly her eyes were dark. "I knew Nathaniel since he colored on my self-portrait in kindergarten and our marriage still failed. I remember when we were six and he suggested we play Peter Rabbit and sneak into our neighbor's garden. Mrs. Black opened the back door and he got scared and ran away." Brigit blotted her mouth with the napkin. "She was very sweet and insisted I come inside for ice cream but he didn't know that. He left me to take the blame.

"Blake and I have so much in common, he's committed to helping end world poverty," Brigit continued. "And he's a perfect gentleman, he always opens my car door and he sends different colored tulips every day of the week. I'm ready for someone who enjoys French champagne and shopping in the men's department at Saks and seeing a Broadway show." She looked at Daisy and her eyes were huge. "I'm twenty-eight, it's time I started acting like a grown-up."

"You'll have a penthouse on Fifth Avenue and a vacation home in Malibu and a Range Rover with matching car seats." Daisy ate a last bite of fluffy egg whites and grilled tomatoes and Gruyère cheese. "You'll give birth to twin boys with blond hair and green eyes and they'll learn to throw a baseball before they're five. You're marrying Blake Crawford! Every woman in America is jealous."

Daisy gazed out the bedroom window at the wide olive trees and pink azaleas and thought Brigit couldn't have picked a more beautiful location. The steep path to the villa was flanked by lemon trees and the air smelled like citrus and honey. Everyone in Santorini was friendly; the taxi driver had given her a bag of figs and the old woman who'd directed her to the villa had insisted she take a bottle of olive oil.

She pictured Nathaniel eating prosciutto and red onions on rye bread in the kitchen and flinched. Nathaniel and Brigit were like two kittens fighting over a ball of yarn. She remembered the first time they met, when Nathaniel was five and crawled under a hole in the fence and appeared in their garden.

Brigit had led him into their parents' dinner party like a new pony. She saw Brigit's mouth pucker when the guests exclaimed over his curly blond hair and long eyelashes and didn't notice her new summer dress or patent leather sandals.

She pictured Nathaniel throughout their childhood: teaching them to use the archery set Brigit received for her eighth birthday;

digging a hole for Goldie, their goldfish, when he jumped out of his fishbowl. She saw him standing over the shallow grave, reciting a poem by Dr. Seuss, and giggled.

She slipped on her cork sandals and remembered when Brigit and Nathaniel burst into the living room of their parents' Park Avenue town house and announced their engagement. She remembered gazing at their white smiles, the Manhattan skyline twinkling behind them, and wondering what it was like to feel so certain about anything.

She thought of all the hours Brigit had spent planning her and Blake's wedding: the pastel bridesmaids' bouquets and six-tier marzipan cake baked by a local baker. She saw the ivory Oscar de la Renta gown and delicate gold sandals and pink pearl necklace. She pictured Brigit's smooth blond hair and large blue eyes and knew she couldn't let Nathaniel ruin her hard work.

Chapter Three

SYDNEY LEANED OUT the bedroom window and gazed at the garden filled with lush bougainvillea and white hibiscus. She saw the steep cliffs and white villas and clear blue sea. She inhaled the scent of oranges and figs and thought she was so happy to be in Greece.

The room was beautiful with a canopied bed and wooden dresser and ceramic vase filled with sunflowers. Her linen dress was flung over a brocade armchair and her sandals sat under the floral bedspread and her silk slip peeked out from the cotton sheets. She pulled the robe around her waist and remembered Francis's mouth on her lips, his hands in her hair, his fingers caressing her breasts.

She pictured Brigit in the dining room straightening the white china plates and gleaming silverware and smiled. Her daughter would have been shocked to know that her parents were upstairs in the villa's sunny bedroom in the middle of the afternoon.

"Come here," Francis had whispered, putting his finger to his mouth and leading her to the bed.

"What are you doing?" Sydney gasped. "The windows are open and Brigit and Daisy will hear us."

Francis walked to the balcony and closed the shutters. He turned and admired Sydney's full breasts and sloping stomach.

"We're in Greece and it's two o'clock in the afternoon." He kissed her. "We have to follow local customs and take a siesta."

The mattress creaked and they dissolved into a fit of giggles. There was a sudden hush when she pulled him on top of her and he plunged deep inside her. Her body tipped and Francis clutched her shoulders and fell onto her breasts.

"Now I know why the ancient Greeks created such great art and literature," he murmured, inhaling her jasmine scent.

"Why?" Sydney felt her heart slow down.

"Because they took the time to appreciate beauty," he murmured.

Now she gazed at the white porcelain bathtub and wished she could spend the afternoon surrounded by bubbles. She imagined eating plump grapes and reading one of the paperbacks she'd brought onto the plane. Francis would return and they would have a romantic dinner on the terrace. She saw Francis dipping calamari into cocktail sauce and drizzling olive oil on Salade niçoise. They would leave their plates half full and climb back into the four-poster bed.

She glanced at her Chopard watch and knew she should be thinking about the caterers and the florists and the harpist. In two hours the villa would be filled with guests from New York and London and Los Angeles. A case of French champagne chilled in the fridge and platters of fresh fruit and soft cheeses waited in the pantry. She took a deep breath and saw Francis's wallet on the bedside table.

After they made love, Francis said he was going into Fira to buy cigarettes and the *Wall Street Journal*. He had zipped up his slacks and buttoned his shirt and slid his phone into his pocket. Then he blew her a kiss and hurried out the door.

She reclined against the silk pillows and thought of all the things she wanted to say: he really had to stop smoking, he could exist one day without reading the *Wall Street Journal,* he must relax, it was their daughter's wedding.

But for the last ten months he had been so preoccupied, coming home from the office late and eating a tuna salad sandwich in his study. Working on Saturdays and only coming out to Summerhill late in the evening. Missing weekends altogether so she had to host their dinner parties alone and make jokes about her husband being a summer bachelor.

She turned the wallet over and thought Francis couldn't buy cigarettes without any euros. He never used to be absentminded; even in the early years when he worked fourteen-hour days he never forgot the girls' school performances or her birthday. She pictured waking up every year to two dozen yellow roses and a blue Tiffany's box. She remembered untying the bow and thinking she was the luckiest woman in the world.

She put the wallet back and smoothed her hair. She was too old to be making love in the afternoon, she would never have time to set her hair and reapply her makeup. She thought about Brigit with her glossy blond bob and Daisy with her long auburn curls and sighed. They didn't realize how precious it all was: being young with everything before them.

She thought about the week that changed everything ten years ago and shuddered. Then she slipped off her robe and turned on the shower. She wasn't going to think about anything except the wedding favors and making sure the caterer knew who was vegetarian. The hot water touched her shoulders and she remembered Francis's mouth on her breasts and shivered.

Brigit entered the dining room and studied the long oak table and bright Oriental rug and mosaic ceiling. She gazed at the deep wine goblets and gold candlesticks and felt a chill run down her spine. It was her and Blake's first proper dinner party and she wanted everything to be perfect.

She folded napkins and polished silverware and remembered Nathaniel eating prosciutto on rye in the kitchen. She hoped he was part of some bad dream caused by jet lag and too much Greek coffee. But then she remembered him handing her the *HELLO!* contract.

Could Blake possibly have forgotten to tell her? Maybe he'd mentioned it in one of their long-distance phone calls and his voice had been drowned out by taxis honking or the loudspeakers at the airport. The last week had been a blur of security checks and duty-free stores and first-class lounges.

She pictured Nathaniel's cropped blond hair and clear blue eyes and straightened her shoulders. She didn't care what the contract said; she wasn't going to let Nathaniel and Robbie join the bridesmaids in the church's anteroom and photograph her putting her dress on. They could sit in the back of the chapel and toss rice at the bride and groom with the other guests. If she had to invite them to the reception, she'd seat them in a corner with Blake's eight-year-old twin nephews.

She heard the front door open and smoothed her hair. If it was Nathaniel she would tell him that he was not swimming at Kamari Beach or hiking the panoramic footpath between Fira and the scenic town of Oia. She rubbed her lips and saw Blake stride into the foyer. He wore a white linen shirt and crisp navy slacks. His dark hair was brushed over his forehead and his cheeks glistened with aftershave.

"You are so beautiful tonight, I can't imagine how you're going to look on our wedding day." Blake's lips brushed her cheek. He smelled of Ralph Lauren cologne and citrus shampoo.

"The dress is Valentino." Brigit flushed as if Blake could tell she had been thinking about Nathaniel. "He sent it with a note saying I was going to be the most beautiful bride since Grace Kelly married Prince Rainier."

"Valentino thinks Grace Kelly was the greatest fashion icon of the twentieth century." Blake raised his eyebrow. "If I didn't know he'd been with his partner, Bruce, for thirty years and owns six pugs he loves more than his mother I'd be jealous."

"The caterers still haven't arrived." Brigit frowned. "If they don't get here soon I'll have to put on an apron and grill the calamari."

"This is Greece, everyone knows we won't eat until midnight." Blake shrugged. "We'll keep their champagne glasses filled and feed them crab cakes and bread rolls. Anyway, they're not here for the ouzo or lamb chops, they came to meet the woman I'm going to marry."

Blake leaned forward and kissed her softly on the mouth. Brigit felt his hand press the small of her back and shivered. She kissed him back and suddenly saw the *HELLO!* contract on the mahogany end table.

"You didn't tell me you talked to Winston." She pulled away.

"Winston?" Blake frowned.

"Winston Powell, the editor of *HELLO!*" Brigit bit her lip. "You signed a contract giving him exclusive rights to our wedding without telling me."

"I must have told you, I remember leaving Winston's office and pulling out my phone. It was pouring rain and I was afraid it would get wet." He rubbed his forehead. "Then I realized it was the middle of night in New York. Christ, did I really not call you back?"

"You didn't." Brigit perched on a high-backed velvet armchair.

"I was so busy, I had to pick up the groomsmen's bow ties and the ring bearer's tuxedo." He sat beside her. "It was a complete surprise, Winston invited me to lunch and I thought he wanted to gossip about Scarlett Johansson's meltdown on the set of *Always Sunday*. But I couldn't turn down two million dollars; I thought you'd be pleased. Think about the libraries the Palmer Foundation can build with that money."

"The money is wonderful." Brigit nodded. "But we wanted to keep our wedding private."

"Winston promised the reporter and photographer wouldn't disturb the guests." Blake took her hand. "Isn't it worth a little discomfort to help achieve our goals?"

Brigit looked at Blake's green eyes and firm jaw and her shoulders relaxed. She knew he must have tried to tell her; they would never keep secrets from each other. Then she pictured Nathaniel's short blond hair and straight nose and jumped up.

"Did Winston tell you the name of the reporter?" She walked to the table and straightened the place cards. She fiddled with the ivory silk tablecloth and rearranged the salt and pepper shakers.

"I don't think he mentioned it but I trust him." Blake wrapped his arms around Brigit's waist. "Let's take advantage of the empty kitchen and have a siesta in the pantry. I've always wanted to make love surrounded by grape leaves and jars of green olives."

"That's tempting." Brigit turned around and kissed Blake hard on the mouth. She fumbled with his zipper and rubbed the crease in his slacks. Suddenly she heard male voices speaking in rapid Greek. She looked up and saw three young men carrying silver salad bowls. They juggled bags filled with red onions and heads of lettuce and cherry tomatoes.

"We're going to have to wait until dinner is over and my buddies polish off two bottles of Grand Marnier and a box of Cuban cigars." Blake groaned, arranging his slacks. "I just hope they don't insist we play Scrabble. Bradley Cooper is a terrible loser and he hides the *j*'s and *q*'s under his cocktail napkin."

Brigit watched Blake walk down the driveway and wished she'd had a chance to tell him about Nathaniel. They had never met but he had seen their wedding photo buried in a box of Christmas ornaments. Brigit remembered Blake studying it carefully and covering it with silver snowflakes. She remembered him kissing her on the mouth and murmuring he was lucky to have found her.

She saw Blake pick up a basket of bread loaves and a warmth spread though her chest. He was a famous movie star but he didn't mind rolling up his sleeves and helping the caterers carry their shopping bags. She turned around and gazed at the ceramic water pitcher and crystal vases filled with yellow and white daisies. She couldn't wait for their guests to arrive; everything was going to be perfect.

Brigit stepped into the garden and wrapped her arms around her chest. The night sky was filled with stars and far below she could see sleek white yachts bobbing in the harbor. A bus climbed up the narrow path and bright lights twinkled in the square.

She heard laughter through the french doors and thought the dinner party had been wonderful. She pictured wide plates of pork wrapped in pastry and tomato sauce. There were platters of artichoke and eggplant and sausage. She remembered the rich chocolate cake and vanilla custard.

She pictured Blake sitting at the head of the table in a dark suit and white silk shirt. Daisy looked lovely in a bright orange dress and gold hoop earrings. Her mother wore a cream Jil Sander sheath and matching pumps and her father was elegant in a pin-striped blazer and tan slacks.

She remembered Blake giving a toast that winning an Academy Award was nothing compared to having Brigit agree to marry him. The best man said she was out of his league and he must have slipped something in her drink to convince her. She remembered everyone laughing and agreeing they were the most beautiful couple since Brad Pitt and Angelina Jolie.

Finally guests started to disperse and Blake and his grooms-men retired to the library to play backgammon and drink Rémy Martin. Brigit's cheeks were flushed from the warm air and Metaxa and she slipped outside and ran down to the garden.

Suddenly she heard footsteps and saw a figure leaning on the stone fence. He wore jeans and a leather jacket and suede loafers. She looker closer and recognized Nathaniel's short blond hair and blue backpack.

"What are you doing here?" she demanded. "I told you it was a private dinner party."

"I had dinner at a tavern in Fira, the chicken souvlaki was delicious and the orzo pasta was better than at the Ithaka restaurant on East Eighty-Sixth Street," Nathaniel replied. "Do you remember we used to sit in a booth and hold hands in the candlelight? The portions were so large we always took home a doggy bag."

"Then why are you here?" Brigit asked. "It's almost midnight."

"I didn't want to go back to the inn." Nathaniel slipped his hands into his pockets. "The mattress on my bed is so thin I may as well sleep on the floor. The monks in the abbey have better accommodations."

"You can't come inside." Brigit glanced at the french doors. "The rest of the guests are leaving and everyone's going to bed."

"What are you doing out here alone?" Nathaniel raised his eyebrow. "Shouldn't you'd be sipping Metaxa brandy in front of a fire while your fiancé whispers in your ear?"

"Blake and his friends are playing backgammon in the library." Brigit flushed.

"And they didn't invite the president of the Dartmouth backgammon society?" Nathaniel asked. "I suppose it takes a real man to be beaten by a woman."

"I haven't played backgammon in years," Brigit replied. "Plus, the smell of cigars makes me dizzy."

"Smoking cigars is a ridiculous habit," Nathaniel agreed. "You may as well park yourself in the cancer ward."

"You smoked a pack of cigarettes a day and drank half a bottle of vodka," Brigit retorted.

"I gave all that up, now I do a cleanse once a month. You should try it, it helps you think clearly." He waved his hand. "Of course then you realize how miserable your life is because you can't afford a decent winter coat or a holiday in Biarritz and you take your last paycheck and spend it on a bottle of Absolut. But at least you know why you're drinking, so it must be healthy."

He stopped and gazed at Brigit's smooth blond hair and diamond teardrop earrings. He admired her pearl necklace and pale pink gown and beige sling backs.

"You do look lovely. I like the way you've let your hair grow, Brigit," Nathaniel mused. "I actually came for a reason, I want to call a truce."

"What do you mean?" Brigit frowned.

"I took this job because I need the money. You don't know what it's like to see your bank account sink into triple digits." Nathaniel dug his heels in the ground. "Sometimes I think if only I worked harder and produced a novel, I'd be holding court in Bushwick surrounded by first-year Columbia grad students."

"You did the best you could," Brigit murmured.

"I slept and breathed that book for two years and ended up with three lousy chapters and a permanent crick in my neck." Nathaniel's blue eyes flickered. "But I want you to know I'm not going to ruin your wedding. If Blake makes you happy, then something good came out of it."

"He makes me very happy." Brigit nodded. "He's honest and hardworking and cares about other people."

"Sounds like an ad for life insurance." Nathaniel rustled in his backpack. "I brought you a gift."

"You didn't have to bring a present." Brigit glanced at the tall box wrapped in silver tissue paper.

"I do remember the rules of etiquette," Nathaniel protested. "Technically I have a year to give a gift but some marriages don't make it to the paper anniversary."

"Blake and I will last fifty years," Brigit said hotly. "If you'll excuse me, I have to say thank you to the caterers."

"Take it." Nathaniel pressed the box into her hand. "It's not much but the Tiffany's soup tureens on your gift registry were out of my price range."

Brigit accepted the box and looked up at Nathaniel's short blond hair and clear blue eyes. She was about to say something and then she hurried up the stone steps and entered the kitchen.

She gazed at the smooth marble counters and dark oak floors and beamed ceilings. There was a silver teapot and porcelain demitasses and pitchers of cream and sugar. She thought it would be lovely to drink a cup of tea with Blake and discuss the delicious seafood and the warm toasts and their friends. But she heard muffled laughter in the library and knew they could play backgammon for hours. She poured a cup of tea and sat at the round wooden table.

She tore the silver tissue paper and opened the box. She took out a yellow plastic bucket and two orange shovels. She gasped and remembered the summer after she graduated from law school. She had just accepted an offer from Bingham and Stoll, and Nathaniel had sold his short story collection. She pictured sharing platters of oysters at the East Hampton Grill and browsing in White's Pharmacy and BookHampton on Main Street.

She and Nathaniel had spent whole days on the beach, reading magazines and licking Good Humor bars. Sometimes he had to drag her into the water because it felt so wonderful to lie in the sun without worrying about torts and rebuttals. At dusk they would wrap themselves in a blanket and eat a picnic of roast beef sandwiches and potato chips and watermelon.

"Who would have imagined that at twenty-four, I'd be a corporate attorney and you would be a serious author," Brigit mused.

It was the last day of summer and they sat on the back porch at Summerhill. She gazed at the house with its gabled roof and thick stone walls and thought she had never been anywhere so lovely. She loved the pond filled with bright orange goldfish and the rose garden with her mother's Princess Diana roses and the sloping lawn with its wide view of the sound.

"I knew you'd be an attorney when we were seven years old and you convinced the woman who sold apples on the roadside to give you everything for a dollar," Nathaniel replied. "You ran back to the house and begged your mother to bake three apple pies. You wrapped them in plastic wrap and put them in a wagon and made me pull it all the way back to the stand. Then you handed the woman the pies and said she could have them for free."

"I was afraid her apples would be rotten and she wouldn't make any money." Brigit frowned. "I thought she'd have a better chance of selling them if they were made into pies."

"You could convince anyone to do anything, you'll be the best associate they ever had." Nathaniel leaned on his elbows. "We don't know if I'm a real author yet. Macmillan may publish my stories and realize they are nothing but smoke and mirrors. I'll be another young writer with glowing potential whose book stinks like old fish."

"I've read your stories and they're wonderful," Brigit insisted. "You're going to be our generation's E. M. Forster or F. Scott Fitzgerald."

"If I sell a single book it's because of you. What would have happened if I hadn't drank too many Irish coffees at winter carnival and confessed I've been in love with you since your tenth birthday party? It had a cowboys and Indians theme and you let me shoot an apple off your head."

"You had great aim and it was a rubber bow and arrow." Brigit smiled.

"I remember thinking you were the bravest girl I'd ever met." Nathaniel reached behind himself and handed her a tall box wrapped in gold paper.

"My birthday isn't until February." Brigit frowned, lifting the lid and seeing a blue velvet jewelry box. She looked at Nathaniel and her hands started shaking.

"I know people will say we're too young but I want to experience everything with you." Nathaniel drew out the jewelry box. "I

want to see the bulls running in Pamplona and trek across the gla-
ciers in Patagonia. I want to watch James Bond marathons on
Netflix and share boxes of Thin Mints Girl Scout cookies. There's
no point waiting when there is no future without you." He dropped
to his knee. "Brigit Emily Palmer, will you marry me?"

Brigit glanced at the pear-shaped sapphire surrounded by diamonds and gasped. She wanted to tell Nathaniel to wait; they had
their whole lives ahead of them. But he had always been in a rush:
insisting they apply early decision to Dartmouth, renting a loft in
the East Village without meeting his roommates, accepting the
first offer on his stories.

Then she thought of her parents who'd married on her mother's
twenty-second birthday. She remembered her mother describing
the formal ceremony at the Cathedral of St. John the Divine and
the elegant reception at the Algonquin and the honeymoon in
Monte Carlo. She pictured her parents drinking Manhattans on
the lawn at Summerhill or curled up in front of the fireplace in
their study. She thought of the way her father knew exactly how
her mother liked her eggs or that they both loved the style section
in the Sunday *New York Times*.

She remembered the summer when she was eight years old and
she and Daisy and Nathaniel spent lazy afternoons on the lawn
making daisy chains. She pictured the crooked chain Nathaniel
had slipped on her finger. She remembered not removing it until
the petals fell off and her skin turned green. Years later she found
it pressed inside a copy of *Little Women*.

If they got married, it didn't mean they would stop spending
weekends browsing in bookstores in East Hampton. They could
still devote whole Sundays to working on the *New York Times*

crossword puzzle or seeing Italian movies at the Roxy. She glanced at Nathaniel's bright blue eyes and knew he was right, she couldn't imagine a future without him.

"Yes, I'll marry you." She nodded.

He slipped the sapphire-and-diamond ring onto her finger and took her in his arms. He kissed her slowly, tasting of roast beef and watermelon. He grabbed her hand and ran to the driveway.

"Where are we going?" she asked as he opened the door of his white BMW.

"To Manhattan to see your parents. They're waiting at their town house with a bottle of French champagne and a platter of Russian caviar."

"I'm starting work tomorrow, I can't go in with a hangover," Brigit protested. "And I never understood how anyone could like fish eggs."

"I can hardly tell my future father-in-law I don't approve of his choice of hors d'oeuvres. When our daughter gets married we'll celebrate with fish tacos." Nathaniel jumped into the driver's seat. "If you douse caviar in salt and wash it down with enough champagne, it's actually quite delicious."

Brigit smoothed her hair and suddenly felt a pit in her stomach. She turned to Nathaniel and frowned.

"How do my parents know we're engaged before I do?"

"You're from one of the oldest families in New York." Nathaniel started the engine. "I couldn't expect your parents to approve if I didn't ask them first. Even if we lived across the lawn from each other since we were five years old, they're giving up their most precious possession."

Brigit gazed at Nathaniel's straight nose and tan cheeks and her shoulders relaxed. They were perfect for each other and Nathaniel understood everything about her.

"What if I had said no?" she asked.

Nathaniel put the car in gear and drove down the long gravel driveway. He stopped under a wide oak tree and kissed her softly on the mouth.

"I would have done everything I could to change your mind."

"I'm an attorney." Brigit was suddenly giddy from the weight of the sapphire and diamond and the feel of Nathaniel's mouth on her lips. "I don't reverse my decision easily."

"I'd spend the rest of my life convincing you if I had to," Nathaniel whispered. "There's nothing I want more."

She remembered the next ten months of black-tie dinners and cocktail receptions. She was so exhausted from her terrifying workload and the never-ending invitations that sometimes she wanted to beg Nathaniel to wait. They needed a couple of years to get settled and then they would plan a wedding.

But he'd bounded into her office with her favorite sesame noodles and brochures of honeymoon destinations and her heart had lifted. She cracked open fortune cookies and thought none of it mattered if they weren't together.

She fingered the plastic bucket and remembered waking up at Summerhill the morning of the rehearsal dinner. She'd slipped on her white cotton robe and sat at the dormer window. She'd gazed at the dew on the grass and the mist hanging on the sound and felt her heart pound.

She wanted to race across the lawn and climb over the stone fence to Nathaniel's parents' estate. She wanted to pound on the door until Nathaniel shuffled downstairs in his plaid boxers. She wanted to say they were too young to get married; they should be focusing on their careers and planning summer holidays in Spain.

She glanced at Daisy asleep in her white-canopied bed and thought it was all slipping away. Just yesterday they used to fight over who could borrow their mother's cream angora sweater.

She tied the robe around her waist and climbed the narrow staircase to the nursery. She gazed at the child-sized table and chairs and the dollhouse with its pink curtains and smiled. She and Daisy hadn't played up there in decades but her mother refused to remove the Nancy Drew books or take down their crayon self-portraits.

She sat on a pink wooden chair and pulled her knees to her chest. She was always so sure about everything: that Dartmouth was perfect because the academics were excellent but it wasn't a pressure cooker like Harvard. That she wanted to be a lawyer because the best way to help people was to give them information.

She gazed at the sapphire-and-diamond ring and wondered why she was nervous. Was she just wistful their childhood was over or was she afraid they were being hasty?

She heard footsteps and saw a figure in a yellow robe and silk slippers. Daisy's hair was tied in a long ponytail and her face was free of makeup.

"Who gets up at seven a.m. on the day before her wedding?"

Daisy yawned. "You're supposed to sleep until noon when your maid of honor pulls you out of bed and drags you to the nail salon."

"I'm sorry I woke you." Brigit sighed.

"I like sharing a room," Daisy replied. "It reminds me of when I was six years old, and I was afraid the tooth fairy wouldn't come. You climbed into my bed and said I should go back to sleep. You'd make sure she wouldn't forget me."

"I had to ask my bridesmaids to stay at Summerhill," Brigit said. "It didn't seem right to make them stay at the Hedges Inn."

"Mom loves having people around." Daisy grinned. "I think it finally hit her that you're leaving. She keeps wiping her eyes and saying her allergies are terrible."

"What if this is all wrong?" Brigit looked up. "Nathaniel and I have never even lived together, what if we can't agree on which cereals to stock in the pantry? And we're so competitive, do you remember the summer when we were fourteen and I beat him in tennis?

"The next day he came down with the flu and couldn't leave his bed for a week. I was so worried, I took him chicken soup and his mother said he was at the club. He'd been taking secret tennis lessons because he couldn't face me until he was sure he would win."

"Do you know why you're competitive?" Daisy asked. "Because when you and Nathaniel are together no one else exists. You might challenge each other but he would defend you against the rest of the world. I hate losing a sister but you are perfect for each other."

"Do you really think so?" Brigit asked.

Daisy picked up a Barbie doll and stroked its blond hair. She looked at Brigit and her eyes were suddenly bright. "I've known it since I was ten years old."

Brigit sat at her dressing table, brushing her cheeks with powder. It was almost seven p.m. and in a few minutes she'd walk over to the Cabots' lawn for the rehearsal dinner. She slipped on diamond earrings and fastened a gold necklace around her neck. She gazed at the blue Dior cocktail dress and tried to stop her heart from racing.

She heard the door open and turned around.

"What are you doing here?" she demanded. "We promised we wouldn't see each other in private until the wedding."

"I brought you something," Nathaniel said. He wore a crisp white shirt and tan slacks. His blond hair touched his collar and he wore a yellow silk tie.

"We're not supposed to exchange gifts until just before the ceremony." Brigit took the square box wrapped in silver tissue paper.

"You know how impatient I am with presents," Nathaniel replied. "I left a dozen roses on your desk in physics class at Dartmouth because I wanted to surprise you on your birthday. Your professor was allergic to flowers and tossed them in the garbage."

"You bought two dozen more and sent them to my dorm room." Brigit smiled.

"Open it," Nathaniel urged.

Brigit untied the silver ribbon and opened the box. She drew out a yellow plastic bucket and two orange shovels.

"Just because we're getting married, doesn't mean we will stop having fun," Nathaniel said. "We can still go ice skating on Town Pond and eat crab at the Chowder House. We can spend whole weekends reading trashy novels and listening to nineties music on SiriusXM."

Brigit glanced at Nathaniel and her eyes filled with tears. He knew her better than anyone and everything was going to be perfect.

"There is something inside," Nathaniel whispered.

Brigit took off the lid and saw a black velvet box. She snapped it open and discovered a diamond-and-ruby pendant with an antique clasp.

"Even when we're eating cotton candy on the Fourth of July, I think you're the most desirable woman in the world." Nathaniel fastened the pendant around her neck. "And a beautiful woman deserves exquisite jewels."

Brigit glanced in the mirror at the glittering diamonds and rubies and gasped. She turned and kissed Nathaniel softly on the mouth. He ran his fingers over her breast and slipped one hand under her panties.

"Daisy could walk in at any minute." Brigit giggled, feeling the familiar warmth spread through her body.

"I told her you have a craving for Ben & Jerry's Pistachio Pistachio ice cream." Nathaniel drew her onto the bed. "I checked, you don't have any in the fridge. She's going to have to go all the way to Montauk."

Brigit heard laughter coming from the library and inhaled the scent of cigar smoke and jumped. She glanced at the yellow bucket and orange shovels and felt a pain in her chest.

Why had Nathaniel been the one who seemed stuck in college? In the second year of their marriage she woke at five a.m. to go to Equinox before she went to the office, while he stayed up watching Jimmy Kimmel and slept until noon.

She pictured him hunched in front of his laptop with his baseball cap pulled over his blond curls and knew it wasn't that Nathaniel was afraid of growing up. He was terrified of failure.

She glanced down the hallway and saw the library door was still closed. She opened the bucket and peered inside. She saw that it was empty and felt strangely disappointed, as if she'd bitten into a custard and someone had removed the cream.

She put the bucket in the box and retied the ribbon. She placed the box on the marble counter and decided she would return it in the morning. She climbed the circular staircase and opened the door of her bedroom.

Chapter Four

DAISY LEANED OVER THE BALCONY and gazed at the sun spreading over the Aegean Sea. White houses gleamed in the morning light and the ocean was a sheet of sparkling diamonds. She saw cliffs spotted with purple flowers and boats pulled up on the shore and thought she had never seen a more beautiful sunrise.

She remembered the dinner party last night and flinched. At first it was intoxicating being in a room with Academy Award winners and U.S. senators and a male model who was on the cover of *GQ*. The crusted feta cheese was delicious and Blake uncorked endless bottles of Moët & Chandon.

But then an old family friend cornered her next to the grand piano and asked if she planned to follow Brigit's footsteps and join the family foundation. Daisy had rolled Santorini cherry tomatoes around her plate and murmured she felt terrible about the conditions in Ecuador but she had no desire to dig houses in the mud.

The costar of Blake's new movie had asked where she could find Daisy's designs and Daisy wanted to reply they only existed on her glass dining room table and in the sewing room of her best friend's brownstone. Instead she swallowed another glass of champagne and smiled, saying that as soon as she returned from Santorini she was lining up meetings with buyers at Bergdorf's and Saks.

She'd glanced around the dining room at the glittering chandeliers and flickering candles and wanted to say she had a terrible headache and was going to bed. But then she caught sight of Blake whispering in Brigit's ear and a warmth spread through her chest.

For the last six months of Brigit's marriage, Brigit had acted like a schoolgirl afraid of failing a math test. When Daisy joined Brigit and Nathaniel at Serafina for their weekly pasta dinner, Brigit's cheeks were pale and her shoulders tensed. She'd wrapped buckwheat fettuccini around her fork and exclaimed it was the best thing she'd ever tasted as if she was enjoying her meal for two. Nathaniel had slumped in his chair with his baseball cap pulled over his ears and sipped his third strawberry basil martini.

But now Brigit's hair was glossy and her skin glowed and a smile played on her lips. She took Blake's arm and introduced him to a Vanderbilt and a DuPont and a cousin of the Kennedys'. Daisy studied Blake's smooth dark hair and tan cheeks and thought they looked like a movie poster.

Daisy gazed at the blue domed roofs and didn't want to go downstairs and bump into any lingering guests eating yogurt with walnuts and honey. She didn't want to explain she hadn't brought a date because she hadn't had a boyfriend since she'd split up with an artist who'd used her tiny apartment to hang his sketches.

She slipped on a yellow blouse and long floral skirt. Her hair was wound in a ponytail and she strapped on leather espadrilles. She ran down the circular staircase and raced down the stone steps into the garden.

The steep path to Fira was crowded with old men leading donkeys. There were racks of brightly colored postcards and stands selling watermelon and apricots. She entered a café and inhaled the scent of cinnamon and vanilla.

She sat at a table by the window and ordered black coffee and fruit salad. She looked up and saw a man with curly hair and brown eyes. He wore a cotton shirt and had a silver camera slung over his shoulder.

"You need to eat more than that." He walked over to her table. "The Corner restaurant serves the best omelets in Fira with feta cheese and bacon and green onions."

"I can't swallow anything until I drink some very black coffee." She grimaced.

"Late night?" the man asked. He had a British accent and a small dimple on his chin.

"You're Nathaniel's friend, the photographer." Daisy started, suddenly feeling as if she'd forgotten to put on a blouse. "I shouldn't talk to you outside of the villa."

"I thought Americans were supposed to be friendly." He pulled out a chair. "Nathaniel went for a hike and I have no one to eat breakfast with. Could I join you?"

Daisy slipped on white oval sunglasses. She didn't want Robbie to report back to Nathaniel that the bride's sister was terribly rude.

"I suppose it's alright," she relented. "I won't be here long, I'm only having coffee."

"Of course you will, there's nothing to do in Santorini except sit at a café and drink iced coffee and eat honey baklava." Robbie smiled. "Then the sun gets so hot you can't walk on the cobblestones, so you go back to your hotel and take a nap. In the evening, you climb to the castle in Oia to watch the sunset and think you didn't know such beauty existed. Then you sit at another café and do the same thing again."

"Have you been here long?" Daisy giggled.

"Nathaniel and I arrived yesterday, but I've spent a lot of time on Greek islands." Robbie shrugged. "You have to think like a local, or you'll end up with a sunburn and blisters."

"I drank too much champagne last night," Daisy admitted. "I hardly ever drink champagne, but everyone kept asking where they could find my dresses."

"How long have you been a designer?" Robbie asked.

"About four months. Before that I was pastry chef and I spent a summer clerking at a law firm." Daisy poured sugar into the ceramic cup. "I was trying to decide whether to go to law school, but I couldn't imagine spending my life sifting through files to find the one sentence that could change someone's life. What if I got it wrong? I'd never forgive myself." She sipped her coffee.

"Have you always wanted to be a photographer?"

"When I was twenty I spent two months between university terms working as a line cook in Provence. Then I traveled around Europe with the Nikon camera I got for my birthday and pretended I was Richard Avedon or Helmut Lang." Robbie grinned. "I thought if I could show my parents I had talent I wouldn't have to go back to London and study trigonometry. One day I walked past the embassy in Istanbul and it blew up. All these people sitting in cafés drinking Turkish coffee or laden with shopping bags were suddenly caught in an international incident.

"I didn't stop to think, I just started taking pictures," he continued. "I never realized life could change in an instant. One minute you're a tourist bartering for a woven jacket, the next you are surrounded by blood and screaming.

"I sold the photos to *Time* magazine and was hooked. I traveled to Tokyo after the tsunami and Nepal to cover the earthquake. I arrived in Paris hours after the attack on *Charlie Hebdo* and I was on the airstrip when soldiers returned from Iraq.

"I photograph other things, of course, but so much of life is focused on acquiring shiny objects. It's important to remember the greatest thing we have is the will to survive." He ran his hands through his hair. "I'm sorry, I didn't mean to get on a soapbox. I've learned having coffee with a pretty girl on a Greek island is as good as it gets."

"You are lucky to be certain about your future," Daisy murmured. "Brigit has always been sure about everything: what kind of puppy we should get when we were children, where to go to college, what brand of lipstick to use. I bring home ten shades of Bobbi Brown lip gloss and have a dozen coffee flavors in my cupboard and every time I find the perfect career I discover something I'd rather do." She fiddled with her napkin. "I love creating sketches and choosing fabric but fashion design is as hard to break into as the Olympics.

"The only constant in my life is Edgar, my French bulldog. But he makes terrible conversation and he drools at dinner."

"Sometimes if you choose your path too early it doesn't work out," Robbie mused. "Your sister got married when she was twenty-four and now she's getting married again."

"How do you know when Brigit got married?" Daisy asked.

"Nathaniel showed me an article in *Town & Country*." Robbie shrugged.

"She knew exactly what she was doing. Brigit and Nathaniel were perfect for each other." She jumped up and grabbed her purse. "I have to go, I have an appointment at the hair salon."

"Daisy wait, I didn't mean to offend you." Robbie stood up.

"This is Brigit's wedding and it's going to be the most wonderful weekend," Daisy said hotly. "Tell Nathaniel if he tries to spoil it, I'll make him wish he never met me."

Daisy hiked up the path to the villa and sat on a wooden bench. She glanced at the hot sun and clear blue ocean and a silver cruise ship. Old women carried baskets of cherry tomatoes and a yellow taxi navigated the narrow road.

She remembered telling Robbie that Brigit and Nathaniel were perfect for each other and flinched. She was determined that Nathaniel wouldn't ruin Brigit's wedding, but how could she say something so foolish? Brigit and Blake were like Cary Grant and Grace Kelly, everyone stopped when they entered a room.

She plucked a daisy from the side of the road and resolved not to talk to Robbie alone again. She pictured his dark curly hair and large brown eyes and sighed. It was unfortunate because he had a lovely English accent and the fried eggs with green onions he'd ordered was delicious.

Sydney stood at the window and let out her breath. Everyone had told her Santorini sunsets were exquisite and she must pack sensible shoes so she could hike to Oia and see the whole caldera lit by a purple flame. But no one mentioned that the sunrises were just as spectacular. She gazed at the shimmering ocean and tile roofs and thought it was as if you'd emptied a paint box and all that was left was blue and orange and yellow.

It wasn't even eight a.m. but Francis had already slipped on a pair of shorts and a shirt and mumbled he was going to make some early morning calls. Sydney calculated the time difference in New York and thought it was unlikely any stockbrokers or bankers would be in their offices at midnight. But he had that look on his face that didn't allow her to ask questions so she turned over and pretended to go back to sleep.

Now she gathered the remnants of last night: a bottle of cognac they'd brought upstairs after the party, a red Armani tie draped over an armchair, the silk nightie Francis had slipped off her shoulders.

She hung her Jil Sander sheath in the closet and pictured the dining room of the villa filled with their closest friends. She had glanced around at Brigit in her pink satin gown and Daisy in a long embroidered dress and Francis wearing an impeccably tailored pin-striped blazer and thought it was easy to be happy.

Daisy really did look beautiful, her hair falling in long curls and tied loosely with a silk ribbon. Sydney bit her lip and hoped her designs would be a success.

She remembered Francis catching her eye while he gave his

toast and for a moment the odd tenseness of the last ten months was erased. The whole night was perfect: dancing with him to Frank Sinatra, the constant sound of laughter and glasses clinking, Brigit's flushed cheeks and sparkling eyes.

It had been so long since she'd seen Brigit with her customary bounce to her step. She pictured her at three years old on the stone porch at Summerhill. She remembered her skipping down the steps until she reached the pond. She'd wobbled on the grassy banks and clapped wildly at the ducks.

She thought about the tennis trophies she won as a teenager and the gold diplomas with the honors tassels from Dartmouth and Columbia. She pictured the afternoon she and Nathaniel burst into the Park Avenue town house flashing the diamond-and-sapphire ring and Sydney thought Brigit looked so in love.

Sydney folded her silk nightie and remembered the time two years ago when Brigit pulled up the driveway at Summerhill. It was a Friday afternoon and Sydney stood on a ladder, trimming the trellises.

"Darling, I wasn't expecting you and Nathaniel until tonight." Sydney climbed down from the ladder. "I've collected vegetables from the garden. We're going to have tomato soup and zucchini lasagna and blackberry tarts for dessert."

"Nathaniel isn't coming." Brigit approached the porch. She wore a beige linen suit and narrow pumps and carried a Tory Burch clutch.

"I know he's been working odd hours on the novel, but I was hoping you'd both join us this weekend. The Whites' daughter is getting married next week and we're invited tomorrow for steak and oysters." She fiddled with a rose. "I thought being married to a stockbroker was difficult. Francis is always getting up with Tokyo and going to bed with Zürich. I can count on one hand the number of breakfasts that haven't been interrupted by a frantic client because the market was closing somewhere and the stocks were plummeting."

"Nathaniel isn't coming at all," Brigit said slowly. "He walked out of the apartment, he's not coming back."

Sydney glanced at Brigit and noticed her cheeks were pale and her blond hair had escaped its clip. She took her arm and led her into the living room.

"Sit down and tell me everything."

"I come home at night and never know his mood." Brigit sat on the paisley love seat. "Sometimes he says his fingertips are on fire and he's going to be the next Faulkner. Lately he's slumped on the sofa with a bottle of whiskey and a comic book.

"Yesterday I suggested he bring his laptop to Summerhill so I could read his new chapters," Brigit continued. "He said there were never going to be any new chapters if I kept hovering over his shoulder like the evil witch in *Snow White*."

"He probably spent the night at his parents' apartment," Sydney replied. "Call him and tell him he can drive out with your father tonight."

"When I came home from work this afternoon his duffel bag was gone and his drawers were empty." Brigit twisted her hands. "He left a note that he was wrong, he'd never be Steinbeck or Thomas Wolfe. He couldn't even write a decent James Patterson thriller."

"Nathaniel has always been temperamental," Sydney mused. "Do you remember when you were children and you got the part of toad in *The Wind in the Willows*? He refused to participate if he wasn't the lead. You finally told the camp counselor you didn't want to wear a costume with warts. The day before the performance he came down with a mysterious stomachache and you ended up playing the part."

"He didn't even know the lines," Brigit murmured. "He would have been a much better frog."

"Once your father lost a good client and wouldn't answer my calls," Sydney continued. "I tracked him down to the King Cole Bar at the St. Regis sampling every kind of Bloody Mary. I ordered steaks and a baked potato to soak up the vodka and took him home."

"That's not all the note said. He told me to keep the apartment," she whispered. "He said it was a gift from his parents to us and it was the least I should have."

Sydney glanced at the dark wood floors and white wool rugs and pink marble fireplace. She saw the high-beamed ceilings and french windows opening onto the lawn. She thought of all the wonderful moments they'd celebrated in this room: Daisy's acceptance into Swarthmore, Brigit's entrance into the law review, her and Francis's twenty-fifth anniversary with a black-tie dinner including the governor of New York.

"Marriage is all about luck." She leaned against the floral cushions. "You tried as hard as you could."

"Marriage isn't anything to do with luck," Brigit retorted. "It's about commitment and love and hard work."

"Of course it's about luck, do you think things would be different if Nathaniel's book of short stories was a success and he was the toast of New York?" Sydney asked. "He'd be giving talks every night at the New York Public Library and the Strand bookstore. You'd attend literary soirees full of Pulitzer Prize winners and congratulate each other on being so clever."

"He's worried about the new novel," Brigit explained. "He can't write a sentence without erasing it."

"He lost his nerve. If the short stories ended up on the *New York Times* Best Seller list, he'd finish this novel faster than a speed typist." Sydney finished her drink. "Marriage is just like life, it needs luck to survive."

Sydney fiddled with her glass and thought of the day her marriage ran out of luck, on her forty-second birthday at Le Bernardin. She glanced at a family portrait above the marble fireplace and remembered when she'd met Francis, at the International Debutante Ball.

It was the most exclusive debutante ball in New York and the Waldorf Astoria ballroom was filled with Astors and Rockefellers and Vanderbilts. Sydney stood in a corner, sipping champagne with crème de cassis. She wore an ivory Oscar de la Renta gown with a pink sash. Her blond hair was brushed to her shoulders and she wore a diamond necklace.

"I can't imagine why your date left you alone when the band is playing 'Fly Me to the Moon.'" A young man had approached her. He wore a white tuxedo and had a pink rose in his buttonhole. "He's practically asking someone to steal you away."

"I can dance with whomever I like," Sydney replied, noticing he was very tall and had a dimple on his chin.

"At the International Debutante Ball?" He raised his eyebrow.

"I read the rule book. Every girl has two dates, a military officer and a civilian, and other men have to ask their permission to dance."

"One of my dates twisted his ankle and the other was allergic to oysters," Sydney admitted. "I seem to have ended up alone."

"In that case, may I?" Francis held out his arm. "I have two left feet when it comes to fast dancing but I'm quite good at a waltz."

After they danced to Frank Sinatra and Nat King Cole they made their way to the buffet. They filled their plates with stuffed mushrooms and glazed duck and sat on the bottom of the grand circular staircase.

"I have one semester left at Harvard and then I'm going to join the family stockbroking firm. It's on the fifty-fourth floor of the Chrysler Building with a view of the East River." Francis nibbled a canapé. "I enjoyed playing football on Boston Commons and eating clam chowder at Boston Chowda in Faneuil Hall but I could never live in New England. The bars close at midnight and everyone talks as if they have a head cold."

"I've lived in the same Park Avenue town house my whole life," Sydney said. "My mother thinks the entire world consists of Saks and the Metropolitan Museum and the dining room at the Carlyle. I like Manhattan but I prefer the country. I'm happiest at Summerhill."

"Summerhill?"

"It's my grandparents' cottage in East Hampton," Sydney explained. "The house is a hundred years old with a barn and a pond. When you stand on the porch you can see the Long Island Sound."

"It sounds wonderful," Francis murmured.

Sydney studied his light brown hair and blue eyes and felt her chest tighten.

"Maybe I can show it to you."

Every weekend in the spring Francis drove his brown Jaguar from Boston to New York. Sydney squeezed her classes at Barnard into four days so they could take long weekends in Vermont and Cape Cod. She sat in the passenger seat with her hair wrapped in a Hermès scarf and thought she really was lucky. She was twenty-two and falling in love.

Francis proposed the day after graduation and they got married on New Year's Eve in the ballroom where they'd met. Sydney stood at the window of her suite at the Waldorf Astoria in her Givenchy gown and saw the Christmas tree in Rockefeller Center and the red and green lights on the Empire State Building and thought the whole city was celebrating their marriage.

Sydney fiddled with her earrings and remembered the night of her forty-second birthday. Brigit had just graduated from Spence and was spending three weeks at a language school in Paris. Daisy had at the last minute decided to be a counselor at a summer camp in Maine.

"Darling, you didn't have to go to all this trouble," Sydney had said, when the maître d' led them to the table.

The gold tablecloth was set with a crystal vase of pink roses and a bottle of vintage Moët & Chandon. A rectangular box was wrapped in gold tissue paper and tied with a pink ribbon.

"Do you remember when we met at the International Debutante Ball?" Francis asked. He wore a white dinner jacket and his salt-and-pepper hair was slicked back.

"Everything in the room was gold and pink: the gold centerpieces and pink-and-gold floral arrangements and gold inlaid china. You wore an ivory silk gown with a pink sash and I thought you looked like a princess."

Sydney opened her mouth to say something but Francis pressed the gold wrapping paper into her hand.

"Brigit is going to Dartmouth and Daisy will graduate in two years," he began. "I've been thinking about the stockbrokerage and it's time to turn it over to someone else."

"You're forty-three," Sydney replied. "You're hardly going to spend your days at the Carlton Club having two-martini lunches."

"I know we contribute to the New York Public Library and the Guggenheim. But I want to do something for children who have never owned a book or seen a painting," Francis said. "I want to start a charitable foundation and travel to Asia and Africa and build schools and libraries."

"You want to leave the firm?" Sydney's eyes were wide and a pit formed in her stomach.

"I've thought about this for a long time. The best part is once Daisy graduates we could travel together." Francis poured two glasses of champagne. "We could see the whole world, not just the lobby of the Grand Hotel in Rome or the dining room in the Connaught in London."

Sydney gazed at the baked snapper and charred green tomatoes and suddenly wasn't hungry. She looked at Francis and bit her lip.

"I'm pregnant."

"What did you say?" Francis gasped.

"It was Mother's Day weekend, you brought me Belgian waffles and strawberries and fresh squeezed orange juice." Sydney looked up. "We left the tray on the bedside table and spent the whole morning in bed."

"But I thought you couldn't . . ." Francis's cheeks turned pale.

"Get pregnant because I'm too old?" Sydney smoothed her hair.

She thought of the years after Daisy was born when they'd tried so hard to have a boy. Francis longed to teach a son to fish and take him to baseball games at Yankee Stadium. But nothing happened and finally they agreed they were too old for diapers and sleepless nights.

Francis ate a bite of pan-roasted monkfish and sautéed mushrooms. He wiped his mouth with a napkin and looked at Sydney.

"Well, that is exciting news." He clutched his champagne glass. "You're as beautiful as you were eighteen years ago, you're going to be a wonderful mother all over again."

"You can still start the foundation," Sydney urged. "I can manage a baby on my own."

"It can wait. You didn't open your gift." Francis pointed to the gold box.

Sydney untied the pink ribbon and took out a diamond bracelet with an emerald charm of a globe.

"It's spectacular." She fastened it around her wrist.

"It was all the places we were going to go." Francis's shoulders tensed and he suddenly looked older. "I'll take it back and get something else."

"Of course I'll keep it." Sydney gazed at Francis's blue eyes and the dimple on his chin and a smile lit up her face. "I can't think of anything I'd like better."

Sydney zipped up a beige Eileen West dress and walked back into the bedroom. She thought of everything that had come afterward and shuddered. A Belgian chocolate wrapper lay on the bedside table and she realized she was starving.

She was going to go downstairs to the kitchen and have dark coffee and fruit and yogurt with honey. She suddenly pictured Francis, his cheeks tan from the Greek sun and his eyes sparkling and thought maybe their luck had changed and everything would be different.

Chapter Five

BRIGIT CLIMBED THE STEEP PATH to the villa and stopped to catch her breath. She gazed at the white houses and sharp cliffs and endless blue ocean. The sun glinted on stained-glass windows and she thought it was going to be a perfect day.

Blake had finally emerged from the library at two a.m. and they sat in the kitchen and talked about the dinner party and Blake's friends and how Ryan Reynolds liked brussels sprouts but hated sweet potatoes.

They crept up the circular staircase to her bedroom and locked the door behind them. Blake unzipped her pink Dior gown and ran his hands over her breasts. Brigit took the clip out of her hair and drew him onto the bed.

She wrapped her arms around his waist and pulled him on top of her. Blake kissed her mouth and her stomach and her thighs. Brigit waited for the warm rush and then the long exquisite release. She tucked herself against his slick chest and felt completely happy.

It was three days before the wedding and in a few hours they would host a picnic on Kamari Beach. She walked back to the villa and suddenly thought of Nathaniel's present on the mahogany coffee table. She wasn't going to give him the pleasure of returning it. She'd ship it back with the other gifts to their new apartment on Madison Avenue or Blake's house in the Hollywood Hills.

She opened the wooden gate and saw a familiar figure sitting on the stone step. He wore navy shorts and a yellow T-shirt and his blond hair was damp with sweat.

"What are you doing here?" Brigit asked.

"I went on a hike and suddenly had a craving for poached eggs and whole wheat toast and grilled tomatoes," Nathaniel replied.

"You're in Greece." Brigit smoothed her skirt. "Every café in Fira serves eggs for breakfast."

"They're more expensive than the Mansion Restaurant on York Avenue," Nathaniel grumbled. "Our bed-and-breakfast was supposed to serve a continental breakfast, but it's a single serving of Froot Loops and a carton of cranberry juice. You know how irritable I get if I don't eat a good breakfast."

"You can't come in." Brigit glanced at the french doors. "Blake will be down soon and he's not meeting my ex-husband over eggs and Santorini cherry tomatoes."

"Isn't it bad luck for Blake to spend the night?" Nathaniel asked. "You wouldn't let me see you before the wedding. I snuck into your room at Summerhill and you almost kicked me out."

"I don't believe in superstitions anymore," Brigit bristled. "I have to go, we're having a picnic on Kamari Beach."

"I'm glad you're having sex. God knows, failure is terrible for the libido. Mr. and Mrs. Glassman in 4A were getting it more than we were," Nathaniel replied. "What's Blake like in bed? I read he's very athletic."

"That's none of your business." Brigit flushed.

"I was just curious how it feels to have someone new leave his hairbrush on the sink and his copy of the *New Yorker* next to the bathtub." He fiddled with his backpack.

"Blake doesn't read the *New Yorker*, and he'd never leave anything on the sink. I'm finally living with a grown-up instead of a child who thinks the nanny is going to make his bed." Brigit looked at Nathaniel. "I'm sure you know what it's like to share your bed with someone new. Just because you can't afford Kobe steaks, I can't imagine you took a vow of chastity."

"Maybe someone to get sweaty with after a few dry martinis at the pub." Nathaniel shrugged. "But no one to wake up with and talk about civil rights and the protests in Baltimore."

"My father asked me to attend a charity ball at the St. Regis and I was seated beside Blake by accident." Brigit adjusted her sunglasses. "I could tell right away he was different from the bankers and stockbrokers I'd met in New York. He drove his own car and walked me to my door to say good night. You'd be surprised how many men stay in their Town Car and wait until I'm in the foyer."

"It's not hard to drive a car," Nathaniel said. "Do you remember I took my father's vintage Ford and drove you and Daisy to Montauk? From the way you two were shrieking, you would have thought you were being kidnapped."

"You were fourteen," Brigit exclaimed. "I was terrified of getting arrested."

"We parked at the beach and went swimming." Nathaniel plucked a blade of grass. "I hadn't seen you in a bathing suit since the previous summer. You stripped down to your bikini and I suddenly felt dizzy."

Brigit looked at Nathaniel sharply. She patted her hair and climbed the stairs.

"I have to go." She opened the french doors.

"Did you say you sat next to Blake by accident?" Nathaniel asked. "That's funny because I ran into your father at Claridge's last summer. I don't know if he mentioned that we met. I was interviewing Gavin Rossdale and Francis was eating a duck egg and asparagus sandwich in the Reading Room. I sat down and said I owed him and Sydney an apology." He paused and looked at Brigit. "I promised him I'd take care of his little girl for the rest of my life and I let him down. I was terribly sorry and hoped he and Sydney would forgive me."

"Oh." Brigit suddenly thought the sun was too bright. "He never told me that he saw you."

"It was very awkward. If we weren't sitting in one of the most exclusive bars in London he might have punched me in the jaw. I felt badly and asked how you were and he said you were pretty low but he'd found you the perfect guy." Nathaniel paused. "His name was Blake Crawford and he was an actor."

"That's impossible," Brigit frowned. "Blake would have told me."

"It doesn't matter, look how well everything turned out." Nathaniel shrugged. "You're madly in love and marrying Hollywood's most eligible bachelor."

"Blake isn't anything like other movie stars." Brigit smoothed her skirt. "He's hardworking and generous and I've never been happier."

"I'm going to find Robbie and borrow some euros for a feta cheese omelet." Nathaniel stood up. "His father is a British lord with a large mansion in Sussex. It's easy to traipse around the globe with a camera and a rucksack if you can go home to baked pheasant and preheated towels."

"Your parents gave you everything," Brigit murmured.

"You mean a Dartmouth degree and a convertible and membership to the University Club?" Nathaniel said. "None of that means anything."

"What do you mean?" Brigit asked.

"The people who love you have to believe in you." Nathaniel's eyes were bright. "The rest you can accomplish yourself."

Nathaniel opened the gate and turned around. "I'll see you at the picnic. Don't forget to wear sunscreen or you'll get more freckles on your nose."

"You're coming to the picnic?" Brigit asked.

"It's on Winston's itinerary." Nathaniel fished a piece of paper out of his pocket and smiled. "I can't wait to meet the groom."

Brigit stood at the enamel sink and her heart raced. Blake and her father couldn't have known each other; one of them would have mentioned it.

She flashed on the time Blake was stopped by reporters at the Hotel Grande Bretagne in Athens. He'd said the luckiest night of his life was when he was seated next to Brigit at the Save the Children foundation gala.

She nibbled a purple grape and thought perhaps Nathaniel was lying. He didn't want Brigit and Blake to be happy and was stirring up trouble. But she sat on the wooden chair and sighed. Nathaniel was stubborn and messy but he had always been brutally honest.

She heard footsteps and saw Blake standing in the doorway. He wore a short-sleeved shirt and tan shorts and leather sandals.

"You slipped out before I woke up." He kissed her on the mouth. "I was going to bring you a tray of yogurt with fruit and thyme honey. I thought we could spend the morning in bed, rehearsing for the wedding."

"I know my vows," Brigit replied. "I memorized them on the flight."

Blake tucked her hair behind her ear. "I was talking about the wedding night."

"You were the one who wanted to stay in separate villas." Brigit giggled.

"It seemed like a good idea while I was in California and you were in New York, but now I want to be with you every minute." Blake sliced a peach. "I met a shopkeeper whose friend runs an orphanage in Thera. Did you know those children have never owned a computer?

"I thought we could send them a shipment of Macs. Can you imagine their faces when they press the power button and see videos of jungles in Africa or ice fjords in Finland?"

Brigit bit her lip. She wanted to tell him what Nathaniel had said but mentioning Nathaniel's name was like bringing in an unwelcome guest. There would be plenty of time to talk about Nathaniel when Blake and Nathaniel met.

She ate another grape and thought there had to be a way to ask if Blake had met her father before the charity gala. She opened her mouth but Blake glanced at his watch.

"God, I forgot." He took her hand. "We have an appointment in Marina Vlihada."

"But we're hosting the picnic at noon," Brigit protested. "I need to shower and change."

"You'd look beautiful in my white Hanes T-shirts and boxers." Blake grabbed a ripe pear. "It's a surprise, I can't wait to show it to you."

Brigit sat on the donkey and gazed at the wide stretch of the caldera. The sun was bright and she could see the volcanic islands of Palea Kameni and Nea Kameni. She studied the sailboats far below and thought she had never seen so many colors. It was as if the whole world had been rinsed in blue and orange and yellow.

They strolled quickly to the square and were greeted by an old man leading two donkeys. Brigit hoisted herself into the saddle and clutched the leather strap. She thought of the glossy ponies she and Daisy used to ride in Central Park and giggled.

She remembered what Nathaniel had said and flinched. Maybe he had gotten the conversation with her father wrong; it was some silly misunderstanding. It was her fault for talking to Nathaniel. She should have told him to eat fried eggs with Kasseri cheese in Fira and she would see him later. Now instead of enjoying the breathtaking view she felt as if there was an insect buzzing around her head.

She gripped the donkey tighter and inhaled the scent of

bougainvillea and hibiscus. She wasn't going to think about Nathaniel, she was going to enjoy being on one of the most glorious islands in the world with the man she loved.

"Isn't it spectacular?" Blake hopped off the donkey. "From Marina Vlihada you can take a private cruise to the coast of Perivolos and the Red and White Beaches. We can snorkel on the island of Aspronisi and go fishing in Therasia."

"We don't have time to take a cruise." Brigit glanced at the white sailboats lining the dock. "We have twenty people including a U.S. Supreme Court judge and an Academy Award–winning screenwriter coming to eat lamb souvlaki and spinach spanakopita."

"Come on." Blake lifted her off the donkey. "This will only take a minute."

Brigit followed him along the dock to a blue catamaran. It had a marble bar and creamy leather upholstery. The steering wheel was smooth walnut and there was an ivory chessboard.

"It's gorgeous." Brigit glanced at the blue-and-gold interlocking *B*'s on the side of the boat and suddenly her heart raced. "Who does it belong to?"

"I wondered why we were in such a hurry to leave on our honeymoon when we're getting married on a Greek island." Blake took her hand and stepped onto the deck. "We can spend a few days sailing to the islands of Sikinos and Anafi. We'll go swimming in Manganari Bay and eat grilled swordfish in Irakleia. At night the whole island is lit up and you can see the tiny village of Imerovigli and the ruins at Firostefani.

"I've lived in Los Angeles for fifteen years and never been on a boat except for a movie premiere on the *Queen Mary* that never left the port." Blake leaned over the railing. "I stood on the deck eating cracked lobster and thought they may as well have held the reception in the ballroom of the Beverly Wilshire. Now we can spend the weekend on Catalina or get ice cream on Balboa Island."

"You bought the catamaran?" Brigit whispered.

"It's your wedding present." Blake grinned, leading her down carpeted stairs. "It comes with a personal chef. We can catch salmon and have it for dinner with fresh vegetables and a summer salad."

Brigit remembered when she was a child and her father bought a wooden sailboat. She pictured Daisy in a striped sailor dress and her mother in white capris and leather loafers. She remembered thinking why would anyone want to grow up, when life was about sailing on the sound and eating corn on the cob and slices of watermelon.

She glanced at Blake's smooth dark hair and green eyes and her heart lifted. She had been wrong; it was wonderful to grow up. She was going to have a handsome, caring husband and her own family.

Blake showed her the salon with polished wood floors and cream walls lined with abstract paintings. The bathroom had a gold-tiled shower and the library was crammed with paperback books by Mark Twain and Hemingway.

She entered a round room with an orange wool rug and turquoise walls. A king-sized bed was covered by a white lace bedspread and littered with pink and yellow pillows. There were ceramic vases and bunches of purple peonies and pink anemones.

"I had it decorated in the colors of Santorini." He unfastened the clip in her hair. "Whether we're sailing in Tahiti or just tied up in Marina del Rey, we will always remember the green cliffs and clear blue water of Santorini."

Brigit inhaled his scent of citrus shampoo and musk cologne and kissed him softly on the lips. She glanced at the cabin door and hesitated.

"What if someone shows up?"

"I told the captain to go sightseeing at the ruins of Akrotiri." He closed the door. "He took a donkey, he won't return for hours."

Brigit unzipped her capris and slipped off her sandals. She unbuttoned Blake's shirt and drew him onto the bed. She felt his mouth on her breasts and gasped. She guided his head between her legs and felt the stirring deep inside her. She pressed herself against him until the waves came and she was almost dizzy. She arched her hips and thought nothing had ever felt so exquisite.

Blake pulled her arms over her head and nuzzled her neck. He opened her legs and slipped inside her. She wrapped her arms around his back and urged him to go faster. She felt his slick chest on her breasts and his thighs between her legs until they came together in one shattering thrust.

"I love you," he whispered, tucking her against his chest. "I'm the luckiest guy in the world."

"I love you too," she murmured, her body still pulsing.

She felt his steady heartbeat and let out her breath. She would ask Blake about her father when he woke up and sort it all out. She gazed at the round white portholes and paneled ceiling and was certain Nathaniel was wrong. It was just like him, to spoil all her fun.

Chapter Six

Daisy glanced at her yellow halter top and long gauze skirt and flat gold sandals. It was early afternoon and the sun was high in the sky. She touched her hair that was knotted into a loose ponytail and fiddled with her coral necklace. She gazed at the women wearing crepe dresses and men in linen shirts and silk shorts and sighed.

She thought a picnic at Kamari Beach meant pita and fava beans and wooden bowls of sun-dried tomato salad. She imagined sitting under striped beach umbrellas and watching Jet Skiers glide across the Aegean.

But she'd arrived a few minutes late because the taxi got a flat tire and she had to make the last half of the trek by donkey and discovered Brigit and Blake had reserved the whole Nichteri Restaurant.

She drifted through rooms with green damask walls and white gauze curtains and chairs covered in striped silk cushions. Round tables were set with bouquets of purple anemones and favors wrapped in white lace and tied with a turquoise ribbon.

Glass sideboards held bowls of orzo pasta and spaghetti with feta cheese and green olives. There were plates of pork filet and beetroot. She gazed at the platters of baked mackerel and steamed mussels and wondered, if this was a simple picnic, what were they going to serve for the rehearsal dinner and wedding?

Then she noticed Brigit in a knee-length Escada dress and smiled. Of course they would have the picnic at the most elegant restaurant on Kamari Beach. Blake and Brigit were going to be Hollywood royalty and guests who interrupted their vacations in Capri or Amalfi wouldn't expect anything less.

Daisy filled her plate with pannacotta with apricots and Greek halva. She saw the mother of an old school friend and suddenly didn't want to hear how her daughter had won the World Equestrian Games in São Paulo.

She ran down to the beach and saw a familiar figure leaning against a thatched umbrella. He wore a striped shirt and had a silver camera slung over his shoulder.

Daisy slipped off her sandals and walked in the opposite direction. The last thing she wanted was to be alone with Robbie and blurt out something she shouldn't about Brigit and Nathaniel's marriage. She hurried along the black sand but suddenly the pebbles were too hot and Robbie approached her.

"The pebbles are made from volcanic formation," Robbie explained. "In the afternoon they get so hot, you have to wear shoes or you'll burn your feet."

"I noticed." Daisy grimaced. "Aren't you supposed to be taking photos of the picnic?"

"Nathaniel had to send an e-mail and said he'd meet me here,"

Robbie said. "I thought I'd wait until he arrives." He glanced at Daisy's halter top and frowned. "Is everyone going swimming?"

"I assumed a picnic meant stuffed grape leaves and hummus on the beach," Daisy replied, gazing at the blue ocean. "It really is gorgeous here, the water is so clear and the sand is like a black pearl necklace."

"Kamari Beach is one of the most popular beaches in Santorini," Robbie said. "In 1956 the whole island was almost destroyed by an earthquake. Tourists stayed away for years and they had to completely rebuild the economy. Now there are luxury hotels and fabulous restaurants and villas with infinity pools and glass patios."

"I've always been happiest at the beach." Daisy nodded. "My parents have a cottage in the Hamptons and Brigit and Nathaniel and I used to spend whole summers building sand castles. Brigit would run to the shore before breakfast because she didn't want Nathaniel to get a head start."

"Brigit and Nathaniel knew each other as children?" Robbie asked.

"We were next-door neighbors." Daisy nodded. "My mother always laughed and said he was going to make some woman happy because he arrived every morning with a basket of red apples or ripe peaches. He wanted to make sure he was invited to lunch; my mother made the best club sandwiches with bacon and avocado and swiss cheese."

"Nathaniel never said anything," Robbie mused. "I would have thought if they knew each other for so long . . ."

"That they would stay married? Brigit worked twelve-hour days at the law firm and couldn't trust Nathaniel to keep their goldfish alive." Daisy's cheeks flushed. "Blake sends yellow roses to Brigit's office and they travel all over the world. They can have an elegant dinner without arguing if Hawthorne was a better writer than Steinbeck and whether most French movies are borderline pornography. I've never seen Brigit so happy and if Nathaniel prints one word about their past I'll make sure he ends up on a kayak without a paddle."

"Of course the bride and groom are in love," Robbie said. "Why else would they be getting married?"

"The sun is too hot and I need a glass of lemonade and a grape-and-hazelnut salad." She walked toward the restaurant.

"I'm going to walk to the beach at Perissa when it gets cooler. Would you like to join me?" Robbie called. "At night Mesa Vouno is lit up and the Red Beach is spectacular."

"I don't think that's a good idea." Daisy turned around. "I'm the maid of honor and I've got a million things to do for the bride."

Brigit filled a ceramic plate with Santorini sausage and quinoa salad. She bit into a feta cheese saganaki and thought she'd never tasted anything more delicious. She glanced at Blake in his navy blazer and white silk shirt and couldn't remember being so happy.

She watched him chat with the British consul and remembered making love on the catamaran. When they were together she felt as if they could accomplish anything: rebuild whole villages and send doctors to places that had never heard of Tylenol or aspirin.

She thought again about what Nathaniel had said and knew her father and Blake would never keep anything from her. As soon as the guests finished the pecan pie with chocolate ice cream she would ask Blake what Nathaniel had meant.

She glanced across the room and saw a man wearing a light blue blazer and tan slacks. His blond hair was neatly combed and his cheeks gleamed with aftershave. Brigit realized it was Nathaniel and flushed. Even if Nathaniel wore the Barneys cashmere blazer she'd bought for his twenty-fourth birthday he didn't belong at a luncheon celebrating her upcoming wedding.

"Blake, it's a pleasure to meet you, Nathaniel Cabot." Nathaniel approached Blake. "I loved you in *The Silk Road*. I haven't seen an actor display so much angst since Liam Neeson in *Schindler's List*."

"Spielberg wanted me to buff up for the part but I said, 'Steven, no one is going to look like they spend every morning at Gold's Gym if they're trekking through the Himalayas eating packets of ramen.'" Blake juggled a plate of chickpeas in one hand and a crystal champagne flute in the other. "I lived on boiled rice and seaweed for a month before we started filming and lost twenty pounds.

"Your name sounds familiar," Blake continued. "Are you a friend of Brigit's?"

"Ex-husband," Nathaniel corrected. "But don't worry, Brigit was an exemplary wife. She made the most delicious tiramisu and never mixed the colors with the whites. Think of it like getting a dealer's car. It's practically brand new but with a few kinks worked out."

Blake put his champagne flute on the glass sideboard and ran his hands through his hair. "This is a very intimate gathering, perhaps you'd better leave."

"You invited me." Nathaniel handed Blake an ivory card engraved with gold letters. "I'm starving, I only had tzatziki yogurt and black coffee for breakfast. The smoked salmon risotto with fennel looks delicious."

"Where did you get this?" Blake waved the invitation.

"Winston sent me an itinerary of events." Nathaniel popped a stuffed mushroom into his mouth. "Has he ever showed you his signed first edition of Madonna's *Sex* book? He only shows it to his closest friends, but for two million dollars he should give you a look. Page fifty-nine is quite extraordinary."

"Nathaniel is the writer hired to write our wedding feature in *HELLO!*" Brigit took Blake's arm.

Blake crumpled the invitation and stuffed it into his pocket. "Winston never told me . . ."

"Think about all the time I'll save not having to learn Brigit's favorite foods or who was her first celebrity crush," Nathaniel cut in. "Can you believe she had a Justin Timberlake poster above her bed?

"I do want to congratulate you, it's rare two generous and intelligent people find each other and I'm sure you will be happy," Nathaniel finished, holding out his hand. "I read that you're from Ohio. I'm a big fan of the Cleveland Cavaliers. Cleveland must be quite a city to convince LeBron James to move from a twelve-million-dollar hacienda in Miami back to his hometown."

"The Cavaliers made the championships two years in a row and they haven't begun to reach their potential." Blake nodded. "But I can't get Leonardo to attend a game, he still roots for the Lakers even though Kobe is washed out.

"I have to say hello to the publisher of *Vanity Fair*." Blake looked up. "We're partnering in bringing literacy to children in the Dominican Republic."

"You've never watched a professional basketball game in your life," Brigit hissed to Nathaniel when Blake strode across the room.

"You said watching sports is like collecting *Star Wars* cards or leaving smelly socks in your gym locker. Guys shouldn't do it after they leave middle school."

"I watch television at the White Horse in Notting Hill." Nathaniel rolled an olive around his plate. "You'd be surprised how many things I miss about America: seeing the Edward Hopper exhibit at the Whitney and eating dark chocolate pralines at La Maison du Chocolat. I even miss our old Thursday nights at the Empire Hotel, even though the french fries were soggy and the guys wore skinny ties and blue jeans."

"That was years ago when everyone watched *Gossip Girl*." Brigit flushed.

"Thankfully you grew out of that phase quickly," Nathaniel mused. "Though you were more poised than any actress playing an Upper East Side schoolgirl."

"If you write one bad thing about Blake you'll be sorry you ever learned to type," Brigit said quietly.

"I told you I called a truce." Nathaniel gazed at Brigit. "I think you picked very well."

"You do?" Brigit asked.

"I watched the way Blake looks at you, he's obviously madly in love," Nathaniel continued. "And he's a gentleman. He refilled your champagne flute and never interrupted your conversation."

"Of course he's a gentleman," Brigit said stiffly. "And he's one of the most hardworking people I've ever met. When we return from our honeymoon he's traveling to East Angola to present an award to Doctors Without Borders."

"Do you remember graduation day at Dartmouth?" Nathaniel poured a glass of sparkling water. "The dry cleaner ruined your dress and you had to wear your mother's pink silk Escada. I found you crying under the rotunda because you said twenty-two-year-olds didn't wear silk Escada in the daytime; it was something your great aunt would do.

"I insisted no one would notice under your gown. You retorted you should be wearing something young and carefree: a paisley Alice + Olivia dress or a design by Stella McCartney.

"Now you're wearing Escada in the daytime and you look perfect." Nathaniel ran his fingers over the rim. "You're all grown up and exactly where you want to be."

"How did you know this is Escada?" Brigit murmured.

"I spent twenty-six years on the Upper East Side." Nathaniel grinned.

Brigit opened her mouth and suddenly saw Daisy cross the room. She wore a long, flowing skirt and gold bangles.

"I'm so glad to see you." Brigit looped her arm through hers. "I thought Molly's mother scared you away."

"It's your pre-wedding luncheon." Daisy smiled. "I wouldn't miss it."

"Nathaniel and Blake were just talking about how much they love sports," Brigit explained.

"I thought the only sport Nathaniel played was backgammon while doing shots of Absolut," Daisy said.

"I haven't touched vodka in two years and I play squash twice a week," Nathaniel replied. "One doesn't keep in shape at my age by eating his green beans and walking to the tube."

A man with dark curly hair stood at the entry and Nathaniel motioned for him to join them.

"Robbie, you remember Brigit and Daisy. Don't they look stunning? British girls have that creamy complexion but they always have that pinched look like their stockings are too tight."

"Daisy and I have met a few times around the island." Robbie smiled.

"Daisy always roamed around East Hampton as a child," Nathaniel said. "Sydney would send Brigit and me out on search parties because she'd go to White's Pharmacy for a packet of Mentos and not come back for hours."

"I like exploring." Daisy smoothed her hair. "Santorini is fascinating, I want to see the ancient villages of Pyrgos and Megalochori."

"Where is Sydney?" Nathaniel asked. "I brought her a box of Fortnum's treacle fudge. I remember how she loved British chocolates."

"She called and said they're running a little late." Brigit glanced at her watch. "You didn't have to bring her anything, you are not a guest."

"It's only polite to bring a hostess gift," Nathaniel insisted. "Sydney is one of my favorite people. Sydney and Francis used to invite me over for lobster ravioli when you worked endless hours at the law firm. Francis would open a Napa Valley cabernet and we'd discuss B.B. King and book banning in school libraries."

"Until you stopped going because you found lying on the sofa and watching *Breaking Bad* more interesting," Brigit murmured.

"I didn't think they'd enjoy my company, I didn't have anything to bring to the conversation."

"If you'll excuse me, I need to make sure we don't run out of Kessarias pasties." she turned to Robbie. "It's nice to see you, please help yourself to some pork filet and white asparagus."

Brigit stepped onto the balcony and took a deep breath. She didn't need to talk to the chef but she wasn't going to spend one of the loveliest luncheons discussing the months Nathaniel wore a flannel bathrobe and played Pac-Man.

She turned around and saw the sun glinting on white gauze curtains. The whole room was like a Seurat painting. The mosaic bar was lined with brightly colored bottles and silver candles flickered on the tables.

Blake caught her eye through the window and his face broke into a smile. He was charismatic and industrious and she was so lucky to be in love. She smoothed her Escada dress and thought Nathaniel was right. She was exactly where she wanted to be and he wasn't going to spoil it.

Chapter Seven

SYDNEY SAT AT THE DRESSING table and dusted her cheeks with powder. She rubbed her lips with Lancôme lipstick and glanced at her Chopard watch. It was almost noon and if Francis didn't return soon they'd be late for the picnic at Kamari Beach.

After she ate a breakfast of yogurt and thyme and berries she walked upstairs and ran a hot bath. She leaned against the white porcelain tub and inhaled the scent of lavender and vanilla. She heard footsteps and saw Francis standing in the doorway.

"What are you doing here?" she asked. "You said you had a conference call with Tokyo."

He hesitated and Sydney saw a strange look in his eye. For a moment she thought he was going to tell her why for the last eight months he'd seemed as if he was never in the same room even when they sipped their morning espressos or read the *New Yorker* in the study.

"I forgot my notes but suddenly I think it can wait," he said, unbuttoning his shirt and stripping off his shorts.

"You never ignore a business call." Sydney gasped as he slid in beside her.

"Don't worry, they'll call back," he whispered, rubbing her shoulders. "When was the last time I discovered my beautiful wife in the bathtub during the day?"

His hands moved down her back and she felt the warm water lap her breasts.

"In that case, I have a better idea," she suggested, a small moan escaping her throat. "It will be much more comfortable and we won't get marks on our backs."

She stepped onto the tile floor and wrapped herself in a white towel. She led him into the bedroom and drew him down on the canopied bed.

He entered her quickly and buried his mouth in her hair. He wrapped his arms around her and pressed his chest against her breasts. Her body opened and all the doubt was replaced by a pleasure so exquisite she'd forgotten it existed.

Now she picked up a mahogany brush and thought she'd better call Brigit and tell her they were running late. She thought of all the activities Brigit and Blake had planned: a private cruise to the Venetian Lighthouse and cocktails at sunset at Oia Castle. She got exhausted thinking about donkey rides and swimming in the Aegean.

But the weekend would be wonderful and their guests would never forget it. She remembered when Brigit had appeared at the town house a few days after Brigit and Blake had announced their engagement. This was the first time Sydney and Brigit were alone since Brigit returned from Crete.

"Darling, how lovely to see you. I thought between jet lag and the long hours at the law firm, you would spend the weekend in your apartment with a copy of *Martha Stewart Weddings*." Sydney stood at the marble island in the kitchen.

The kitchen was her favorite room in the Park Avenue town house. The walls were turquoise plaster and the floor was polished wood and the backsplash behind the stove was blue mosaic tiles. The decorator had hesitated when Sydney suggested putting a mirror above the walnut desk but Sydney laughed and said with three females in the family, someone was always fixing their hair or reapplying their lipstick.

"I've only been engaged for five days. I haven't begun to think about dresses or flowers," Brigit replied. "It was so sudden, I didn't expect Blake to propose."

"You look like you did before you gave the graduation speech at Spence." Sydney sipped her coffee. "You entered my dressing room and said you were supposed to talk about the future but you'd been at the same school your whole life and were terrified of what came next.

"I suggested you speak from your heart and you stood at the podium and said many students attended Spence because it guaranteed they got into Yale or Princeton but you were grateful for the friends and experiences you had along the way." Sydney paused. "You got a standing ovation and there wasn't a dry eye in the auditorium."

"When Nathaniel and I got married it felt inevitable. We didn't know what we were doing but we had to do it anyway." Brigit fiddled with her gold earrings. "Now I'm a grown woman and I don't want to make a mistake. Blake is handsome and caring but we've only known each other for six months."

"People think love and passion are the most important parts of marriage but they're wrong." Sydney buttered a slice of toast. "Passion can't survive dirty diapers and late-night feedings and even love is challenged when you discover you can't stand the way your spouse gargles in the shower. Marriage is like life; it has to move forward. As long as you're moving in the same direction, you'll be fine."

Sydney dusted crumbs from her slacks and remembered the day she felt she and Francis were moving in opposite directions. She pictured sitting in the paneled study with a cup of chamomile tea and an *Architectural Digest*. She remembered gasping and knowing something was terribly wrong.

Sydney had placed the cup on the porcelain plate and clutched her stomach. The dull ache that had started in the small of her back was now a jagged pain. She was only five months pregnant so it was too early for contractions and she hadn't been lifting any boxes or doing strenuous exercise.

She picked up the phone and put it down. Francis was in an all-day meeting and she couldn't disturb him just because being pregnant at forty-two meant she had more odd twinges.

She closed the magazine and flinched. When she was pregnant with Brigit and Daisy, every night she brought color swatches for the nursery or some new toy that was necessary for a newborn. But now she studied photos of nurseries in magazines and didn't dare suggest turning the upstairs den into a baby's room.

At night they sipped tomato juice and talked about parents' weekend at Dartmouth and Daisy's latest boyfriend and Francis's new client in London. She studied his salt-and-pepper hair and the lines on his forehead and knew he was uncertain about having another baby.

Her face turned pale and the pain dug into her back. She picked up her phone and called the doorman.

"Oscar, it's Sydney Palmer. Could you call a taxi? I think it's an emergency."

Sydney entered the living room and glanced at the marble bar. She would give anything for a gin and tonic but these days no one drank when they were pregnant except for a glass of champagne to celebrate news and an occasional red wine at dinner.

She was lucky Dr. Ogden had seen her right away. It was only after he performed the ultrasound and showed her the healthy fetus that her shoulders relaxed.

She heard the front door open and was glad she hadn't told Francis. Perhaps they could go to dinner at Four Seasons or the St. Regis. She pictured wide plates of quail breast and pink blush asparagus in hollandaise.

"You are home early." Sydney looked up. "I thought we could go out. I'm dying to sit at the King Cole Bar and nibble chicken croquettes and sip a virgin Bloody Mary."

"I ran into Robert playing squash at the club," Francis said. "He mentioned you visited his office."

"It was nothing." Sydney smoothed her hair. "Just normal back pain."

"He said you were certain you were losing the baby," Francis replied.

"You know how hysterical pregnant women can be," Sydney mused. "Remember when I was pregnant with Daisy and got stung by a bee? I was positive I did some terrible harm to the fetus."

"What if it had been something serious?" Francis asked. "I should have gone with you."

"I wasn't sure how you felt," Sydney murmured.

"What do you mean?" Francis walked to the bar and poured a glass of scotch.

"When I was pregnant with Brigit and Daisy you called from work every day to see if I craved Zabar's lemongrass chicken soup," Sydney began. "Now the only time we discuss the baby is to talk about whether you'll be at the economic summit in Davos on my due date.

"Brigit is at Dartmouth and Daisy is wrapped up in boys and you have conferences all over Europe," she finished. "I feel like everyone is moving forward and I'm starting at the beginning."

"We're starting at the beginning," Francis corrected.

"We can't go to Aspen after Christmas and we'll never give dinner parties because I'll always be listening to the baby monitor." She paused. "The worst part is I can't wait to spend my days running baths and folding baby blankets. I adore babies and I feel so selfish."

"Robert congratulated me on having a boy." Francis finished his scotch. He poured another and took a small sip. "He thought I already knew."

"You know I didn't want to find out the sex. But I was so relieved the baby was alright, I couldn't help looking at the screen." Sydney flushed. "I was going to tell you tonight at dinner."

"I'll finally get to use those Yankee tickets." Francis fiddled with his glass. "I'll teach him how to sail and maybe he'll go to Harvard and join the Delphic Club." He looked at Sydney and smiled. "I guess we all want to pass on a little of ourselves."

He reached into his suit pocket and handed her a blue Tiffany's box.

Sydney unwrapped the gold ribbon and snapped it open. She discovered a diamond-and-sapphire pendant and gasped.

"You've never looked more beautiful." He fastened it around her neck. "I'm going to get dressed and then we'll eat prime rib and roasted potatoes and warm chocolate cake for dessert."

Sydney watched Francis climb the marble staircase and let out her breath. Francis was happy about the baby; she'd worried for no reason.

She fiddled with the diamond pendant and wondered if he would be so thrilled if it wasn't a boy. She straightened her skirt and thought it didn't matter why he was excited. They were going to have a healthy baby and everything was going to be fine.

Sydney fastened diamond earrings in her ears and slipped on her sandals. Francis was probably in the villa's garden on a phone call to New York. She would tell him they had to leave now or they'd miss the luncheon altogether.

She spritzed her wrists with Estée Lauder perfume and gazed

at the towel draped over the chair and the cotton sheets bunched together on the bed. She remembered Francis stepping into the bath and running his hands over her breasts.

Maybe all they had needed was to go somewhere completely new. She dropped the towel in the hamper and hoped she was right. Something had to change or she couldn't bear it.

Chapter Eight

BRIGIT RAN DOWN the circular staircase into the living room. She had two hours before the private tour of Akrotiri and she was going to sit in the garden and read the paperback book she'd brought on the plane. Sometimes she wondered if they'd packed too many events into the weekend.

The picnic at Kamari Beach had been delightful but now they had the private tour of the ruins and this evening was the welcome dinner at Kasteli Castle. But then she thought about how they were on a fabulous Greek island with their closest friends. They wanted to show their guests the ancient villages and amazing views and spectacular sunsets.

She heard a male voice in the kitchen and walked to the doorway. Blake paced around the tile floor, clutching his phone. He wore the navy slacks he'd worn at the luncheon but his jacket was missing and his shirt was open to the third button.

"I didn't know you were here." Brigit sat at the round kitchen table. "You said you had to go back to your villa and send some e-mails."

"I was too upset about your ex-husband to worry about the movie." Blake kissed Brigit on the mouth. "I can't imagine how it feels to have Nathaniel at your wedding. If Winston had told me, I wouldn't have allowed it."

"Don't worry, I'm used to ignoring Nathaniel." Brigit tried to smile. "I was very upset when he appeared in Santorini, but it's not your fault Winston gave him the assignment. Think of all the good that will be done with the money *HELLO!* donates to charity."

"I called Winston and asked him to assign another reporter but it's impossible." Blake ran his hands through his hair. "Nathaniel signed a contract and we could never get another journalist to Santorini so quickly. Apparently getting Nathaniel was quite a coup, he's up for an award for a series in the *Guardian* about Britain's council projects."

"Is that so?" Brigit looked up. "He didn't mention it."

"I wish you had told me the minute he showed up at the villa, it's not something you should handle by yourself." Blake pulled out a wooden chair. "I once had an old girlfriend get a small part in a movie I was in. I spent three weeks trying to be courteous so we didn't get into a raging fight in the middle of the Australian outback."

"Between last night's dinner and today's luncheon, we haven't had time to talk about anything." Brigit smoothed her skirt and took a deep breath. "Nathaniel mentioned you and my father knew each other before the St. Regis gala. He ran into Francis in London and Francis said he'd found the perfect man for me."

Blake stood up and walked to the fridge. He took out a bottle of milk and poured a small glass.

"I met Francis at a fund-raiser at Warren Buffett's chalet in

Jackson Hole." Blake nodded. "We started talking about his recent trip to Ghana. It's not often you meet someone who gets on a plane and visits impoverished children in Africa. Most CEOs of charity foundations act as though third world countries are part of a movie that only exists on the screen.

"He told me his daughter was joining the foundation and I should meet her. He invited me to speak at the gala and I couldn't say no.

"I'd seen your photo in *Town & Country*," Blake continued. "You wore an ivory satin gown and your hair was held back with a diamond clip. You looked like a young Grace Kelly."

"You said we were seated next to each other by accident." Brigit felt something hard pressing on her chest. "You never told me you knew my father at all."

"I've had friends trying to marry me off for years," Blake began. "I know how awkward it can be to move grilled halibut around your plate and having nothing to say except the wine is smooth and the cold cucumber soup is delicious. I didn't want to put you in that position.

"But I knew before we finished the spring salad, you were special. The whole time I was at the podium I was afraid you would get bored and leave." Blake grinned. "My publicist was furious I forgot to thank the Whitneys but all I wanted was to return to my seat."

Brigit remembered the St. Regis ballroom with its crystal chandeliers and huge bouquets of pink and yellow roses. She pictured Blake's wavy dark hair and green eyes and white smile. She remembered catching his eye across the room and a tingle running down her spine.

"You should have told me." She twisted her hands. "You can't keep secrets in a relationship."

"I could have bumped into you on the subway or in line at Pinkberry and I would have fallen in love." Blake touched her cheek. "Does it really matter how we met? We're in Santorini and about to have the wedding of the year."

"Honesty is the most important thing," Brigit said quietly. "Without it you don't have anything at all."

"Do you remember the first weekend we went away, to the Ralph Lauren Polo Classic in Palm Beach?" Blake asked. "We were standing in the lobby of the Breakers hotel and a group of photographers approached us.

"I never understood how movie stars can hate photographers, it's like a pastry chef saying he doesn't like sugar." He finished the glass of milk. "But when they asked if you were my new girlfriend, I insisted we were just friends and they should photograph Johnny Depp and his new wife.

"If I told them you were the most beautiful woman I'd ever met and I couldn't concentrate on the match because all I wanted was to learn your favorite books and movies, they wouldn't leave us alone.

"When your father suggested I sit next to you at the gala, I jumped at the chance," he continued. "But I didn't want you to think I'd asked you out because he set us up. I never meant to mislead you, but I wanted to win you over by myself. Not because your father and my publicist thought we were a good match.

"Sometimes a little white lie is necessary," Blake finished, wrapping his arms around her waist. "We're on a spectacular Greek island with our closest friends. This afternoon we're taking a private tour of a two-thousand-year-old temple and tonight we'll eat grilled pork and stuffed eggplant on a marble balcony overlooking the Aegean." He stopped and kissed her softly on the mouth. "The first time I saw you in that silver Dior gown, I knew you were a princess. I'm the luckiest guy in the world."

Brigit kissed him back and tasted milk and chocolate. She inhaled the scent of his musk aftershave and thought Blake was right. It didn't matter how they'd met. What was important was they were together.

She thought about everything they had to look forward to: a three-week honeymoon in Aix-en-Provence and Paris. The new apartment on Madison Avenue and Blake's house in the Hollywood Hills. Visiting villages in New Guinea and being greeted by children with wide eyes and extended stomachs.

"I can't wait to get married," Brigit said, kissing him. "I'm just tired from the hot sun and listening to Mrs. Fitzpatrick say it was lovely to meet a bride who still wanted a church wedding with flowers and a buttercream wedding cake. Her daughter eloped in a sailboat off Nantucket and she is heartbroken." She walked to the fridge. "I'm going to pour a glass of grapefruit juice and lie on a chaise lounge in the garden. I love you and I'm having a wonderful time. Everything is perfect."

"I love you too, I wish I could join you." Blake glanced at his watch. "But if I don't send Ang my script notes, he'll replace me in the movie with Matthew McConaughey."

Brigit filled a glass with ice cubes and gathered a peach and a ripe nectarine. She heard footsteps and turned around and saw

Nathaniel leaning against the marble counter. He wore a white T-shirt and navy shorts and his blond hair was slicked back.

"What are you doing here?" Brigit asked. "The tour of Akrotiri isn't for two hours."

"Winston wanted a photo spread of the Palmers relaxing in their Greek villa." Nathaniel took a plum from the fruit bowl and rubbed it on his sleeve. "Robbie is changing camera batteries so I thought I'd come ahead and scout locations."

"My parents are shopping in Fira and Daisy hiked to the village of Firostefani." Brigit sipped the glass of grapefruit juice. "You'll have to come back later."

"It's not a big island, I can wait." Nathaniel perched on a wooden chair. "You really picked a gorgeous villa. Sun-filled rooms with high ceilings and tall french doors. I thought Blake would be here, making love to you in one of the upstairs bedrooms."

"It's none of your business, but he just left." Brigit flushed. "He said you're up for a journalism award; you didn't tell me."

"Being nominated for a prize for a thousand-word piece on council politics didn't seem worth mentioning when the *New Yorker* once wrote: 'Cabot might achieve the unholy trifecta of producing a commercially successful novel that is nominated for the Pulitzer Prize and makes a difference in social reform.'"

"That was after they published your short story, 'A God for the South,'" Brigit murmured.

"I'm sure the reporter wanted to swallow his words." Nathaniel shrugged. "I don't mind living on a journalist's salary. It reminds me of when we used to eat instant oatmeal and yogurt-covered raisins in your dorm room because it was too cold to walk to the cafeteria.

"Though I imagine it's more fun being a movie star and nibbling duck foie gras at black-tie dinners," he continued. "Did Blake mention who'd invited him to the St. Regis gala?"

"We discussed the whole thing," Brigit replied. "He didn't tell me my father invited him because he didn't want to put me in an awkward position. He wanted me to get to know the real Blake Crawford. He wanted me to accept his invitation to dinner and the theater because I enjoyed being with him, not because my father set me up with a movie star."

"That's noble of him." Nathaniel nodded. "Funny he didn't explain when he put that stunning Neil Lane diamond ring on your finger or before you planned your honeymoon."

"Sometimes things aren't black and white." Brigit fiddled with her glass.

"Do you remember when we had to declare our majors and you couldn't decide between applied math and comparative literature?" Nathaniel asked.

"We went to the screening of *To Kill a Mockingbird* at the Hopkins Center and you decided you wanted to be a lawyer. I groaned that every twenty-year-old college coed falls in love with Atticus Finch.

"You said it had nothing to do with Gregory Peck's smoldering eyes and dark hair. You wanted to be a lawyer because law was like math—it only dealt with the truth. But instead of solving logarithms in a textbook, you could help people."

"It's easy to be idealistic when you live in an ivory tower," Brigit retorted. "When you grow up, things become more complicated. Maybe if we hadn't been so honest, it would have been different."

"What do you mean?" Nathaniel raised his eyebrow.

Brigit pictured Nathaniel grumbling that if she didn't spend all her time dusting the coffee table and straightening the sofa she might enjoy herself. She remembered seeing Nathaniel reading *Look Homeward, Angel* and saying he would realize he had as much talent as Thomas Wolfe if he sat down and typed. She remembered him walking out the door and the empty pit in her stomach.

Brigit put the carton of grapefruit juice in the fridge and sighed. "We would have realized we weren't suited for each other much sooner."

"Daisy, there you are." Nathaniel looked up. "I thought you were sitting in the square, breaking the locals' hearts. Those young Greeks don't stand a chance with one of the Upper East Side's most desirable twentysomethings."

"I haven't had a serious boyfriend in two years." Daisy entered the kitchen. She wore a gauze skirt and leather sandals. "I'm hardly likely to catch the bridal bouquet."

"You have to extend your horizons," Nathaniel suggested. "Not all eligible men wear Brooks Brothers suits and spend every evening drinking Orange Peels at the Penrose."

"I don't have time to meet men." Daisy twisted her ponytail. "I'm trying to launch my clothing line. Unless you're Ralph Lauren's daughter or related to Tory Burch it's impossible to get noticed."

"Do you remember the summer you and Brigit made lemon crepes with honey and cottage cheese?" Nathaniel opened the fridge. "Everyone said they were delicious so we rode our bikes to

Martha Stewart's cottage and left a plate of crepes with the housekeeper.

"You were so sure she would feature them on her television show you made three new batches. She finally sent a note saying they looked scrumptious but she wasn't allowed to sample anything that didn't come through her production company." He ate a handful of chickpeas. "Sydney served them at her garden party and one of the guests offered to pay you to make them for her daughter's sweet sixteen party."

"But we decided it was too hot in the kitchen and we'd rather spend the day at the beach." Daisy grinned.

"Daisy, I'm sure your dress designs are going to be hugely successful. The Palmer sisters always accomplish what they set their minds to," Nathaniel mused. "Brigit is going to marry a movie star and jet around the world with matching Louis Vuitton luggage. Photographers will wait at Heathrow and JFK and her photo will be on the cover of *Vogue*."

"We're going to travel to India and Asia in blue jeans and sneakers." Brigit bristled. "If you'll excuse me, I'm going to sit in the garden."

"You can't leave now." Nathaniel glanced out the window. "I see Robbie and Sydney."

"Nathaniel!" Sydney entered the kitchen. She wore a crepe Nina Ricci dress and beige sandals. Her blond hair was tucked behind her ears and she wore diamond earrings. "What are you doing in Santorini and who is the young man lurking around the gate with a camera?" she demanded. "Your name wasn't on the guest list. This is Brigit's wedding and her ex-husband is the last person she wants anywhere near her."

"You don't look a day older than when I snuck under the fence at Summerhill when I was five." Nathaniel jumped up and kissed Sydney on the cheek. "Didn't Brigit tell you? *HELLO!* magazine is doing a cover story on the wedding and I'm the journalist."

"That's impossible." Sydney turned to Brigit. "Blake would never allow it."

"I do think your family has to get to know your fiancé better," Nathaniel murmured.

He turned to Sydney and smiled. "I can't tell you how wonderful it is to see you. London doesn't have any women as elegant as Sydney Palmer, though I've always admired Jackie Collins. She's an excellent writer and wears fabulous jewels."

"Blake sold the rights to the wedding for two million dollars," Brigit explained. "All the money will go to the Palmer Foundation to fund various charities."

"That is quite exciting; does your father know?" Sydney asked. "He stopped in Fira to buy cigarettes."

"If you'll excuse me, I need to help Robbie set up some shots." Nathaniel walked to the door.

Daisy walked upstairs to change and Sydney went to her bedroom to freshen her makeup. Brigit put the glass in the sink and tossed apricot pits in the garbage. She heard the wooden gate open and her shoulders relaxed. Blake had returned to say he was sorry. He should never have lied to her and it wouldn't happen again.

She glanced out the window and saw it was only the housekeeper. She gazed at the shimmering ocean and clusters of white houses and thought she was being silly. Blake had explained why he didn't tell her Francis had invited him to the gala.

She wouldn't let Nathaniel put doubts in her mind. She was

going to go upstairs and change into a red Theory dress and Prada sling backs. She was going to fasten sapphire earrings in her ears and rub her lips with red lipstick. Then she was going to pose for Robbie's photos because she was about to have the wedding of the year on a spectacular Greek island.

Chapter Nine

DAISY TIED HER PONYTAIL with a purple ribbon and adjusted her sunglasses. She gazed at the wide stretch of Aegean and white sailboats far below. She turned and saw the ancient buildings covered in lava and brilliant red and gold frescoes and thought maybe she was glad she'd come to Santorini after all.

She had imagined the tour of Akrotiri would be like the school field trips to the Frick or the Natural History Museum. You could never hear the tour guide and the most interesting part of the day was gossiping about boys on the subway.

But the guide explained that Akrotiri was part of the flourishing Minoan civilization. It was built high on a cliff with abundant fruits and vegetables. There were elegant villas and paved streets and a drainage system.

In 1450 B.C. a large earthquake was followed by a volcanic eruption and the town was demolished. Akrotiri lay under mounds of ash until it was discovered two hundred years ago.

But then one of Blake's friends said Daisy must see the Buddhist temples in Chiang Mai and a *Sports Illustrated* model insisted the underwater caves in Vietnam were spectacular. Suddenly the sun was too hot and Daisy couldn't breathe. She strode down a narrow path and perched on a stone outcrop.

"You're missing the tour of the House of Ladies, it has authentic furniture and pottery from 1600 B.C." Robbie approached her. He wore a white short-sleeved shirt and tan shorts and his silver camera was slung over his shoulder.

"I'm tired of explaining that the only places I've visited are Big Ben and the Eiffel Tower and the Vatican." Daisy sighed. "My parents loved showing us the European capitals but now everyone goes on extreme adventures to stand near water buffalos in Nairobi and swim with tiger sharks on the Great Barrier Reef.

"Brigit was always the one leaning against the railing at the top of the Empire State Building or demanding to ride the Eye in London," Daisy continued. "I still read the safety manual on airplanes and won't go anywhere I need a malaria shot because I'm terrified of needles." She stopped and gazed at the black outline of the caldera.

"The tour guide said the volcano on Santorini caused tsunamis in Crete that decimated the island. Citizens came down from the mountains to rescue survivors but every thirty minutes there was a new tidal wave." She looked at Robbie. "Some people are so brave; I would have raced in the other direction."

"You're very brave." Robbie picked a yellow tulip. "Most people stay in the same job even if the only thing they look forward to is the Friday rugby pool. It's easy to go to work in the morning if you know you have to write ten reports followed by a salad sandwich and a Coke for lunch."

"You fly to Istanbul and Bangkok to photograph bombings

and riots." Daisy fiddled with her gold earrings. "I try to decide on the length of a skirt hem."

"But I have a boss telling me what he wants," Robbie insisted. "All I have to do is point and click the camera."

"The only time I ever saw Brigit afraid was when Nathaniel walked out," Daisy mused. "They had their whole lives mapped out: buying a six-room apartment on the park and a ski cottage in Maine. Having two children before she was thirty-five and taking a year's sabbatical in France. When Nathaniel left, Brigit spent five days in bed before she put on her favorite Donna Karan suit and returned to the law firm."

Daisy realized what she'd said and her cheeks went pale. She jumped up and smoothed her skirt. "We should go, the bus is leaving for Fira."

"I thought I'd go swimming before dinner and wash off some of this three-thousand-year-old ash." Robbie grinned. "Would you like to join me?"

"I can't." Daisy shook her head. "I have to help Brigit with the place cards."

Robbie reached out and touched her arm.

"I've spent most of the last few years eating at McDonald's in airport terminals because I don't know whether there will be food and running water at my destination," Robbie began. "The last time I ate at a decent restaurant was five days after the earthquake in Nepal when we took a break and had pork dumplings and buckwheat noodles in a café in Kathmandu. Halfway through the chicken chow mein there was a large aftershock and we piled into the street. By the time we returned to our table, the chow mein was cold and the noodles had congealed." He stopped and looked at Daisy. "I might not be very good at it, but I'm asking you on a date."

Daisy opened her mouth and then closed it. She twisted her ponytail and fiddled with a gold bangle.

"We really have to go," she said finally. "I don't want to mess up the schedule."

"Will you think about it?" Robbie asked.

Daisy's face broke into a small smile. "Yes, I'll think about it."

Daisy sat in the back of the bus and gazed at donkeys lumbering down the steep path. She saw old women carrying baskets of figs and purple grapes. The blue Aegean glittered far below and she had a sudden desire to splash in the ocean.

She remembered what she'd said about Nathaniel walking out on Brigit and flushed. She should never have mentioned that to Robbie; what if he told Nathaniel and he wrote about it in the article?

Nathaniel leaving was the best thing that had happened to Brigit because she was marrying someone bright and caring and handsome. Blake and Brigit had an apartment on Madison Avenue and a home in the Hollywood Hills and friends who were movie stars and directors.

Daisy bit her lip. She was in Santorini to make sure Brigit had the wedding of her dreams and she wasn't helping by saying foolish things to the photographer.

If Robbie asked her out again she would say she couldn't concentrate on anything except the silver centerpieces and making sure Brigit's ivory crepe veil wasn't crumpled. After the wedding he could have her number and if he was ever in New York, they could drink vanilla lattes at Joe Coffee.

She looked out the window at white stone churches and beds of pink azaleas and let out her breath. Santorini really was lovely; coming to the wedding had been a good idea.

Sydney poured cream into the enamel cup and added a spoonful of honey. She never put sugar in coffee but Greek coffee was so dark, she had to make it sweeter. It was midafternoon and the square was full of tourists buying gold jewelry and cotton scarves and soft leather sandals.

After the tour of Akrotiri, Francis had suggested they relax at a café in Fira. They sipped glasses of Agiorgitiko wine and Sydney fiddled with her sunglasses. She gazed at Francis's salt-and-pepper hair and thought this was a good time to suggest they spend a few days in Mykonos before they returned to New York.

"I didn't realize I would enjoy the Greek islands so much," she began. "The fish is delicious and the scenery is breathtaking. I was thinking . . ."

"Oh, God, I was sure I turned this off," Francis interrupted, taking his phone out of his pocket. "For half an hour I wanted to sit across from my gorgeous wife and enjoy a local glass of wine and plate of olive tapas." He stood up and pushed back his chair. "But this time I have to take it. Do you mind if I step away for a few minutes?"

"Of course you do." Sydney tried to smile. "Don't worry, we have plenty of time."

But his call lasted for ages and finally he sent her a text saying he had another conference call in ten minutes and he would have to go back to the villa. She traded her glass of wine for a cup of coffee and pushed away the tapas.

Now Sydney fiddled with the cup and thought about Nathaniel. It had been such a surprise seeing him at the villa; she couldn't imagine how Brigit felt. Having your ex-husband report on your wedding wasn't the ideal for a romantic, carefree weekend.

But she pictured Brigit strolling through the ruins in a floral Lilly Pulitzer dress and white sandals and smiled. She was as relaxed as Jackie Kennedy patting elephants in India.

Sydney nibbled a bite of honey baklava and remembered when Brigit had twisted her ankle before a school tennis tournament. Brigit didn't tell anyone because she was afraid she would have to forfeit the match. She won two sets before the smile pasted on her face was replaced by a gasp of pain.

She never turned in a homework assignment late even when she had pneumonia and appeared at breakfast on the morning of her AP statistics exam with her hair perfectly brushed and her cheeks lightly powdered.

Sydney remembered the Thanksgiving after Brigit and Nathaniel got married. Brigit was assigned to a high-profile case and Nathaniel's book of short stories had just received a stinging review in the *New York Times*. She pictured Brigit standing in the galley kitchen of her Lexington Avenue apartment with her mascara smudged and her dress rumpled and felt her chest tighten.

"I didn't put the turkey in the oven in time, and now I've got eight people coming to dinner and nothing to feed them except stuffing and grilled asparagus." Brigit twisted her hands. "And I don't have any canned pumpkin so they'll have to eat berries and whipped cream for dessert." She stopped and her eyes filled with sudden tears. "I wanted our first Thanksgiving to be perfect. Instead it's going to be like the tea parties I served to my American Girl dolls but on our wedding china."

"Where's Nathaniel?" Sydney glanced at the normally pristine counter littered with jars of gravy and a bottle of cranberry sauce.

"I told him I didn't want help and he should go to the New York Public Library," Brigit admitted. "I didn't realize Alistair would insist I work fifty hours on the Chevron case the week of Thanksgiving. Zabar's was closed when I got off work, so I couldn't pick up my order."

"You should have asked Nathaniel to pick it up." Sydney rinsed cherry tomatoes.

"You always prepared the most delicious Thanksgiving feast with stuffed Cornish hens and roasted sweet potatoes and caramelized onions." Brigit fiddled with her diamond ring. "And Nathaniel's mother serves warm goat cheese salad and rack of lamb with herb confit on Christmas Eve. I don't want to be one of those working wives who show up thirty minutes before a dinner party to see if the caterer left the chicken in the oven.

"Anyway, Nathaniel knew how much I've been working. He could have offered to help." She opened the fridge and took out a head of butter lettuce. "He's too busy moaning about how the book reviews in the *New York Times* are written by frustrated English professors who think good writing is about grammar and syntax."

"Do you remember the summer you turned sixteen and tried out for the girls' cross country team? Nathaniel offered to come over and run with you at six a.m. before it got too hot." Sydney sliced shallots. "You said you were perfectly capable and didn't want him to get up that early. One morning you bumped into him on Town Pond in his jogging shorts and running shoes. He didn't want to admit he was trying out for cross country too in case he didn't make the team." She paused. "Sometimes we all need a little help, we just have to ask."

"When Nathaniel wrote his short stories I had to put a turkey sandwich and bag of chips under his nose or he would forget to eat," Brigit said. "I'd wake up in the morning and the whole apartment smelled of freshly ground coffee because he got up at five a.m. to start typing.

"Since the review came out, he hasn't written a word of his novel. He reheats the same cup of coffee all day because he's too tired to drink it," she continued. "Sometimes I come home and find him dunking a Nerf ball in the fruit bowl. If I ask him to wait in line at Zabar's the night before Thanksgiving, it means I know he isn't accomplishing anything."

"Marriage is about communication. If you need something you have to ask." Sydney gazed out the window at the soft snow covering the cars. "If you don't, you could lose everything."

Sydney glanced around Summerhill's living room with its thick plaster walls and floral Oriental rugs and brightly colored silk sofas. The marble fireplace was littered with Christmas cards and crystal vases were filled with white and red roses and a giant Christmas tree reached the ceiling. She inhaled the scent of pine leaves and cinnamon and thought how much she loved Christmas at Summerhill.

Many of their friends flew to Bermuda and stayed in pink villas and drank Tom Collinses on the beach. But Sydney insisted the family celebrate Christmas at Summerhill. She pictured the long mahogany table set with platters of baked ham and roast beef and grilled vegetables. She imagined the snow falling softly on the pond and hot apple cider simmering on the stove.

Brigit was coming from Dartmouth and Daisy was bringing a school friend and even Francis had promised to take a week off. He had suggested she wait and they drive to Summerhill together but Sydney wanted to get the house ready.

The best part really was seeing everyone's faces when they saw the wreath on the door and silver lights flickering on the porch and heard Bing Crosby singing, "White Christmas" on the stereo.

Now she gazed at boxes of Christmas ornaments and thought maybe she should have taken Francis's advice. Decorating the tree was exhausting when she was six months pregnant. She remembered when she was expecting Brigit and Daisy and loved digging in the garden and furnishing the nursery. This time her whole body ached and all she wanted to do was drink cups of sweet tea and read paperback books.

She thought of the new baby's room with its glossy white crib and blue bedding and her chest tightened. Some days she was so impatient for him to be born she felt like a child waiting for a birthday party.

But Francis worked endless hours and often didn't come home

for dinner. All fall he'd avoided joining her at Summerhill on the weekends and she arrived home on Sunday nights and found him hunched over his desk with a glass of scotch and a half-eaten sandwich.

She gazed at his blue eyes and salt-and-pepper hair and wanted to ask if he was really buried in work or if he didn't want to talk about the baby. But he would kiss her on the cheek and say he didn't know where the time went and go upstairs to bed.

She selected a clay ornament Daisy had made in kindergarten and thought she didn't have time to worry about Francis. She had to finish decorating the tree and make sure everyone had an equal number of presents. She remembered when Brigit was four and learned to count. Sydney came downstairs on Christmas morning and found Brigit sitting at the oak table in the kitchen, her eyes filled with tears.

"Darling, what's wrong?" Sydney asked. "It's five a.m., you should be asleep."

"I woke up because I was starving," Brigit said. "I was too excited last night to finish my ice cream."

"I hope you didn't come downstairs," Sydney replied. "Santa Claus wouldn't come if he thought you and Daisy were awake."

"Of course not, Santa Claus would never climb down the chimney if he thought someone was watching," Brigit insisted. She wore red-and-white-striped pajamas and red felt slippers.

"Then what's wrong? There are a dozen presents under the tree and the cookies and carrots are gone," Sydney said. "Santa and his reindeer must have been here."

"I counted the presents." Brigit's lips trembled. "Daisy got three more than I did. Santa Claus likes her more than me."

Sydney tried to hide the smile that flickered across her face and looked at Brigit. "That's impossible, maybe Santa left them on the roof. You go back to bed, I'll have your father check."

Sydney glanced at the brightly wrapped presents and smiled. Ever since then, she was careful to buy an equal number of gifts for Brigit and Daisy. Even now, when they were eighteen and sixteen she checked the American Express bill to make sure Brigit didn't receive an extra cashmere sweater or she hadn't bought Daisy an extra silver bracelet.

She entered Francis's study and flipped through the credit card statements. She liked to pick up Christmas presents all year long—a paisley skirt for Daisy at Bloomingdale's summer sale, boating shoes for Francis from the Ralph Lauren store in Southampton.

She scanned the list and frowned. There was a charge on Francis's card for a three-week African safari. She looked closer and saw the departure date was in March.

Why did Francis book a vacation when she would be home warming baby bottles and folding blankets? And if he planned on going alone, why hadn't he told her?

Maybe he'd realized everything he was missing: attending intimate dinner parties, traveling to exotic places, starting his foundation.

She entered the living room and took a glass ornament out of the box. She couldn't blame him, all their friends were buying apartments in Italy and the south of France. They'd stopped planning their lives around school plays and flew to Rome for the weekend.

She climbed onto the ladder and hung a glass ball. If Francis wanted to go to Africa she wouldn't stop him. She could handle all of it herself: applying to preschools and attending children's birthday parties and making orange cupcakes for Halloween. Francis could play squash at the club and go fishing in Montana or Wyoming.

She perched on the top rung and thought she would talk to him when he arrived tomorrow. He had worked hard for thirty years and now it was time to do what he liked.

She reached up to hang the last ornament and heard a male voice. It was only when she turned and saw Francis wearing a Burberry overcoat and clutching a blue Tiffany's box that she lost her balance.

"Sydney," Francis called, setting down his briefcase. "I couldn't wait to get to Summerhill so I drove out early. I bought you something special. Do you think the girls will mind if I give it to you before Christmas?"

The ladder tilted and she grabbed the tree. She tried to find the step but there was only air under her feet. She clutched her stomach and heard the clatter of metal. The hard wood smacked her ribs and then everything went black.

Sydney ate the last bite of baklava and shivered. Why was she thinking of that time now? It was so long ago. She pictured all the things she tried not to think about: what happened afterward, the empty spaces in the last ten years, the afternoon at Summerhill eight months ago when suddenly her whole word looked different.

She gazed at the whitewashed buildings and thought she was too busy planning the rehearsal dinner and preparing for the wedding to dwell on old memories. Brigit was perfectly happy; you could tell when she entered a room. Her skin glowed and her eyes sparkled like a young Lauren Bacall.

She pictured Nathaniel standing in the villa's kitchen and remembered all the summers at Summerhill. He always complimented Sydney's hair or her dress and said she had the best-stocked pantry in East Hampton.

Nathaniel and Brigit may be divorced but they had been best friends since kindergarten. Nathaniel wouldn't intentionally hurt Brigit; it wasn't in his nature.

She drained her coffee cup and wondered why she still felt uneasy. She suddenly remembered the young photographer with his silver camera and put her hand over her mouth. She grabbed her purse and hurried down the street.

Chapter Ten

BRIGIT GAZED AT the tall stone turrets and pink and yellow lights and waiters carrying silver trays. Round tables were covered with gold tablecloths and set with flickering candles. She saw men in silk tuxedos and women in shimmering evening gowns and thought it looked like a movie set.

Brigit had hesitated when Blake suggested holding the welcome dinner in the ruins of Kasteli Castle. The castle was in Pyrgos on the highest point of the island. Their guests had had a full day with the picnic at Kamari Beach and the private tour of Akrotiri. Would the women really want to hike up a gravel path in four-inch stilettos?

Now Brigit gazed at the sky turning orange and purple and the sea like a blue velvet cloak and was glad she'd agreed. They were so high up it was like being on a magic carpet in a Disney movie.

Brigit patted her hair and smoothed her turquoise Givenchy gown. She had felt silly fastening a sapphire pendant around her neck and diamond earrings in her ears. They were going to eat lamb skewers and fava beans in a six-hundred-year-old ruin. The dress code should be sweaters and slacks and comfortable shoes.

But now she inhaled the scent of French perfume and expensive cologne and was glad Blake had insisted on black tie. She felt like a princess and it was going to be an unforgettable night.

"I'd say you were the most beautiful bride in the world but your mother might get upset." Her father approached her.

He wore a black silk tuxedo and white tie. His salt-and-pepper hair was slicked back and he wore gold cuff links. "She really was the most beautiful bride I'd ever seen. I stood at the altar of St. John the Divine's and thought I was the luckiest guy in New York."

"She did pretty well herself." Brigit grinned. "A Harvard graduate with a family stockbroking firm on Wall Street."

"But your mother is Old New York," Francis mused. "Her great-great-grandmother was friends with Edith Wharton and Henry James. Edna used to roll up Fifth Avenue in a horse-drawn carriage."

"I can't believe how many people flew in from Manhattan." Brigit nibbled a tomato keftedes. "It looks like the roof deck of the Plaza. I'm glad you invited your old friends."

"I didn't invite anyone." Francis shook his head. "You and Blake took care of the guest list."

"Blake has never met the Forbeses or the Eisenhowers." Brigit frowned. "Why would he invite them to our wedding?"

"Excuse me, darling." Francis touched her hand. "I see the consul of Tunisia, I've been trying to obtain a visa for months."

Brigit accepted a glass of champagne from a passing waiter and saw a familiar figure wearing a black dinner jacket and white bow tie. She swallowed her champagne and ducked behind a stone outcrop.

"I'd say you were avoiding me but that's not the Brigit I know," Nathaniel said. "Do you remember you asked for Emily Post's book of etiquette for your sixteenth birthday? You said you were lucky to be born into a society where people use a different fork for every course and you didn't want to get it wrong."

"The rules of etiquette are like brushing your hair or your teeth," Brigit replied. "If everyone follows them, life is more civilized."

He gazed at the pastel-colored love seats littering the lawn and the lights twinkling in the olive trees and smiled. "You've done a wonderful job, it looks like a scene from *Sabrina*."

"It does look lovely," Brigit agreed. "And everyone seems to be enjoying themselves."

"I didn't know you invited so many New Yorkers, it's like standing at the bar of the Colony Club."

"Blake created the guest list." Brigit suddenly felt queasy, as if the champagne formed a pit in her stomach. "I only invited a few school friends and sorority sisters from Dartmouth."

"I didn't know Blake was friends with the deputy mayor and the CFO of Payne Whitney," Nathaniel mused. "I would have thought his pals were more like characters in an *Entourage* episode."

"Blake is one of the most successful movie stars in the world." Brigit's eyes flashed. "I'm sure he has friends who are artists and bankers and politicians. Now if you'll excuse me. I'm going to grab a plate of delicious lamb giovesti and eggplant moussaka."

"I did some background research on Blake for *HELLO!*" Nathaniel followed her across the courtyard. "He grew up in Sandusky, Ohio and his father owned an outdoor furniture store. He dropped out of Ohio State and hitched a ride to Los Angeles with two hairdressers driving a yellow Buick."

"He didn't drop out, he took a semester off to try his luck in Hollywood." Brigit turned around. "And he didn't hitchhike, he caught a Greyhound bus. He'd dreamed of being an actor ever since he saw Robert Redford in *All the President's Men* and didn't want to miss his chance."

"Whichever version you want to believe." Nathaniel filled a plate with round cherry tomatoes and stuffed grape leaves. He popped a tomato into his mouth and looked at Brigit.

"Do you ever worry you're making a mistake?" he asked. "You've only known each other six months and you come from different worlds. While you were studying advanced Latin and volunteering at the Frick, Blake was learning first-year Spanish and selling lawn chairs to Midwesterners in seersucker suits."

"I've never been more certain about anything." Brigit fiddled with her champagne flute. "Blake knows exactly what he wants and he's not afraid to work for it. Not all of his movies are sequels to *The Hunt for Red October*; he's starring in Scorsese's remake of *Metamorphosis*. And we're going to bring computers to villages in Laos and Kenya. In ten years children in Asia and Africa will be able to consider a career in programming."

"You always were sure of yourself." Nathaniel ate pork rolled in filo pastry. "Do you remember when you read your first Nancy Drew book and came racing down to the boathouse? You said you'd finished the best book in the world and I had to read it.

"I replied I didn't want to read about a teenage female detective. You pushed the book into my hand and said you weren't interested in Nancy Drew, it was her father, the attorney, who was inspiring."

"You spent the whole summer flipping through *Mad* magazines," Brigit murmured. "I was trying to improve your reading."

"I've only been certain of two things in my life." Nathaniel stuffed his hands in his pockets. "That all I wanted was to marry you. And that I had to leave."

"I see Henry Astor." Brigit's cheeks flushed and she turned away. "I have to go say hello."

Brigit gazed at the sideboard set with platters of fried zucchini and tomato balls. There were plates of Santorini cucumbers and sausage dressed in olive oil. She ate a bite of grilled octopus and her stomach clenched.

Why had Blake added to the guest list without consulting her? She saw him across the courtyard. He looked incredibly handsome in a black silk tuxedo and shiny Ferragamo loafers. Of course everyone wanted to come to their wedding; he was one of the most famous movie stars in the world.

She poured another glass of champagne and thought she wasn't going to let Nathaniel spoil her evening. He was like a splinter that got stuck under your skin.

"How can the most beautiful woman in Greece be standing by herself?" Blake crossed the courtyard.

"I was admiring the buffet," Brigit murmured. "The caterers did a wonderful job."

"Wait until you see the desserts." Blake grinned. "The chef prepared baklava and chocolate soufflé with vanilla ice cream."

"I thought we'd completed the guest list together," she began. "I haven't seen the Rothschilds since my kindergarten graduation and the only time I met the Winthrops was at a debutante ball at the Waldorf." She stopped and looked at Blake. "Why did you invite them to our wedding?"

"I gave my assistant a few more names last week." Blake shrugged.

"They're lovely people but we wanted the wedding to be intimate." Brigit hesitated. "Just our family and closest friends gathered on a magical Greek island."

"Do you really want to know why I invited them?" Blake asked.

He drained his glass and ran his hand through his hair. "The press have been saying for years that I'm a confirmed bachelor and I'll never make it to the altar. They print stories about me proposing to a model I met in line at Starbuck's. Every month *People* says I jilted some young actress or broke my high school girlfriend's heart.

"I never minded because it was part of the business. But then I met you and I couldn't believe my luck. You're bright and beautiful and I want the whole world to know we're getting married.

"We're going to spend a lot of time in New York and I didn't want the CEO of Sotheby's or the curator of the Guggenheim to think we're another Hollywood couple who shucks oysters with Calvin Klein in Southampton." He took her hand. "I thought if they were sitting in the church of Panagia Episkopi and saw us recite our vows they would know the truth. That I'm crazy in love with you and I'm going to spend the rest of my life making you happy."

Brigit gazed at the glass bar lined with brightly colored bottles and felt almost dizzy. She reached up and kissed Blake softly on the mouth.

He kissed her back and she tasted lemon and honey. She felt his hand on the small of her back and wanted to race down the narrow path to the villa. She wanted to unsnap her sapphire pendant and slip off her gown and lie on the canopy bed. She wanted to feel his chest on her breasts and the cotton sheets tangled between their legs.

"I can't wait to do it all again on our twentieth anniversary," Blake whispered. "It will be on a private island in the Bahamas. Our children will give a toast saying their dad may embarrass them at school dances and make the worst blueberry pancakes, but he did one thing right. He gave them the best mother they could imagine."

Brigit ate a bite of lemon cheesecake and gazed at the black sky and silver stars and dark ocean. The desserts were delicious and the aged cognac was superb and it had been a wonderful night.

But now her feet ached and she longed to go back to the villa and climb into bed. She glanced at guests nibbling honey baklava and thought it wouldn't be polite if she were the first person to climb into a taxi.

She strolled through the courtyard and saw a familiar figure leaning against a stone wall. Nathaniel's bow tie was loosened and he clutched a shot glass.

"I thought you stopped drinking." She gazed at the amber liquid. "And you should never drink whiskey. It always made you crazy."

"That was when I was nineteen and a freshman at Dartmouth." Nathaniel looked up. "A senior dared me to streak across the quad during Winter Carnival. I had to drink the whiskey for courage."

"You could have said no," Brigit murmured.

"I was trying to impress you," Nathaniel explained. "He was a coxswain on the crew team and spent the whole night showing you his muscles."

"You looked ridiculous running through the fountain naked."

"It was minus ten degrees," Nathaniel retorted. "Your fiancé offered me the whiskey. I couldn't say no."

"Blake offered you a drink?" Brigit raised her eyebrow.

"Winston said I had to get an in-depth interview with the groom." Nathaniel nodded. "Don't worry; we didn't talk about you. Did you know Blake was voted Best Hair in high school?" He took another sip. "He's seen all the Star Wars movies and he's a brown belt in karate."

"You're tipsy." Brigit frowned. "You should go back to your hotel."

"I can't leave in the middle of an interview." Nathaniel looked at Brigit. "You're the one who always said work comes before anything."

"Getting up every morning and going to the office is what most Americans do," Brigit said quietly.

"Perhaps you didn't realize you were marrying a writer when you accepted my grandmother's diamond ring," Nathaniel replied.

"Fitzgerald completed *The Beautiful and Damned* sitting poolside at a villa in Nice and Hemingway never left his fifth-floor Paris walk-up."

"You're the one who gave it up and became a reporter for trashy magazines." Brigit fiddled with her gold earrings.

"Sometimes you have to let things go even when they're important to you." Nathaniel drained his glass. "And *HELLO!* is not a trashy magazine. Winston has a vision. He wants to bring the reader closer to celebrities. Sort of like communism in pop culture."

"You could have done so much more," Brigit said quietly.

"And miss writing about the royal family?" Nathaniel waved his glass. "Last week I did a story on Princess Kate's nanny. The requirements of the job include knowledge of three languages and certification from a Swiss finishing school. Princess Charlotte is two years old but her nanny has to be able to teach her how to speak French and hold a teacup."

"It's never too early to learn manners." Brigit smoothed her skirt. "I have to say good-bye to our guests."

"There you are." Blake wrapped his arm around her waist. "I was just saying good-bye to Alec Baldwin, he gave us matching bicycles as a wedding present."

"I had a couple more questions." Nathaniel took a notebook out of his tuxedo pocket and turned to Blake. "You have backstage access to Victoria Secret's fashion shows and a standing invitation to *Sports Illustrated* swimsuit photo shoots. You're not going to lose your looks for another twenty years." He drained his shot glass. "What made you decide to settle down?"

Nathaniel gazed at Brigit's glossy blond hair and continued. "Brigit does have eyes like sapphires and the loveliest heart-shaped mole behind her ear but she's terribly bossy and she sleeps with her socks on."

Blake's cheeks turned pale and his eyes flickered. He dropped the bottle of whiskey and grabbed Nathaniel's collar.

"You're drunk and you should leave," he muttered, releasing Nathaniel and stuffing his hands in his pockets. "I'm going to get someone to clean up this glass."

Brigit watched Blake stride across the square. She glanced at Nathaniel and her lips trembled.

"How dare you start a fight at our welcome dinner," she stammered.

She walked to the stone arch and turned around. "And I haven't worn socks to bed in years. You would have known that if you ever came to the bedroom."

Chapter Eleven

Daisy rinsed a bowl of Santorini cherry tomatoes and placed them on the marble counter. She added a wedge of feta cheese and a white aubergine. She took a bowl of fava beans out of the fridge and a shiver ran done her spine.

She pictured Robbie at the welcome dinner in a black dinner jacket and white bow tie. His dark hair touched his collar and his cheeks glistened with aftershave. She remembered his brown eyes and warm smile and thought he looked so handsome she almost didn't recognize him.

She sliced a cucumber and remembered watching couples twirl across the dance floor. Her father wore a perfectly cut black tuxedo and her mother was stunning in a floor-length ivory gown. Daisy had suddenly wanted to put down her plate of stuffed dolmades and ask Robbie to dance.

But then she heard glass breaking and saw Blake cross the courtyard. She watched Brigit gasp and Nathaniel clutch a shot glass. The last thing Brigit needed was for Daisy to appear on the arm of Nathaniel's friend.

Now it was morning and Brigit was still in bed. Daisy was going to cook eggs and whole wheat toast. Whatever had happened last night, Brigit would feel better with a fluffy egg-white omelet and fruit salad.

There was a knock at the door and she turned around. Robbie juggled an olive baguette and a bag of nectarines. He wore a navy T-shirt and tan shorts and his dark hair was freshly washed.

"What are you doing here?" Daisy asked.

"I got up early and went to the market." Robbie placed the bag on the round kitchen table. "The vendor gave me an extra bag of nectarines and I thought you might like one."

"Thank you, I did the same thing." Daisy pointed to the basket of mushrooms and ripe plums. "We must have missed each other."

"That smells delicious." Robbie walked to the stove. "Would you like some help? I worked as a line cook in Provence one summer. My back ached and I got blisters on my hands but I learned how to use butter and garlic."

Daisy inhaled the scent of Robbie's musk shampoo and thought it would be lovely to slice fruit together in the sunny kitchen. It would be wonderful to drink Greek coffee and talk about his photographs and her designs.

But she pictured Brigit's flashing eyes when she'd arrived at the villa. Her cheeks were pale and she'd raced upstairs to her bedroom.

Brigit would never admit Nathaniel upset her. But how would she feel if she appeared in the kitchen and found Robbie standing at the sink?

"I can handle it." Daisy twisted her ponytail. "Shouldn't you be taking location shots of the view from Firostefani or the churches in Therasia?"

"Actually I came to ask you a question," Robbie said slowly. "After Santorini I'm going to explore Mykonos and Crete. I was wondering if you'd like to join me. We'd stay in hostels in separate rooms." He ran his hands through his hair. "We'll visit the ancient city of Knossos and swim at Paraga Beach."

"I thought you only traveled to places that suffered bombings and earthquakes," Daisy replied.

"A photographer has to have an eye for beauty." Robbie gazed at her large brown eyes and auburn hair. "And I've always wanted to photograph the windmills and the ruins at Delos."

Daisy collected a jar of Kalamata olives and her heart raced. She'd promised herself she wouldn't see Robbie until after the wedding, but what stopped her from traveling to Mykonos and Crete?

She tossed capers into the pan and pictured whitewashed buildings and blue lacquered doors. They would eat oysters in quaint cafés and take long walks along the beach. She pictured sharp cliffs and bright beds of flowers and drinking pineapple daiquiris at the Belvedere bar.

Then she thought of her living room littered with fabrics. Sketches covered the glass dining room table and floral skirts hung in the shower. She'd finally found something she loved to do and she couldn't put it off to trek around the Greek islands.

"It sounds wonderful but I can't." Daisy shook her head. "My former roommate works at Tory Burch and she promised to get me an interview."

"It can wait three weeks," Robbie persisted. "The palace of Knossos was the center of Minoan civilization and had private villas and shrines and banquet halls. It was discovered in 1896 and almost completely restored with gold columns and mosaic ceilings."

Daisy fiddled with her hoop earrings and pictured summer in New York with its sizzling sidewalks and stifling subways. Her apartment didn't have air-conditioning and she had to perch on the fire escape to catch the evening breeze.

But if she waited, all the important buyers would be on vacation in Majorca or Capri. By the time they returned, they would be busy with Fashion Week and the winter collections. If she didn't get her line in stores now, she would miss her chance.

"Maybe another time." She turned off the stove. "I have to go upstairs and wake Brigit. She'll be furious if she oversleeps and misses my omelet and your delicious nectarines."

Robbie walked to the door and turned around.

"Last month Winston sent me to Paris to photograph Lady Gaga," he began. "She stayed in a flat in the first arrondissement and paparazzi snapped photos of her buying croissants or going to the gym. Every day her security guards got rid of photographers and the next day there were more.

"One evening she arrived in sweats and sneakers and asked why I didn't take a picture. I said I was waiting until she wore a pretty dress and makeup. I wouldn't leave, but I couldn't take a photo she wasn't happy with.

"The next night she appeared in a gold lamé gown and diamond-encrusted stilettos. She was on her way to the Crillon and let me take the first photo.

"I'm persistent and I'm not going anywhere." His face broke into a smile. "Eventually you have to say yes."

Daisy filled a ceramic plate with eggs and berries. She poured a glass of orange juice and pictured Robbie's dark curly hair and wide shoulders. Was she really in a hurry to return to Manhattan or was she afraid something might happen? She couldn't fall in love now; that would ruin everything.

She wiped her hands on her skirt and climbed the circular staircase. There was no time to think about Robbie. She had to make sure Brigit ate a healthy breakfast so in two days when she walked down the aisle her cheeks glowed and her eyes sparkled.

Sydney hung her ivory Dior gown in the closet. She folded Francis's bow tie and tossed his silk shirt in the laundry. She gazed at her reflection in the mirror and thought it had been a wonderful night.

She and Francis had stood at the edge of Kasteli Castle and watched the sunset over the caldera. Pink and purple clouds had drifted over the ocean and Sydney had thought it really was possible to be happy. Francis had wrapped his arm around her waist and she wanted to stay there forever.

They nibbled vegetable croquettes and filo kasseropita. Francis poured glasses of Moët & Chandon and they danced to Ella Fitzgerald and Frank Sinatra. He whispered in her ear that they should get out of there and she felt like a young girl escaping from her senior prom.

They took a taxi to the villa and entered the tile foyer. Francis sat at the round kitchen table and Sydney prepared bowls of pistachio ice cream. She gazed at his clear green eyes and remembered when they were first married and could talk for hours.

Now she picked up her wooden hairbrush and remembered Brigit's face when she came home from the dinner.

Sydney was thirsty in the middle of the night and slipped down to the kitchen. She discovered Brigit clutching a glass of warm milk and honey. Her Givenchy gown was crumpled and her blond hair had escaped its diamond clip.

Brigit explained she'd had too much champagne and she'd be fine after a good night's sleep. She grabbed a pear and climbed the staircase to her bedroom.

Sydney thought Brigit was probably just nervous. In two days she would stand at the altar and her whole life would change. She had a new life in New York and Hollywood and friends who were movie stars. Paparazzi would snap her photo and she would always worry about her hair and makeup.

Sydney rubbed her lips with lipstick and thought she would go downstairs and make a pot of coffee. She and Brigit could talk about selecting roses for the bridal bouquet and making sure the baker made enough strawberry cupcakes. Sometimes the best way to face the future was to concentrate on today.

She remembered when Brigit arrived at Summerhill six months after Nathaniel left. She had deep circles under her eyes and her crepe suit and leather pumps were replaced by jeans and sneakers.

"Darling, I wasn't expecting you until this evening." Sydney walked down the stone steps. "I'm going into town to pick up a banana cream pie from Crumbs. I invited the Buchmans for dinner and we're having baked halibut and sautéed green beans."

"I took the day off," Brigit explained. "I had a sudden desire to jog around Town Pond and drink a cappuccino at Hampton Coffee Company."

"You could run in Central Park and Joe Coffee serves better espresso than anything you find in East Hampton." Sydney studied Brigit's pale cheeks. "You haven't taken a full day off since you sprained your ankle at the company tennis tournament and the CEO insisted you stay home and keep your foot up."

"When Nathaniel left I was so relieved it felt like a holiday," Brigit began. "I didn't have to worry if he liked the James Bond movie I chose on Netflix or remembered to order takeout from Up Thai on Seventy-Third Street. The living room was spotless and I kept fresh daisies on the dining room table.

"I love working at the law firm and it's heavenly to come home and slip on socks and curl up with a paperback book." She took a deep breath. "But sometimes I feel like I boarded the wrong train and I can't remember the name of the station. We always knew exactly where we were headed and now my whole future is different." Brigit bit her lip. "I'm not unhappy, but I'm afraid I will be tomorrow."

Sydney took Brigit's arm and led her into the kitchen. She poured two cups of fresh coffee and added cream and sugar. She handed one to Brigit and sat on a suede stool.

"When you and Daisy were babies I was so happy, even though each day was torture. I barely had time to shower and brush my hair before you needed a bottle or bath. But when you took your afternoon nap and I had two hours to myself it was like having a seaweed wrap at an Elizabeth Arden spa.

"But when Daisy started kindergarten and I had the whole afternoon to myself I didn't know what to do. Those free hours needed to be filled with volunteering at the Met or St. Luke's hospital. Instead of falling into bed at night, sometimes I couldn't sleep.

"Focus on the things you have to do: preparing a deposition or buying a gift for Daisy's birthday. Eventually something will change, that's the way life is." She clutched the porcelain cup and her cheeks were pale. "Then you might wish things had stayed the way they are now."

Sydney arranged lilies in the crystal vase and placed them on the glass coffee table in the town house's living room. She glanced at the high plaster ceilings and dark wood floors and plush Oriental carpets. She stood at the window and saw women in bright spring dresses and the lush green of Central Park and wondered what it felt like to be happy.

It was six months since she fell off the ladder and lost the baby. Dr. Ogden had explained it was a terrible accident: if the baby's lungs had been more developed or if something other than the hard metal ladder had broken her fall . . .

She knew she only had herself to blame. She'd noticed the trip to Africa on Francis's American Express statement and decided to hang the Christmas ornaments herself. If she'd known he had booked the safari before she was pregnant and forgot to cancel it, she would have waited until Francis came home to help.

She had been determined to prove that nothing would change because they were having a baby. It was stupid to climb that ladder and she wished she could do it all over again.

Every morning Sydney made Francis fresh coffee and poached eggs and fruit. She waited until he left and then she sat in her sitting room of the Park Avenue town house and reread *The Age of Innocence* and *Anna Karenina*.

She kept vases filled with lilacs and orchids and bought pumpkin soup and baked chicken at Zabar's. She never allowed herself more than one glass of wine at dinner and tried to make interesting conversation. Francis usually pulled out his briefcase after dessert and said he had to catch up on work in his study. She murmured she'd left her paperback book on the bedside table and climbed the stairs to their bedroom. Then she slipped under the beige satin bedspread and wondered how she could do it again tomorrow.

Brigit came home for spring break and they went shopping at Saks and Bloomingdale's. She listened to Brigit talk about her new relationship with Nathaniel and suddenly felt lighter. Then they walked along Fifth Avenue and saw a mother pushing a stroller. The baby had wispy blond hair and was wrapped in a soft blue blanket.

Tears streamed down Sydney's cheeks and she rushed into the store. It wasn't fair to let Brigit or Daisy or Francis see her grief, she had to be a good wife and mother.

Now it was June and they would spend the summer in Summerhill. She imagined making endless turkey sandwiches and jugs of lemonade in the sunny kitchen. Brigit and Daisy would drift in and out, gathering sunglasses and towels and suntan lotion.

How could she be around Brigit and Daisy for two months without them noticing her despair? How could she pile Swiss cheese on whole wheat bread knowing if it weren't for her stubbornness, a baby would be asleep in the nursery?

She would concentrate on the things she had to do: call White's pharmacy and order Daisy's acne prescription and Francis's cholesterol pills. Remind the housekeeper to keep the town house stocked with milk and bread for the nights Francis spent in the city.

The front door opened and Francis entered wearing a pinstriped suit and black tasseled shoes. His salt-and-pepper hair was smoothed back and he clutched a leather briefcase.

"You're home early." She looked up. "Would you like a gin and tonic?"

"I saw Harley Adams at the club." He set his briefcase on the sideboard. "His daughter got accepted to the Royal Ballet's summer program, and his wife thinks she's too young to be on the other side of the Atlantic. They're renting a flat in Belgravia for the summer."

"That's terrific, Sally is a wonderful dancer." Sydney filled a glass with gin. "Tell them we'll miss them on the Fourth of July."

"They weren't going to spend the summer in East Hampton." Francis loosened his tie. "Margot rented a house in Provence but they're not going to use it."

"Why don't they stay in Provence while Sally is in London?" Sydney handed him the glass.

"Harley wasn't very keen. There's no decent Internet and he's on a diet, so he can't eat crepes or soufflés. He convinced Margot she'd be happier shopping at Harrods and attending Wimbledon and Ascot." He sipped his drink and looked at Sydney. "He wondered if we would like it."

"A villa in Provence?"

"The house has stone floors and a pool and tennis court. The girls could practice their French and we could visit wineries and galleries."

"Brigit just started seeing Nathaniel and Daisy has a new boyfriend. They'd be miserable if we carted them off to France." Sydney twisted her hands. "You never spend more than four nights at Summerhill in a row and if the Internet is spotty you couldn't work."

"I thought it might be better . . ." Francis began.

"If we didn't go to Summerhill this summer?" Sydney asked. "Do you really think it will be different if we're cooped up in a villa in a foreign country?"

Sydney turned away so he couldn't see the tears in her eyes. She filled a glass with soda water and took a small sip.

"Why don't you go by yourself," Francis said suddenly. "Not for the whole summer, but for a couple of weeks. You could collect recipes and go for long walks."

"Leave Brigit and Daisy at Summerhill?" Sydney hesitated.

"Brigit is a college student, she's perfectly capable of grilling a burger. And I'd keep an eye on Daisy, she can't get into too much trouble without a car or license." He ran his hands through his hair. "I played squash with Robert the other night and he thought it might be good for you to go somewhere new."

"You spoke to my doctor about me?" Sydney started.

"I watch you fold laundry and do dishes as if you're completing a military exercise," Francis said softly. "Daisy would be fine without her school shirts perfectly pressed and I can grab a coffee and a bagel on the way to work." He touched her hand. "What we need is you."

Sydney bit her lip and whispered, "I'm not sure that's possible."

"You adore France," Francis urged. "Robert said a change of scenery is healthy."

Sydney pictured a gabled cottage in Provence. She imagined bicycling on gravel paths and nibbling croissants at outdoor cafés. She smoothed her skirt and turned to Francis.

"I think I'd like to go."

"That's wonderful!" Francis beamed. "I'll have my secretary book you a first-class ticket to Paris. Maybe you can spend a night at the Ritz on the way home and go shopping at Chanel."

"I have a million things to do." Sydney straightened a pile of magazines. "I have to make sure the freezer at Summerhill is stocked and the gardener knows when to pick the peaches."

"I'll go upstairs and change and then we can open a bottle of champagne." Francis paused and his voice was low. "Maybe when you come home, we can share a bedroom."

Sydney stood on the balcony and gazed at the whitewashed houses and sparkling blue Aegean. Why was she remembering all that now? It was so long ago.

Perhaps it because she was somewhere new and it was exciting to explore the quaint villages of Santorini. Or maybe it was because in the last eight months everything they'd accomplished in the last decade seemed to be slipping away.

She glanced down and saw a tall man open the gate. She realized it was Nathaniel's friend, Robbie, and frowned. She walked inside and thought maybe she was remembering it for a different reason altogether.

Chapter Twelve

BRIGIT SAT ON THE BALCONY of Café Classico and gazed at the silver cruise ships lining the harbor. It was midmorning and the ocean was a sheet of diamonds. Waiters carried enamel plates of mushroom omelets and sliced melon.

She sipped dark coffee and thought she should have known Nathaniel would humiliate Blake; he had been too pleasant. Then she pictured Blake lunging toward Nathaniel and shuddered. Journalists would always ask intimate questions; Blake couldn't threaten them because they commented on Brigit's blue eyes or slender neck.

She moved fava beans around on her plate and wished she and Blake had spent the night together. If only they had been able to talk about the wonderful parts of the evening: the spectacular location and elegant centerpieces and Blake's speech to all their friends.

But Blake had to return to his villa and make sure the grooms-men didn't play poker all night and miss today's cruise to the island of Therasia. She remembered him pulling her close in the taxi and whispering he'd see her in the morning and wanting to tuck herself against his chest.

She stabbed a pineapple wedge and saw a familiar figure leaning against the railing. He wore a short-sleeved shirt and navy shorts and leather sandals.

"There you are." Nathaniel approached her. "Daisy said you'd gone out. I searched every café in Fira."

"I'm having a quiet breakfast by myself." Brigit turned away. "Please leave me alone."

"You don't want to turn into one of those brides who only cares about herself." Nathaniel pulled out a chair. "Daisy made you an egg-white omelet and fruit salad. You left without telling her."

"She did?" Brigit asked. "I'll have to apologize, I needed some fresh air."

"It's a fantastic view." Nathaniel shielded his eyes from the sun. "If I didn't feel like I was trampled by a donkey, I would appreciate it."

"Of course you're hungover. I told you not to drink whiskey." Brigit's eyes flashed. "How dare you start a fight in front of our friends?"

"I'm really sorry, I didn't mean to cause trouble." Nathaniel fiddled with a sugar packet. "We may not be married, but I'll always want to protect you." He paused. "I didn't accept the assignment just for the money. I wanted to make sure Blake was good enough for you."

"When you walked out the apartment door and took off your wedding ring I stopped being your responsibility," Brigit retorted. "And how dare you question if Blake is good enough for me? He's one of the best people I've ever met."

"Blake might be a movie star, but you're Brigit Palmer," Nathaniel said. "You're like one of those priceless jewels they keep in a special room at Tiffany's.

"But then I read his article in *GQ* about poverty in Cuba and realized he's not just a prettier Sean Penn. He understands third world crises," he continued. "Most importantly he was ready to punch a guy to defend his fiancée's honor." He ran his hands through his hair. "I think you're making the right decision."

"You do?" Brigit looked up.

"You can't stay single, that would be like covering the Statue of Liberty in a shroud. Your name should be on a plaque at the New York Public Library and Carnegie Hall.

"You have so much to offer and it's impossible to accomplish it alone," Nathaniel finished. "I approve, you and Blake are going to be very happy."

"Of course we're going to be happy. I told you I was in love, he's everything I dreamed of." Brigit looked at Nathaniel and her cheeks flushed. "And I don't need your permission to get married. Blake and I worked for months planning the perfect wedding in Santorini. If you do anything to ruin it, I'll never forgive you."

"You have my word. From now on I'll do everything to make it the best weekend of your life." Nathaniel picked up the menu. "God, I'm starving. The best cure for a hangover is eggs and sausage and bacon."

Brigit blinked in the bright sun. She sprinkled pepper on her eggs and pushed the plate toward him. "You can share mine, I'm not really hungry."

Brigit turned onto Ypapantis Street and gazed at the jewelry stores with their lacquered front doors and brightly colored awnings. It was nicknamed "the gold street" and was one of the most famous shopping streets in Greece.

She remembered Nathaniel saying he'd searched every café in Fira for her and thought she should be happy. He had apologized and promised not to cause trouble. But there was still an uneasy pit in her stomach, as if she'd drank too much dark coffee.

She saw a couple strolling hand in hand and wished again Blake had spent the night at the villa. Then she adjusted her sunglasses and sighed. Of course he'd had to go back to his groomsmen, they had flown across the world to attend the wedding.

She stopped in front of a large gold window and thought Nathaniel was right, she was becoming one of those brides who only thought about herself. Daisy had dropped everything to come to Greece and she'd barely spent time with her. She would surprise her with a pair of aquamarine earrings or a lapis pendant.

She entered the store and saw a man leaning against a glass case. His dark hair was slicked back and he wore silk shorts.

"Blake, what are you doing here?" Brigit asked.

"This is a surprise." Blake flushed. He turned to the man behind the counter and smiled. "Yiorgos, this is my fiancée, Brigit Palmer. Now you understand why I was in such a hurry. Isn't she the most beautiful woman in Santorini?"

"It's a great pleasure." The man bowed. He wore a blue suit and thin black tie. "If you'll excuse me, I'll be right back."

"Why are you here? I thought you'd be having breakfast with your groomsmen." Brigit gazed at the black-and-white marble floor and gold-lacquered ceiling. Glass cases were scattered around the room and the walls were covered in blue damask.

"Poniros is one of the most famous jewelry stores in Greece," Blake explained. "Yiorgos made a bracelet to go with your turquoise Givenchy dress but the clasp didn't close, so I brought it here after the party." He rubbed his chin. "He promised he'd get it back first thing this morning."

"You came here last night?" Brigit gasped. "It was after midnight."

"I met Yiorgos's father, Dimitrus, years ago in Athens," Blake continued. "He made the most exquisite black diamond cuff links for my first Academy Awards. We've been friends ever since and Yiorgos is as talented as his father."

"You already gave me a sailboat," Brigit spluttered. "We're not giving each other any more gifts until the morning of the wedding."

"I commissioned Yiorgos to create a piece to commemorate every event." Blake stuffed his hands in his pockets. "It's such a magical weekend, I don't want to forget it."

"You didn't have to do that," Brigit insisted.

He handed her a gold box. "It's from Yiorgos's Thalassa collection, I hope you like it."

Brigit snapped it open and discovered a sparkling bracelet set with pink and blue diamonds. It had a platinum clasp with a yellow amethyst.

Brigit looked at Blake and her doubts faded away. He was always thinking about her and she was the luckiest girl in the world.

"You can wear it this afternoon for the cruise to Therasia."

Blake fastened it around her wrist. "We'll sneak into a stateroom and make love while everyone is gazing at the volcano."

"We can't leave our friends." Brigit giggled, suddenly feeling light and warm and happy.

Blake leaned forward and kissed her softly on the lips. She kissed him back and inhaled his scent of cologne and peppermint aftershave.

"We can do anything we want," he whispered. "It's our wedding."

Blake went to pick up crepes for his groomsmen and Brigit lingered in Poniros, picking out topaz earrings for Daisy and a gold bangle for her mother.

She slipped on her sunglasses and stepped onto the pavement. The sun was warm on her shoulders and she saw the whitewashed buildings and blue domed roofs.

She gazed at the pink and blue diamond bracelet and thought about the rehearsal dinner at Amoudi Bay and the wedding in the stone church above Megalochori. She remembered Blake's mouth on her lips and shivered. It was going to be a magical weekend and she'd never forget it.

Chapter Thirteen

DAISY TWISTED HER PONYTAIL and strolled along the cobblestone street in Firostefani. She gazed at boutique windows filled with bright cotton dresses and leather espadrilles and thought wouldn't it be wonderful to see her designs in a store window.

Daisy had gone up to Brigit's bedroom and discovered she'd left without having breakfast. She wasn't upset that Brigit slipped out without telling her. She must have so much on her mind: lengthening the flower girl's dress because she had a sudden growth spurt and making sure the three-year-old ring bearer could balance the ring on the satin pillow.

She remembered the events of the last couple of days and thought Brigit looked gorgeous in her pink Dior dress and turquoise Givenchy gown. Her hair was glossy and her skin was creamy like a fashion spread in a magazine.

She pictured Brigit and Blake twirling across the dance floor and felt a small twinge. She wasn't jealous Brigit was getting married. She didn't want to be responsible for taking her husband's shirts to the dry cleaners and making sure they used enough starch. She enjoyed eating Life cereal and an apple for dinner and watching reruns of *Sex and the City*.

But then she pictured the way Blake put his hand on the small of Brigit's back and thought they looked so in love. She remembered the summer after Nathaniel proposed and she'd helped Brigit pick out linens and place cards. The oak kitchen table at Summerhill was scattered with fabric swatches and card stock.

"How do you know what you want?" Daisy fingered an emerald silk tablecloth.

"I've always wanted to get married at Summerhill." Brigit scribbled on a notepad. "The reception will be outside so everything should be emerald and pink and yellow."

"I don't mean the wedding colors," Daisy corrected. "I mean how did you know you wanted to get married?"

Brigit put down her pencil and looked at Daisy. "You know when you discover a signed copy of *Catch-22* at the Strand and can't wait to give it to him," she mused. "Or you suddenly have an interest in the Spanish Civil War and reread *The Sun Also Rises*. You buy the crunchy peanut butter at Whole Foods even though you've always eaten the creamy. Suddenly the checkout line seems to take forever because it's almost eight p.m. and you haven't seen him since you snuck out of the office for a tuna sandwich at Carnegie Deli."

"But how do you know it will last forever?" Daisy demanded.

Brigit gazed at the silk fabric swatches and lace bags of

Jordan almonds. Her mouth trembled and she looked like a small child about to jump in a swimming pool. Then she smoothed her hair and turned the page of her notebook.

"You just do." She smiled. "You don't even have to think about it."

Daisy reached the cliff and gazed at white stone churches and beds of pink bougainvillea. Firostefani was a ten-minute hike from Fira and had one of the most spectacular views in Santorini. She watched tall sailboats glide over the Aegean and thought Brigit and Nathaniel knew each other their whole lives and still didn't stay together.

Daisy was perfectly happy with Edgar, her French bulldog and her one-bedroom apartment on East Seventy-Third Street. She liked being on a first-name basis with Steve, the barista at Starbucks and occasionally eating donut holes for breakfast.

But she suddenly pictured Robbie's dark hair and brown eyes. It was crazy, but she couldn't stop thinking about him. She remembered seeing him at the welcome dinner in a white dinner jacket and tan slacks and black shiny shoes. His cheeks glistened with aftershave and she'd longed to ask him to dance.

What if she accepted his offer to travel to Mykonos and Crete? Bergdorf's and Bloomingdale's would be there when she returned. She so enjoyed being with him, what if she never felt this way again?

Then she pictured the twinkling lights strung over the castle's courtyard and thought maybe she was swept up by the romance of the weekend. She would feel differently sharing a seat on a sweaty tour bus or sleeping on a lumpy mattress in a hostel in Crete.

She wished she could ask Brigit's advice but she still didn't know what had happened last night. Now wasn't the time to mention Robbie.

She suddenly saw a familiar figure stride up the steep path. He wore a short-sleeved shirt and navy shorts and leather sandals.

"Nathaniel," she exclaimed. "What are you doing here?"

"I had breakfast with Brigit and thought I'd walk off fried eggs and bacon." He sat beside her on the stone bench. "I don't know how old Greek men trudge up and down these hills. I hiked two miles and I'm ready for a nap."

"You had breakfast with Brigit?" Daisy asked.

"Technically we were both at Café Classico and I sat down at her table." Nathaniel shrugged. "But she did offer to share her feta cheese omelet and fruit salad. She's much more generous than when we were children. Do you remember she never gave me a bite of her Carvel chocolate drumstick?"

"That's because you ate the whole thing and left her with the nuts," Daisy replied.

"Nuts don't belong in ice cream." Nathaniel picked a purple daisy. "I actually apologized to Brigit, I told her I won't cause any more trouble."

"You did?" Daisy raised her eyebrow.

"You think I'm here to spoil the wedding, but landing this assignment is like getting an interview with Philip Roth. I couldn't pass it up," he replied.

"I don't quite believe you," Daisy said slowly. "You must be here for another reason."

"Marriage is hard enough without doing it twice. I just wanted to make sure she's happy." He stopped and looked at Daisy. "Even though at the end I would have happily switched places with a Benedictine monk, I don't regret a minute of it."

"If you're trying to win Brigit back—"

"I'd rather watch a *Star Trek* marathon than have Brigit color coordinate my dress shoes and socks," Nathaniel cut in. "I'm worried about you."

"Me?" Daisy gulped.

"Do you remember the summer you and Brigit were supposed to go to sleepaway camp and at the last minute she got allergies and canceled?" Nathaniel rubbed his chin. "I heard Sydney talking to my mother. Brigit refused to go because she was afraid she would get homesick.

"And remember when you started participating in gymkhanas and you suggested Brigit compete? She said she was too busy with tennis and cross country." Nathaniel looked up. "She was terrified of horses."

"Why are you telling me this now?" Daisy asked.

"Brigit isn't as perfect as you think she is," Nathaniel explained. "You've been so busy keeping up with her, you haven't stopped to enjoy being Daisy."

"I'm perfectly happy," Daisy insisted. "I have a lovely apartment and a wonderful dog, and I'm going to launch my clothing line in the top department stores in Manhattan."

"Then why don't you let yourself fall in love?" Nathaniel asked. "Robbie said he's falling in love with you but you want nothing to do with him."

"He said that?" Daisy felt something pressing on her chest.

"He asked you to go to Mykonos and Crete and you said no."
Nathaniel pointed to the silver sailboats and dark outline of the
caldera. "Are you really in a hurry to leave all this and go back to
Manhattan?"

"You had a book of short stories reviewed in the *New York
Times* and Brigit was an associate in a law firm and is about to
head an international foundation." Daisy fiddled with her hair ribbon. "The only thing I've accomplished in the last four years is
training Edgar not to jump on the sofa and knowing the best use
of cinnamon." She paused and gazed at the shimmering ocean. "If
I don't go back now, the buyers will be booked until Christmas.
How can I traipse around the Greek islands with a British photographer I just met, when I finally have a chance for a career?"

Nathaniel stood up and dusted his shorts. He stuffed his hands
in his pockets and looked at Daisy. "If you're in love, how can you
do anything else?"

Daisy entered a newsagent and gazed at the glossy postcards of Oia
and Perissa. Glass cases were filled with sweets and she thought
Robbie might like a Cadbury Flake bar.

She selected a packet of Life Savers and glanced at the clock
behind the counter. It was almost noon and she had to dress for
the cruise to Therasia.

She remembered what Nathaniel had said and felt a sharp jolt.
If Robbie was falling in love with her, she couldn't go back to New
York without seeing if they had a future.

She gathered a guidebook to Mykonos and a bag of English
toffees and handed them to the man at the cash register. She

walked into the street and gazed at the striped awnings and lacquered window boxes and thought she was glad she had come to Santorini.

Sydney sat on the terrace of Café Mezzo and ate stuffed tomato with rice and seafood pasta. She dipped bread into olive oil and gazed at the wide band of ocean. The sky was pale blue and the clouds were a thin line of white and she thought it would be the perfect place to bring Francis for a romantic dinner.

Brigit and Daisy had gone out so she'd decided to hike to Imerovigli. The village had whitewashed houses and plaster churches with stained-glass windows. Narrow streets were filled with galleries and views of the Skaros castle.

The waiter brought a platter of prawn moussaka and she had to laugh. Everything on the menu had looked delicious, but now she couldn't eat half of it. She wrapped spaghetti around her fork and thought of the last few days. Sex improved your appetite and made you feel twenty years younger.

Sydney sipped sparkling water and thought of the all nights she'd waited for Francis to come to bed but he'd fallen asleep on the sofa in his study. She remembered attending elegant dinner parties and feeling the delicious buzz between them. By the time they got home and Francis hung up his tuxedo and she slipped off her gown, it had fizzled like a warm glass of champagne.

She nibbled capers and remembered the early days of their marriage, when Francis would lead her upstairs while the ice was still fresh in their martinis. Sydney would unzip her dress and they would fall onto the king-sized bed. It was only later, when they were both flushed and sweaty that she realized she'd forgotten to put the chicken in the oven.

They would run down to the Second Avenue Deli and buy pastrami sandwiches and egg salad. They carted shopping bags through the art deco lobby and hoped no one was in the elevator. Finally they tossed their purchases onto the kitchen counter and raced back up to the bedroom.

Maybe all that was disturbing Brigit last night was she hadn't found time alone with Blake. Sydney would remind Brigit on the cruise to Therasia that their friends could entertain themselves. The only people they should think about were each other.

She scooped up risotto and remembered when Brigit burst into her dressing room a few weeks after she'd started dating Blake. Her blond hair was cut in a new bob and she wore pink lipstick.

"Darling, there you are." Sydney looked up from her dressing table. She was meeting Francis at Per Se and still needed to do her hair. "I called your phone all weekend. I wondered if you and Blake would like to join us for dinner tonight."

"I left it at my apartment," Brigit explained. "Blake surprised me with a trip to Palm Beach."

"Palm Beach?" Sydney raised her eyebrow. "Isn't that a little soon? You've only been dating a few weeks."

"We stayed at the Breakers and had Citroën lemonade and

grilled Atlantic salmon at the Beach Club," Brigit continued. "Blake insisted on buying me a Lilly Pulitzer dress and I got my hair done at Salon Margrit."

"Your hair is gorgeous, you belong on the cover of *Vogue*." Sydney nodded. "I just wonder if you're rushing things."

"Blake is handsome and intelligent and we care about the same things." Brigit fiddled with her gold earrings. "Why shouldn't I go away with him?"

"I'm glad you're enjoying each other's company." Sydney brushed her hair. "But when you're nibbling Godiva chocolates in a suite at the Breakers, you might make the wrong decisions."

"I'm hardly a virgin, I've been married," Brigit said hotly. "I don't think I'm going to ruin my reputation by sharing a hotel key."

"I'm not worried about your reputation." Sydney put down the hairbrush. "The closest my mother and I came to discussing sex was the length of my gloves at my cotillion. But sex can change the way you look at things," she continued. "Every couple is perfect when they only have to worry about whether to order room service or share a steak at the hotel bar."

"Every evening I can't wait for Blake to appear at the office," Brigit mused. "We can spend hours drinking a bottle of pinot noir and the maître d' at Gramercy Tavern had to kick us out before we finished our chocolate tiramisu."

"That's the thing about sex. You can walk for hours without getting tired and the simplest tomato soup tastes delicious." Sydney stopped and her eyes clouded over. "It makes you believe everything is wonderful. It's like sitting at an outdoor café in the glorious countryside, and not looking up at the clouds and realizing it's about to pour."

Sydney nibbled pain au chocolat and turned the pages of her paperback book. She had only been in Gordes for four days, but she couldn't get over the beauty of the French landscape. Everywhere she looked there were fields of lavender and vineyards and thick forests.

The village of Gordes had cobblestone streets and a small square built in the shadow of a twelfth-century castle. There was a florist and grocery store that sold French cheeses and Belgian chocolates.

The whole way to the airport, Sydney thought of all the reasons she couldn't go. Brigit would forget to put sliced apple in the Fourth of July potato salad; Daisy would never remember to wear a hat. But she'd gazed at Brigit's glossy blond hair and Daisy's auburn curls and knew she couldn't spoil their summer.

By the time she arrived in Paris, she knew she had made a terrible mistake. Without Francis's shirts to pick up and Daisy's lunches to prepare, she had nothing to do to help her forget. She pictured sitting in the cold kitchen of a French farmhouse and feeling completely alone.

But the minute the yellow taxi pulled up in front of the château, the hard clamp on her chest loosened. She put the key in the lock and entered a stone foyer with yellow plaster walls and a circular wooden staircase. The living room had floral sofas and french doors opening onto a garden.

Each morning she ate muesli on the porch and swam laps in the pool. She spent the afternoon bicycling or exploring Sénanque Abbey. She bought posies at the outdoor market and felt almost happy.

A raindrop fell on her book and she glanced at the sky. Gray clouds hung over the castle and rain splattered the sidewalk. She grabbed her purse and ran to her bicycle.

She cycled along the lane, hoping to reach the château before it began to pour. She heard a clap of thunder and the sky opened up and sheets of rain drenched the fields.

Sydney leaned her bicycle against the gate and hurried to the front door. She fumbled in her purse and shuddered. She had gone out the back door and left her key on the kitchen counter.

"You're very wet," a male voice said.

Sydney looked up and saw a man in his early twenties. His blond hair was stuck to his head and he wore a checkered shirt and denim shorts.

"I've done something very silly." Sydney bit her lip. "I locked myself out."

The man fiddled with the lock and frowned. He walked around the house and Sydney suddenly heard the sound of glass breaking.

"I had to break a window," he explained. "I'll climb inside and let you in."

"You shouldn't have done that," she said when he opened the door. "My landlord will be furious."

"You couldn't stay outside, you'd catch cold," he insisted. "Though it would be wise to carry an extra key."

"I'm sure the landlord left one somewhere." Sydney entered the kitchen. She glanced at the oak counters and large silver stove and mosaic backsplash. "I arrived a few days ago and haven't explored the whole house."

The man walked to the pantry and grabbed a set of keys from a gold ring. He handed them to Sydney and smiled.

"How did you know where they are?" Sydney gasped.

"I'm Oliver Ford, your landlord." He held out his hand and his green eyes sparkled. "I'm sopping wet and I'd give anything for a cup of tea."

"It doesn't usually rain in June, but sometimes the mistral noir blows in." Oliver sat on a chintz sofa in the living room. "Tourists think the mistrals are just strong winds with clear skies but the mistral noir can blanket the whole valley in rain."

"I hope they don't blow in this week." Sydney stirred honey into hot tea. "I love visiting the outdoor markets and strolling through the vineyards."

She had found a box of English breakfast tea and a packet of madeleines. She added a pitcher of cream and a jar of honey and placed them on a silver tray.

"I rather enjoy them." Oliver dunked a madeleine into his tea. "All the perfect weather and breathtaking views can get boring."

"You're very young to be a landlord," Sydney mused. She had run upstairs and slipped on a cashmere sweater and pleated skirt. Her hair fell smoothly to her shoulders and she wore beige pumps.

"My father actually owns the château. I stay at a hostel in Gordes and he pays me to look after it," he explained. "I'm sorry I wasn't here when you arrived. I usually bring a basket of fruit and cheeses."

"You shouldn't apologize, you saved me from catching pneumonia," Sydney replied. "Though I must pay for the window."

"Don't even think about it." He stopped and a smile lit up his face. "I spent five hours on a train from Paris with an apple and a bag of chips. Do you think I could get a sandwich?"

They moved to the kitchen and Sydney took out a loaf of bread and a wedge of goat cheese. She added sliced ham and green olives. She poured a glass of milk and placed it in front of Oliver.

"I marvel at how much young people eat." She perched on a stool. "I have two daughters, and when their friends come over I'm always running out of roast beef and tuna salad."

"My mother used to say I ate poached eggs faster than the chickens could lay them." Oliver wiped his mouth with a napkin. "My father is a food writer. He met my mother at a restaurant opening in Avignon and thought it would be romantic to live in a château in a vineyard." Oliver's eyes dimmed. "My mother died a few years ago and he hasn't written another book. He rents the house out during the summer and stays with friends in Paris."

"You must have had a wonderful childhood." Sydney nibbled a baguette.

"I collected truffles in the forest and helped my mother make quiche and bouillabaisse." Oliver nodded. "I thought I might be a chef but every kid who read James Beard thinks he's going to open a one-star Michelin restaurant.

"My roommate works at a restaurant near Gordes. He spends

ten hours a day in a sweaty kitchen and the closest he comes to creating interesting dishes is making sure the china isn't smudged." He scooped up aioli. "I took my father's advice and went to architecture school. People will always need a place to live and you can't throw up a building because you read a cookbook."

"My oldest daughter is at Dartmouth and she's terribly ambitious," Sydney mused. "I wouldn't be surprised if she became chief justice or ran for president."

"And what about you?" Oliver asked.

"Me?" Sydney started.

"What did you want to be?"

"I studied art history at Barnard and wanted to open a gallery in Manhattan." She sipped her tea. "But then I met my husband and we got married right after graduation."

"So you never did anything for yourself?" Oliver asked curiously.

Sydney pictured Summerhill with its wide lawn and view of the Long Island Sound. She remembered dinner parties filled with delicious foods and French wines and music filtering through the sound system. She pictured Francis in a black dinner jacket and white bow tie leading her onto the dance floor.

"I have a wonderful husband and two gorgeous daughters." She placed her cup on the porcelain saucer. "That's all I ever wanted."

Sydney loaded dishes into the sink and stood at the window. Oliver had left and she'd made herself another cup of tea.

What was she doing in Provence when Francis and Brigit and

Daisy were at Summerhill? She remembered the long winter in the Park Avenue town house and the constant ache deep inside her.

She folded the dish towel and thought about the last few days of swimming and bicycling and eating crepes. She hadn't really been happy; it was just an illusion. She watched the rain blanket the vineyards and let the tears run down her cheek.

Sydney sat in the château's living room and turned the pages of her paperback book. It was almost noon and rain pounded on the gabled roof.

She heard a knock at the door and stood up to answer it.

"I thought I may have eaten all your bread and cheese yesterday." Oliver stood outside. He wore a bright yellow raincoat and juggled two paper sacks. "You can't go to the market in this weather and my father would be furious if his tenant went hungry."

"You didn't have to come in the rain." Sydney glanced at the crusty baguette and wedge of Camembert and realized she hadn't eaten anything except a pear at breakfast.

"It was either that or sit in my room and study structural engineering." Oliver took off his raincoat and hung it in the foyer.

Sydney gazed at his blond hair and smooth cheeks and suddenly thought he looked like a young Robert Redford.

She grabbed the bag and blushed. "That's very kind, I can put them away."

"The kitchen at the hostel is crowded with Australians eating Marmite sandwiches and Tim Tams. I'd give anything to cook an omelet with avocado and sliced tomatoes." He gestured to the floral sofa. "Why don't you sit here and I'll make lunch."

"Why not?" She shrugged. "But please don't use red onions, they always make me cry."

They sat at the mahogany table in the dining room and ate mushroom omelets and berries with brown sugar. Sydney spread tapenade on toast and thought she'd never tasted anything so delicious.

"When my mother was alive, she was always in the kitchen crushing garlic and whipping cream." Oliver ate a roasted potato. "My father grumbled he gained five pounds when he walked in the door. But he ate everything she prepared and always asked for more."

"We have a cottage in East Hampton and the family spends the summer there." Sydney sipped creamy coffee. "My favorite moment of the day is before everyone comes down to breakfast. The kitchen is completely quiet and smells of butter and syrup.

"Then my husband wants to know who took the business section of the *New York Times* and the girls start arguing over who gets the first waffle and I complain I'll never get any peace." She smiled. "But I wouldn't want it any other way."

"Why did you come alone?"

"Excuse me?" Sydney asked.

"My mother wasn't happy unless the porch overflowed with friends nibbling canapés and my father kept the door of his study open so he wouldn't miss a funny story," Oliver said.

"Since my mother died, he has a steady flow of visitors. I have to wear earplugs because they stay up all night playing chess and drinking Pastis." He ate the last bite of eggs. "Why didn't your family join you?"

"East Hampton has quaint shops and it's only two hours from Manhattan," Sydney replied. "Brigit and Daisy adore the beach and my husband loves being close to the office."

Oliver put his napkin on his plate and leaned back in his chair. "If it's perfect, why did you come to Provence?"

Sydney gazed at the platter of sliced capers and soft cheeses. There was a plate of fig tarts and white nougat.

"I had a craving for ratatouille and nougat."

Sydney strolled through the outdoor market in Gordes and ate a juicy plum. She was going home in two days and wanted to buy a silk scarf for Brigit and hoop earrings for Daisy and a bottle of burgundy for Francis. She tossed the plum pit in her basket and thought she would miss the Tuesday market with its jars of preserves and slices of pork.

The mistral had lasted two days and then the Luberon valley was bathed in sunshine. She spent the week swimming and riding her bicycle. Sometimes she gazed at the fields of purple lavender and felt a pleasant warmth. Then she would remember losing the baby and double over in pain.

She selected a patterned scarf and handed it to the vendor. She heard a male voice behind her and turned around.

"There you are," Oliver said. "I haven't seen you in days, you're all brown."

"I did a lot of walking." Sydney smiled. She reached into her purse and took out a fifty-euro note. "I'm leaving in a couple of days and wanted to pay for the window."

"It's been fixed but you can do something for me," Oliver replied. "My roommate is the line cook at Hotel Les Bories, it has one Michelin star and overlooks the whole valley.

"It usually takes months to get a reservation but he got a table for tonight. If I go alone, I won't be able to sample all the dishes. Will you join me?"

"I'm sure you can find a more suitable dinner partner," Sydney mused.

"All my friends are in Nice or Paris for the summer," Oliver pleaded. "You can't leave Provence without eating at Les Bories. The guinea fowl with amandine mashed potatoes is delicious."

"I'll go if you let me pay for dinner." Sydney put the euro note back in her purse. "It's the least I can do for breaking the window."

"It's a deal." Oliver grinned. "I'll pick you up at seven p.m."

They sat at a table on the terrace overlooking the rolling hills. It was almost sunset and the sky was a muted orange. Sydney saw stone farmhouses and green hedges and felt like she was in a Monet painting.

The restaurant had wood floors and plaster walls and a long marble fireplace. The booths were covered in white damask and littered with purple silk pillows.

The waiter brought duck liver pâte and stuffed artichoke with yellow egg. There was lamb in honey and mustard and summer vegetables. Sydney sipped a Château Sainte Marguerite and thought it was the best rosé she'd ever tasted.

"This is delicious but you should have brought a date," Sydney said, after they'd ordered lemon meringue for dessert. "You must have a girlfriend."

"All the girls in Provence either get married when they're twenty or go to Paris and never return." Oliver shrugged.

"Why do you come back?" Sydney asked.

"When I started university, I couldn't wait for the train to leave Gordes," he replied. "My mother had just died and I never wanted to return. But I sat in my flat in Paris and knew being away wasn't the cure. It sounds silly but Provence is like a warm blanket."

"It doesn't sound silly at all." She ate a bite of meringue. "I know exactly what you mean."

They drank shots of Pastis and talked about Oliver's plans and Brigit and Daisy. Sydney opened her purse to pay the bill and realized she'd left her credit card at the château.

"Don't worry, I'll take care of it." Oliver reached into his pocket and took out two fifty-euro notes.

"I'm terribly embarrassed." Sydney flushed. "I'll pay you when we reach the château."

Oliver went to pay the check and a young man approached the table. He couldn't have been more than twenty and wore a white linen apron.

"I'm not usually allowed to leave the kitchen but I wanted to make sure you enjoyed your meal," he said.

"You must be Oliver's roommate." Sydney held out her hand. "It was delicious, I've never tasted such sweet vegetables."

"I'm glad you like it," he replied. He had dark hair and a British accent. "Oliver said he had a very important date and the ratatouille had to be perfect."

Sydney opened the door of the château and entered the kitchen. She took two fifty-euro notes out of a drawer and heard footsteps behind her.

Oliver crossed the stone floor and touched her shoulder. He pulled her toward him and kissed her on the mouth.

"What are you doing?" Sydney spluttered.

"You're like a photo in a fashion magazine but you're completely real," Oliver said. "I can't stop thinking about you and I've never wanted a woman more in my life."

"I'm married," Sydney exclaimed. "I've never cheated on my husband."

"But you forgot your credit card." Oliver ran his hands through his hair. "I thought you did it on purpose, you wanted me to come here."

"I had a wonderful time." Sydney smoothed her skirt. "But you have to go."

"Could I have a cup of coffee?" Oliver asked.

"I don't think that's a good idea." Sydney held out her hand. "Thank you for everything, I had a lovely stay in Provence."

Sydney waited until the front door closed and sat in the living room. She heard a door open and looked up. Oliver stood in the entry, clutching a bouquet of lilies.

"I forgot to give these to you." He entered the living room. "They would have wilted in my car."

She tried to stand but suddenly her legs were unsteady. Oliver sat beside her and took her face in his hands. He kissed her slowly, tasting of sugar and liqueur.

He took her hand and led her up the wooden staircase. She glanced at the canopied bed and was seized by a terrible panic. She started to say something but his hand reached under her dress. His fingers brush her thighs and she gasped.

"Come here," he moaned. "I've wanted this since the first moment I saw you."

She unzipped her dress and slipped off her sandals. He drew her onto the bed and she opened her legs and guided him inside her. She clung to his back and suddenly thought of everything she was giving up. Then her whole body opened and she thought she would die of pleasure.

Oliver clasped her shoulders and buried his mouth in her hair. He pushed faster until he came with a terrible force. He groaned and collapsed against her breasts.

"I knew you were beautiful," he whispered, pulling the sheet over them. "But I never thought anything could be so exquisite."

"Neither did I." Sydney felt his slick thigh on top of hers. "It was almost too good."

She waited until he fell asleep and then she pulled on a cotton robe and sat at the dressing table. She glanced at her pale cheeks and tousled hair and shuddered. Losing the baby had been an accident and Francis had already forgiven her.

She picked up a wooden hairbrush and brushed her hair. He could never forgive what she'd done now. If he found out she would lose everything.

Sydney pushed away the plate of risotto and gazed at the white-washed houses and deep blue Aegean. Of course she recognized

Robbie, he was Oliver's roommate! She pictured him standing at the table of the restaurant in Gordes and could barely swallow.

It had been ten years; she must look different. Her hair wasn't as blond and she had new wrinkles on her forehead. Why would he remember an American tourist he'd met for a few moments?

Then she thought of Oliver saying he couldn't stop thinking about her. Oliver was like an eager puppy; he wouldn't keep secrets from his roommate.

She'd spent the last two days around Robbie and he hadn't said a word. He probably didn't remember anything about it and she had nothing to worry about.

She put a twenty-euro note on the table and stood up. Her legs were shaky and she felt almost dizzy. What if Robbie thought he recognized her but couldn't quite place her? If he suddenly remembered, everything she loved would be taken away.

Chapter Fourteen

BRIGIT GLANCED AT THE YACHT'S mosaic tile floor and sleek wood paneling and thought it was like something in a James Bond movie. The plush sofas were creamy leather and the coffee tables were rich walnut and there was an ivory chess set.

She saw ceramic bowls filled with mangoes and a marble bar lined with brightly colored bottles and had never been more excited. They were going to cruise to the ancient island of Therasia and tour the volcano.

Brigit had selected a turquoise shift dress that matched Blake's pink and blue diamond bracelet. She remembered eating breakfast with Nathaniel at Café Classico and bumping into Blake at Poniros jewelry store and thought now she could relax. Nathaniel had promised he wouldn't cause any trouble and he would keep his word.

Her mother stepped on board wearing a patterned dress and gold sandals. Her cheeks were dusted with powder and she wore a sapphire necklace. Her father wore a pin-striped blazer and they both looked relaxed and happy.

Brigit saw Daisy in a yellow caftan and white espadrilles. She wore the topaz earrings Brigit had given her and her auburn hair was tied with a yellow silk ribbon. Her arms were golden brown and Brigit thought she'd never looked so beautiful.

"You are more stunning every day." Blake approached her. His dark hair was slicked back and he wore suede loafers. "I can't imagine how you'll look on our wedding day."

"I feel like a Greek shipping magnate." Brigit grinned. "I've been on yachts all my life, but I've never seen one with a casino."

"The yacht belongs to Johnny Depp, he usually docks it in Monaco. He couldn't be here for the wedding but he wanted us to have it for the cruise to Therasia."

"I'm going to have to send him a big thank you." Brigit giggled.

"Maybe we'll have to buy one." Blake kissed her on the mouth. "I like to see you so happy."

"I'm just excited everyone is here." Brigit sighed. "My parents look so in love and Daisy's cheeks are glowing. It's going to be a wonderful weekend."

"There are only fifty-two hours and thirty six minutes left." He glanced at his black TAG Heuer watch.

"Until what?" Brigit asked.

"Until the priest pronounces us husband and wife." Blake tucked Brigit's hair behind her ear. "People told me for so many years I'd never get married, I started to believe them. I see now I would have missed out on the most important thing in the world. Johnny can keep his yacht and Leonardo can have his plane, as long as I have you I don't need anything else."

"You can repeat that to me on our wedding night," she whispered. "Now we should welcome our guests."

Blake drifted off to chat with a producer and Brigit saw two men leaning against the railing. Nathaniel wore a short-sleeved shirt and held a plate of steamed mussels.

"This is quite a boat, it must have cost Blake a fortune." Nathaniel whistled. "The fixtures have more gold than Tutankhamun's tomb."

"It belongs to a friend of Blake's." Brigit turned to the other man and held out her hand. "I'm Brigit Palmer, I don't believe we've met."

"It's a small world, this is Peter Martin. We were in Miss Chadwick's fifth grade English together," Nathaniel explained. "We both had a crush on her and held a duel with our light sabers. It was a tie and we agreed to give her up and save our friendship." He smiled. "Now he's Blake's banker in California."

"My parents were horrified when I moved to Malibu," Peter said. "They think everything that is destroying society comes from California: Facebook and Twitter and iPhones."

"It's lovely to meet you," Brigit replied. "I don't know enough of Blake's friends."

"I'll leave you to get acquainted," Nathaniel cut in. "I want to make sure Robbie photographs the van Gogh in the salon."

"Have you known Blake long?" Brigit asked.

"I've been Blake's personal banker for two years. Most movie stars just hand you their paychecks and tell you to invest them. Blake is very opinionated. I was nervous when he insisted on investing two million dollars in the Palmer Foundation," Peter mused. "But with his face on the foundation and your father's connections I think it will be a success."

"What did you say?" Brigit asked.

"I'm sorry, I shouldn't talk business." Peter sighed. "I've always been terribly boring, I only know how to discuss statistics and capital returns."

"You're not boring at all," Brigit replied. "Why don't I find you a glass of Veuve Clicquot and a small plate of chickpea meze."

Brigit ran down the steps to the main cabin. She closed the door and tried to stop her heart hammering in her chest.

Blake and her father had never mentioned he'd invested in the foundation. And her father had plenty of money; he didn't need anyone else's funding.

She poured a glass of scotch from a crystal decanter and thought she would have to ask Blake. But then she remembered asking him whether he knew her father before the St. Regis gala and why he'd invited people he hardly knew to the wedding. He had an answer to everything and it all made sense.

She heard a male voice and turned around.

"Brigit Palmer drinking scotch in the middle of the afternoon." Nathaniel whistled. "If I didn't see it with my own eyes, I wouldn't believe it."

"What are you doing here?" Brigit demanded.

"Taking notes on the yacht," Nathaniel replied. "The wine cellar has a bottle of 1956 Château Lafite Rothschild, and there's a sushi station serving sashimi. Why would you eat raw fish flown in from Japan when you're sailing on the Aegean?"

"If you print one word that I was drinking alone in the cabin . . ." Brigit's eyes flashed.

"I told you I wouldn't cause trouble." Nathaniel paused. "Though I do remember you hiding my bottle of Absolut and saying it was for my own good."

"You kept it next to the breakfast cereal," Brigit retorted. "You know I never drink except for a martini or glass of wine at dinner."

"Then why are you starting now?" Nathaniel raised his eyebrow.

Brigit sank onto a cream leather sofa and her mouth trembled. "I can't tell you."

"Do you remember when we were nine and you saw your housekeeper break your mother's porcelain vase at Summerhill?" Nathaniel asked. "You didn't want to tattle on Inez but you felt terrible your mother had lost her favorite vase.

"I finally convinced you to tell her the whole story. You discovered Inez had already confessed and Sydney wasn't upset at all." He paused. "Nothing is as terrible as it seems if you tell the truth."

Brigit fiddled with her diamond bracelet and took a deep breath.

"Blake's banker said Blake invested two million dollars in the Palmer Foundation," she said. "Blake nor my father never mentioned it."

"Two million dollars." Nathaniel rubbed his chin. "Not bad for a boy from Ohio who couldn't afford airfare to California."

"It's not the amount of money, it's that he didn't tell me," Brigit explained. "He's excited about everything the foundation will accomplish but he never said he was already involved."

"He's certainly full of surprises," Nathaniel mused.

"You promised you wouldn't say anything bad about Blake," Brigit snapped. "He could spend his money on expensive artwork and flashy cars, instead he cares about issues and does something about it."

"Everyone's definition of success is different but that doesn't mean he's doing the right thing," Nathaniel said softly.

"What do you mean?" Brigit asked.

"Whatever reasons Blake has for hiding things, they are not as important as telling the truth."

Brigit pictured romantic dinners at Per Se and the Four Seasons. She thought of their plans to build libraries in Asia and Africa. She remembered Blake whispering he'd never thought he'd get married and now he knew it was the most important thing in the world.

"There has to be a reason." She jumped up. "I'll go ask him."

"I have a better idea," Nathaniel said suddenly. "Why don't you ask your father?"

Brigit gazed at her crystal shot glass and flinched. Her father had always been proud of her accomplishments. He'd rarely missed a tennis tournament and took her to lunch at the Metropolitan Club after her law school graduation.

But when Brigit was unsure about a boy or did badly on a test, she went to her mother for advice. She didn't want her father to think she and Blake weren't madly in love and everything was perfect.

"I guess I could." She hesitated.

"Your father is one of the most honorable men I know." Nathaniel ran his fingers over a marble bust. "I'm sure he can explain everything."

"I've been so busy planning the wedding, I've hardly seen my father since we arrived in Santorini." She bit her lip. "I'll talk to him right now."

Brigit put the shot glass in the sink and smoothed her skirt. She walked to the stairs and turned around.

"Did you forget something?" Nathaniel asked.

Brigit smiled. "I was just going to say thank you."

Brigit walked onto the deck and saw her mother leaning against the railing. She held a crystal champagne flute in one hand and a porcelain plate in the other.

"Darling, you've outdone yourself," Sydney exclaimed. "The mulberry treats are delightful and the eggplant moussaka is delicious."

"I'm glad you're enjoying yourself." Brigit stood beside her. "Have you seen Dad? I wanted to ask him a question."

"He had to send an urgent e-mail." Sydney sighed. "Apparently the yacht has a communication room with computers and a dozen phone lines."

"Oh, I see," Brigit murmured.

"Was it important?" Sydney asked.

Brigit gazed at the steep cliffs and beds of pink azaleas. She saw blue domed roofs and white stone churches. In two days she was getting married on a spectacular Greek island and it was going to be the happiest day of her life.

"It can wait." She turned to her mother and smiled. "You're right, everything smells heavenly. I think I'll get a plate of Santorini cucumbers and lamb skewers."

Daisy glanced around the yacht at women wearing emerald and ruby bracelets and sapphire necklaces and felt like she was in an ad for Van Cleef & Arpels. She had never seen so many diamond teardrop earrings and amethyst pendants and lapis rings.

She touched her new topaz earrings and thought when she'd boarded the yacht she'd felt so confident. She was going to tell Robbie she'd love to visit Mykonos and Crete. But then she saw women wearing silk tunics and jeweled sandals and wondered if Nathaniel was wrong. There were so many beautiful women in Santorini, why would Robbie be in love with her?

She sipped a glass of champagne and thought she didn't want to talk about skiing in Gstaad or camel races in Dubai. She wished she were sitting in her living room with Edgar and the latest Jane Green novel.

"There you are." Robbie approached her. "I've been busy taking pictures, I couldn't find you."

"There are so many gorgeous women to photograph." Daisy sighed, gazing at two women wearing metallic bathing suits. "I always forget Blake's friends all belong on the cover of *Vogue*."

"I did see a model wearing a see-through jumpsuit and five-inch stilettos." Robbie grinned. "I don't know how she'll ride a mule in Therasia."

"I thought we were just going to circle the island and nibble feta cheese and Kalamata olives," Daisy said.

"Therasia is a fascinating spot." Robbie leaned against the railing. "According to Greek mythology, King Thera gave it to his daughter, Therasia as a birthday present. In 1866 they used soil from Therasia to build the Suez Canal and unearthed pottery and a human skeleton. That led them to excavate on Santorini and discover the ruins of Akrotiri and Thera."

"I can't wait to get off the yacht," Daisy said miserably. "I'm afraid someone will ask whether I bid on Elizabeth Taylor's pink diamond ring at Sotheby's."

"They're not all bad, a lot of these people donate money to charity." Robbie laughed. "Your father started his own foundation."

"He doesn't pick up a Porsche in Germany or keep his passport in his suit pocket," Daisy replied. "I heard one woman say she has a home on each continent. She must spend more time on airplanes than in her own bedroom."

"My sister and her husband have a flat in Notting Hill and a villa in Portugal and an apartment in Paris." Robbie nodded. "I asked why she needed so many houses and she retorted I was going to inherit the family estate. I didn't have to worry about my future."

"Nathaniel mentioned you grew up in the English countryside." Daisy fiddled with her hair ribbon.

"Grayhaven has forty rooms and a moat. We used to spend rainy afternoons trying on armor in the throne room." Robbie grinned. "The nanny would chase us out and say we couldn't use priceless artifacts in our production of *Ivanhoe*."

"It sounds like our childhood." Daisy giggled. "Brigit and I put on my mother's floaty dresses and pretended we were characters in *The Great Gatsby*."

"We're almost at Therasia." Robbie pointed to the dark volcano. "Maybe we could explore the town of Korfos together. There are some wonderful swimming spots and the black sand beach at Riva is spectacular."

Daisy was about to answer when Nathaniel waved for Robbie to join him. Robbie strode across the yacht and Daisy's shoulders relaxed. As soon as they arrived at Therasia she would tell him she would love to go to Mykonos and Crete. He was handsome and charming and when they were together the sun seemed brighter.

She gazed at platters of grilled squid and fried zucchini and realized she was starving. She picked up a plate and stood next to a woman wearing a chiffon dress and silver sandals. Her blond hair was knotted in a low chignon and she wore diamond earrings.

"I see you know Robbie," the woman said. She had lavender eyes and a soft British accent. "It's such a small world, I didn't know he was the photographer."

"I'm Daisy Palmer, the bride's sister," Daisy replied. "Are you a friend of Blake's?"

"I was the ingénue in his first movie." She laughed. "I thought acting would be fun. But you spend all your time sitting in a trailer and having your cheeks plastered with makeup. I gave it up and joined my mother's design firm in London."

"How do you know Robbie?" Daisy asked.

"We grew up riding ponies and playing badminton," she replied, eating a plump fig. "Now he's becoming a young Richard Avedon."

"He's very talented." Daisy nodded. "I can't wait to see photos of the wedding."

"I haven't seen him in years, I'm glad we ran into each other," she continued. "After the wedding we're going to Mykonos and Crete."

"What did you say?" Daisy asked.

"He suggested it this morning and I said of course I'd go." She gazed at sleek motorboats and the clear blue water. "Why would I trade sailing on the Aegean and watching the Greek sunset for London in July?"

Daisy excused herself and ran across the deck. She sunk into a leather love seat and her cheeks flushed. Robbie wasn't in love with her; he just wanted a travel partner to share calamari and the price of a taxi.

She caught sight of Brigit standing at the bar. Her hair was pinned in a loose chignon and she wore pink lipstick. Of course Blake wanted to marry her. Her eyes sparkled and her skin was creamy and she was radiant.

Daisy pictured the sketchbooks piled in her galley kitchen. Why had she considered going to Mykonos and Crete when she was excited about her designs? She was going to be the next Stella McCartney or Tory Burch.

She sipped her champagne and thought about how she was in Santorini to make sure Brigit had a wonderful wedding. As soon as it was over she would go home and schedule an appointment with the buyer at Bergdorf's. Everyone knew too much sun and salt water was terrible for the skin.

Sydney sat at an outdoor café in Korfos and gazed at the pebble beach and curved inlet. The yacht had docked at Therasia and all the guests rode mules to the town of Manolas. But Francis was still in the communications room and Sydney wasn't going to climb on a donkey and be led up a sheer cliff without him.

She sipped a glass of lemonade and felt like she was unraveling. She was terrified Robbie might recognize her and Francis would discover her indiscretion.

She fiddled with her sapphire necklace and thought she could tell Francis the truth. She had been out of her mind with grief and guilt over losing the baby; she hadn't been herself and was terribly sorry. She fleetingly thought of the afternoon at Summerhill eight months ago when she'd arrived unexpectedly and saw his Audi in the driveway and wondered if really there was a point.

But even if she wanted to tell Francis, she couldn't approach him now. They were in Santorini to celebrate Brigit's wedding. It wasn't the time to reveal long hidden secrets like a character on a daytime soap opera.

She could confess to Robbie and beg him to keep it to himself. It was so long ago and she didn't want to hurt Francis or Brigit or Daisy. But what if he told Nathaniel and it ended up in the pages of *HELLO!*?

She wished it were evening so she could sip a stiff Campari. She pictured watching the orange sun slip behind the caldera and thought she should be savoring every moment of being on a Greek island with the people she loved most.

These days they were all together so seldom: Summerhill for the Fourth of July and Labor Day, a long weekend in Bermuda in February. Francis and Brigit were always working and Daisy had difficult hours and they never seemed to be in the same place.

She suddenly pictured Daisy clutching her champagne flute and Brigit saying she needed to ask Francis a question and frowned. They both seemed tense; as if there was something they weren't telling her.

Relationships were so difficult. How could she protect her daughters from getting hurt? Daisy was beautiful and talented but she questioned her own decisions as if she needed someone else's approval.

Brigit usually moved like an actress in a 1950's movie who

knew she could have anything she wanted with a tilt of the head. The last couple of days she'd seemed as if she was trying to solve a difficult algebra problem.

Maybe she should tell Brigit her marriage didn't have to consume her; she still had her career and family and friends. But was that really possible? Of course you had to put your husband first, that was the point of the whole exercise.

She gazed at wooden fishing boats and thought even when you tried to do the right thing, you often failed. You buy your husband's favorite macaroons at Bouchon only to discover he's given up sugar, or make reservations at the St. Regis and learn he spent the afternoon entertaining clients and craves a quiet evening at home.

It was a wonder more people didn't get divorced. You can be so confident you know everything about your spouse when you don't know anything at all.

She remembered when Brigit appeared at the Park Avenue town house the spring before Nathaniel walked out. She'd worn an Ella Moss dress and her hair was held back with a gold clip.

"Darling, it's lovely to see you." Sydney stood at the marble kitchen counter. She and Francis were having a dinner party and she was making coq au vin and peach cobbler for dessert. "I thought you were buried in depositions and you and Nathaniel couldn't make it."

"We can't come to dinner." Brigit perched on a suede stool. "I left work early and made reservations at the Pierre."

"Isn't that a little pricey on an associate's salary?" Sydney asked.

"I have big news for Nathaniel and wanted to go somewhere special," Brigit explained.

"You're not . . ." Sydney glanced at Brigit's flat stomach.

"No, but that's part of it." She took a deep breath. "I've been offered a position at another firm. They mostly do pro bono work so the pay will be a lot less but I won't work eighty hours a week. The head is a woman with three children and she believes in putting family first. I could leave work at five p.m. and eventually have Fridays off."

"You're only twenty-six and you're on the partner track at your firm." Sydney hesitated. "You might not want a baby for years, it seems a lot to give up."

"If I stay at Bingham and Stoll I'll always work impossible hours," Brigit continued. "The senior partners still have dinner served in the board room and usually appear on Saturday mornings with a bag of croissants and the *Wall Street Journal*. We'll never take a proper vacation and when we do have a baby, we'll have to hire a live-in nanny."

"Have you discussed this with Nathaniel?" Sydney rinsed cherry tomatoes.

"He's always wanted a big family." Brigit twisted her hands. "When we were children he envied James Finnegan because he had more siblings than the *Partridge Family*.

"After we got engaged he said he wanted a cottage in East Hampton filled with bicycles and surfboards. He imagined children slamming in and out of the house, carrying buckets and plastic shovels." She stopped and her eyes were bright. "Lately I think he feels I'm so wrapped up in work. I have to show him I want children's artwork on the fridge and action figures stuck under the sofa."

"You need to talk to Nathaniel before you make a big decision. He might still want a large family or he might want something completely different." She gazed at the ripe peaches and vanilla ice cream. "We think because we share Egyptian cotton sheets we know our spouses better than anyone. But often we keep our most important thoughts to ourselves." Her eyes clouded over. "Then we discover we don't know anything at all."

Sydney sat in the bar at Daniel and gazed at the paneled walls and blue Brazilian marble. It was one of her favorite restaurants in Manhattan and usually she loved sipping a Golden Girl and waiting for Francis to arrive. But tonight her heart raced and she fiddled with the hem of her silk Dior dress.

Ever since she'd returned from Gordes three months ago she tried to eat out as often as possible. She picked at a salade niçoise at Le Bernardin and wished she were eating a bowl of pumpkin soup in their kitchen. But anything was better than sitting across from Francis at the mahogany dining room table, sipping a dry martini and trying to make light conversation.

Everything about Francis seemed different: his cologne, the way he wore his hair, the lines on his forehead. It was only when she caught sight of her reflection in her dressing room mirror she realized she was the one who had changed. Her hair was dull and her Chanel suits hung loosely on her body.

On the flight from Paris she'd rehearsed how she was going to tell Francis what happened. She never kept secrets in their marriage and she had to tell him the truth. But when they arrived at Summerhill and she saw Brigit's tan shoulders and the new freckles on Daisy's nose, she couldn't do it. How could she spoil their summer to assuage her guilt?

Now Brigit was back at Dartmouth and Daisy was applying to colleges and the space between them grew wider. One evening Francis suggested they make love and she followed him up to the bedroom. She unzipped her dress and stepped out of her panties and suddenly panicked. She hastily pulled on a robe and murmured she wasn't ready and would sleep in the study.

"You look stunning." Francis entered the bar. He wore a navy suit and red silk tie. His salt-and-pepper hair was slicked back and he wore black tasseled shoes. "We must be celebrating something special. Daisy got an early acceptance to Vassar or you were named head of the Robin Hood Foundation winter ball."

"Nothing that exciting. I had a craving for the seviche and I know you love the caramelized veal shortbread." She looked up. "Our table is ready, why don't we move to the dining room."

Francis ordered an Anderson Valley pinot noir and they ate lobster with mango coulis. Sydney nibbled duck foie gras but it got stuck in her throat.

"Brigit is busy with school and Nathaniel, and we never see Daisy except when she tosses her school clothes in the hamper. It's a perfect time for you to resign and start the foundation." She fiddled with her wineglass. "We could plan a trip for next summer to Ghana or Haiti. The girls are perfectly capable of being alone at Summerhill and we don't have to hurry home."

"The foundation?" Francis asked. "I haven't thought about it since . . ."

"You wanted it so much. Now we don't have to worry about years of private school tuition." She paused. "I've sat on every charity board in Manhattan and you've entertained enough clients at the Colony Club, it's time we went on an adventure. I can't wait to build schools in Africa and South America."

Sydney saw the gleam in his eyes and her shoulders relaxed. She would wait until they were in a remote village in Nepal and then she would tell him what happened. He would be so grateful he was doing what he loved; he would eventually forgive her.

"I don't think it's a good idea." He shook his head.

"Why not?" Sydney asked.

"I didn't want you to go to Provence, but Robert insisted you needed a change," he began. "When you returned you were so pale, I thought you'd contracted a disease and I'd never forgive myself. But once you arrived at Summerhill you bloomed like one of your hothouse roses. I watched you make tuna sandwiches for Brigit and Nathaniel, and help Daisy with her summer reading and knew that's where you belonged.

"Brigit is always calling you about something and Daisy hopes to get into Swarthmore or Vassar. She'll probably come home every other weekend. I don't want to cart you off somewhere there isn't a phone or it takes days to reach an airport," Francis finished. "You belong with your family."

"But this is the perfect opportunity to do what you want," Sydney urged.

"Eventually Brigit and Daisy will have their own homes and won't eat Thanksgiving dinner at the Park Avenue town house or spend all summer at Summerhill." He leaned back in his chair. "We've been so fortunate. What I want more than anything is for the striking blond debutante I fell in love with twenty years ago to be happy."

Sydney dropped her fork on her plate. Her cheeks were pale and she felt dizzy.

"Are you alright?" Francis asked.

She smoothed her hair and rubbed her lips. She took a deep breath and a small smile lit up her face.

"I always forget how much alcohol is in a Golden Girl." She picked up the menu. "I need something sweet. Why don't we share the Bing cherry custard for dessert?"

Sydney glanced at the yacht bobbing in the harbor and suddenly longed for a cigarette. It was impossible to calm your nerves these days when everything was bad for you.

She had to tell Francis the truth before Robbie discovered it first. She thought of the last few days in the bedroom of the villa and shivered with desire. They had been together for thirty years; surely their marriage could survive one indiscretion.

She finished her lemonade and put a five-euro note on the table. She would tell Francis the whole story, and at the same time she would ask him about that afternoon in Summerhill when she thought he was in Manhattan and saw him on the porch.

Everyone made mistakes, what was important was being honest. Francis had to forgive her. She adjusted her sunglasses and prayed he hadn't done something she wouldn't be able to forget.

Chapter Fifteen

BRIGIT STEPPED INTO THE VILLA'S garden and gazed at the black velvet sky and silver stars. The moon glinted on the dark Aegean and white sailboats drifted in the port.

After the guests returned from the village of Manolas, they boarded the yacht and ate beetroot salad and mozzarella risotto. There were platters of fried calamari and tiramisu. Brigit gazed at the pink and orange sky and turquoise water and thought she'd never seen a more beautiful sunset.

The yacht docked in Santorini and guests dispersed to boutique hotels perched above Fira. The cool air settled on her shoulders and she longed to curl up in the living room with a cup of hot tea. But she had to ask her father why he hadn't told her Blake had invested in the foundation. She crossed the grass and inhaled the smell of cigarettes.

"I thought you were giving up smoking as my wedding present," she said lightly, joining her father at the stone fence.

"Greece is the only country where smoking is as natural as brushing your teeth." Francis stubbed the cigarette with his shoe.

"Even the old men with their donkeys keep a packet of Marlboros in their shirt pocket."

"I won't be one of those brides who expects everyone to change just for me." She linked her arm through his. "But you have to promise you'll cut down before Blake and I have children. You can't push a stroller through Central Park if you have trouble breathing."

"That's a deal." Francis nodded. "What are you doing out here? I thought you'd be chatting with Daisy or planning the rehearsal dinner menu with your mother."

"I was looking for you actually," Brigit explained. "We've barely had a chance to talk since we arrived in Santorini."

"People think weddings are relaxing, but they can be more grueling than a high-powered merger. Your mother spent sixteen months planning our wedding. The altar at St. John the Divine was decorated with thirty dozen South African tea roses and the ballroom of the Waldorf Astoria resembled the main salon at Versailles."

"It sounds exhausting." Brigit sighed. "I'm so grateful you and Mom came to Santorini, I know you're terribly busy."

"And miss riding a mule or eating pork souvlaki?" Francis smiled. "I hope you're enjoying yourself. It can't be easy having your first husband appear at your wedding."

"I'm used to Nathaniel showing up where he's not invited." Brigit shrugged. "Do you remember when he arrived at my ninth birthday party? It was an American Girl party and the other girls were horrified, they'd never had a boy at a party.

"Nathaniel said he didn't want to miss pin-the-tail-on-the-donkey and chocolate ganache birthday cake. Then he saved

Elsie's doll from being chewed by our golden retriever, and by the end of the party all the girls wanted to be his best friend."

"Are you sorry your marriage didn't work out?" Francis asked.

"Nathaniel and I were like two fabrics that rubbed the wrong way." Brigit shook her head. "Blake is everything I've dreamed of. He's intelligent and hardworking and we care about the same things.

"But there is something I want to talk to about." She fiddled with her gold earrings. "Nathaniel mentioned he ran into you at Claridge's last summer. You said you'd met the perfect guy for me and he was an actor named Blake Crawford.

"I asked Blake and he admitted you'd met in Jackson Hole and you invited him to speak at the St. Regis gala." She stopped and looked at her father. "I thought Blake was seated next to me by accident. You both lied to me."

Francis tapped a cigarette onto his palm and lit it with a pearl lighter.

"Do you remember when you were eighteen and knocked on the door of my study?" he began. "It was just before finals and I thought you wanted to talk about your interview at Harvard. Instead you said you wanted to come out at the International Cotillion.

"I was so surprised, I spilled coffee on my annual report," he mused. "You'd always been so focused on school and tennis. I thought the last thing you wanted was to parade around the Waldorf Astoria ballroom in a white satin ball gown.

"You explained you knew you wanted to go to Harvard or Dartmouth and study pre-law or pre-med. You wanted an apartment in Manhattan and a cottage in the Hamptons and two children before you were thirty-five. All that was easy, you just had to set goals and achieve them.

"Meeting the right husband was harder, you couldn't control falling in love." His voice wavered. "You wanted to attend the cotillion because you wanted to marry someone like me. What better place to find that man than at the same ball where your mother and I met?"

"Then Nathaniel offered to be my date and no one asked me to dance." She grinned. "He admitted later he'd told everyone my dog had died and I was overcome with grief."

"I know the last couple of years have been difficult and you gave up finding the right man," Francis finished. "When I met Blake I couldn't let him disappear. He suggested being seated with you at the gala. He said the fastest way to kill a romance is to know you've been set up."

"He told me and I understand . . ." Brigit hesitated.

"It turned out better than I imagined." Francis blew a thin smoke ring. "You'll have homes on two coasts and travel all over the world. And anyone who sees Blake can tell he's madly in love with you."

"There's something else." Brigit took a deep breath. "I met Blake's banker on the yacht. He said Blake invested two million dollars in the foundation."

Francis's shoulders tensed and he stubbed out his cigarette. "He was very impressed with my vision. He wanted to be involved."

"I'm about to become chief counsel and you never told me?" Brigit gasped. "Don't you think I'd like to know my future husband is an investor?"

"That's what these financial summits are about," Francis replied. "Everyone sits around eating fresh fish and drinking fine wine and discussing how they can make a difference in the world. I told Blake about the library we were building in Bangladesh and his eyes lit up."

"So he wrote you a check over grilled trout and corn on the cob?" Brigit asked.

"He sent it to me later." Francis shrugged. "You know better than anyone how serious Blake is about improving health care in third world countries."

Brigit inhaled the scent of hibiscus and tried to stop her heart from racing.

"Why didn't Blake tell me?" she demanded.

"Most men win women with diamonds and furs, not with a desire to erase world hunger."

"We agreed the Palmer Foundation wouldn't accept outside donations." Brigit twisted her hands. "If you accept checks from Pepsi you have to install a soda machine in a village in Kenya. And if Frito-Lay becomes a sponsor, you have to teach malnourished children in Fiji that potato chips are part of a healthy diet."

"Blake's a movie star. He was hardly going to hand out DVDs of the sequel to *The Hunt for Red October*." Francis smiled. "This is different, he was practically family."

"It's the principle," Brigit insisted. "Someone should have told me."

"I was about to fly to India and you were working eighty-hour weeks and Blake was promoting his movie." He put his arm around her shoulder.

"I'm the luckiest guy in the world having my daughter work

beside me. From now on I promise I won't make any decisions without consulting you." He walked toward the villa. "And I would be a terrible father if I let you catch cold before your wedding. Why don't we open a bottle of Rémy Martin and toast the future of the Palmer Foundation?"

Brigit stood on the balcony and gazed at the lights twinkling in Fira. Daisy had gone to the square for a cup of hot chocolate and her parents were in their bedroom. Brigit heard muffled laughter and smiled.

Lately when she stopped by the Park Avenue town house, her mother had seemed strangely distracted. As soon as she saw Brigit she fixed her makeup or smoothed her hair but Brigit noticed new lines around her mouth.

But in Santorini she was like a young girl. Her eyes sparkled and her cheeks were flushed and she gazed at Francis as if they were on a first date.

Brigit pictured Daisy's auburn curls and thought there was something odd about her since they'd returned from the yacht. It was as if she'd eaten a bad piece of fish and had a mild stomachache.

She walked inside and unzipped her dress. She slipped off her sandals and thought there was something her father said that made her uneasy.

She was too tired from the cruise and cognac to remember what it was. She climbed into the four-poster bed and thought she'd figure it out in the morning.

Chapter Sixteen

DAISY TUCKED HER KNEES to her chest and gazed at the sharp cliffs and beds of yellow tulips. The sun glinted on turquoise roofs and lingered over the caldera. She saw silver cruise ships lining the harbor and felt a jolt of excitement.

She had tossed and turned all night, picturing the woman on the yacht with her blond chignon and soft British accent. She was glad she hadn't made a fool of herself and told Robbie she would love to go to Mykonos and Crete. When she saw him she would be polite and distant; they were just friends.

She woke early and slipped on a floral dress. She stood on her balcony and saw the sky explode with color. The clouds were pale pink and the ocean was bright blue and suddenly she felt a tingle run down her spine. She grabbed her sketchbook and ran down the steep path to Fira.

Now she flipped the page and fiddled with her colored pencil. She had been sketching all morning; long skirts and blouses in the colors of Santorini. She glanced at the illustration of an emerald-green dress and a smile lit up her face.

She looked up and saw Robbie striding toward her. He carried a paper sack in one hand and his silver camera was slung over his shoulder.

"What are you doing here?" Daisy asked.

"It's my favorite spot to take photos." He sat beside her. "You're welcome to share a pastry. The Corner restaurant makes the best filo pastry with ricotta in Santorini."

"No, thank you." Daisy shook her head. "I'm not hungry."

"I miss a proper English breakfast of fried eggs and rashers and bacon. In European hostels you're lucky to get a glass of juice and a muffin." He glanced at Daisy's sketch pad. "What are you drawing?"

"It's nothing." Daisy hesitated. "I saw the sunrise this morning and suddenly had an idea for a line of clothing in all the colors of Santorini. There'd be burnt-orange skirts and green chiffon blouses and dresses with pink and purple flowers."

"Can I see?" Robbie asked.

"They're very basic." She handed him the sketch pad. "I won't be offended if you don't like them."

Robbie studied the drawing and turned the page. He flipped through the notebook and handed it back to Daisy.

"What do you think?" Daisy asked.

"They're the best things I've ever seen."

"Do you really think so?" Daisy flushed. "I thought I'd call them Santorini Daisies. I'd pair them with floppy hats and leather espadrilles. There will be straw purses and silk hair ribbons."

Robbie picked a tulip and fiddled with the stem. He ran his hands through his hair and looked at Daisy.

"We were going to explore the beaches at Riva and you disappeared. I stopped by the villa last night but you weren't there. I thought . . ."

"I had a headache and stayed on the yacht," she explained. "Last night I walked to the square in Fira for hot chocolate."

"Let's walk along the beach now," Robbie urged. "We can ride donkeys to Old Port and eat tzatziki at an outdoor café on the harbor."

"I have to go back to the villa and help Brigit finish the place cards for the rehearsal dinner." Daisy shook her head.

"Your sister is perfectly capable of arranging place cards." Robbie grinned. "I promised Winston some photos of Old Port and they would look better with a model. There are only so many images you can take of wooden fishing boats."

Daisy fiddled with her topaz earrings and thought Robbie was right, Brigit didn't need her help. The ivory place cards were arranged in neat piles and the Tiffany favors were tied with satin ribbons. She had the whole day to herself and nothing to do.

But how could she spend time with Robbie when he was taking another woman to Mykonos and Crete? Then she remembered nothing had happened between them and they were just friends.

"Alright." She closed her sketch book. "But you have to ride on the first donkey. I'm always terrified the donkey will slip and tumble down the hill."

"The main port of Athinios is too small for cruise ships," Robbie explained. "They drop anchor next to the volcano and wooden boats bring tourists to shore. Or the ships berth in Old Port but the only way to get to Fira is by donkey or cable car or up a flight of five hundred and eighty steps."

"I'm glad we took the donkey." Daisy grinned, gazing at rocks dotted with purple hibiscus. "I wouldn't like to hover above the cliff in a cable car."

They shared peach gelato at an ice cream stand and sampled fish roe at the outdoor market. An old man gave her a bag of oranges and a basket of figs.

"Wait there." Robbie approached a flower stall. He gave the vendor a five-euro note and handed Daisy a bouquet of purple lilies. "Now look up and smile."

Daisy glanced up and the camera clicked.

"What are you doing?" she asked.

Robbie clicked the camera again and grinned. "I'm photographing a pretty young American exploring an exotic Greek island."

They strolled along the promenade and Daisy bought a packet of halva and a selection of postcards. They passed a tavern with fish nets hanging from the ceiling.

"Sirtaki Tavern has been in the same family for seventy years." He took her arm and led her inside. "Most tourists get off the ship and take the cable car straight to Fira and miss the freshest fish on the island. Nico makes the spiciest tomato balls and the grilled sardines are delicious."

They sat at table next to the window and ate fried aubergine and grouper fish. There was a Santorini salad with feta cheese and green olives.

"How do you know so much about every place we visit?" Daisy

asked. "You told me the history of Therasia and the dates of the excavation of Akrotiri and the exact number of steps to Fira."

"Most people go to Venice to see St. Mark's Square and the Doge's Palace but they never discover palazzos that have been there for six hundred years. Or they visit the Eiffel Tower in Paris but miss the boulangerie on the Left Bank that serves the richest crème brûlée," Robbie began. "I don't want to just visit the pages of a guidebook, I want to eat the local foods and learn the history.

"It's the same reason I take photographs. When you stand behind a camera you don't just see the glossy surface, you look inside a person." He found a picture of Daisy clutching a purple flower and handed her the camera.

"You might see a young woman with light freckles and brown eyes," he mused. "I see someone who thinks she's afraid of trying new things but she's wrong. She rode a donkey down a cliff and shared her sketches with a man she barely knows." He paused. "I think she's the bravest girl I've ever met."

Daisy clicked through the images and saw photos of Kasteli Castle. There were pictures of the yacht and the view from the village of Manolas. Suddenly she saw a photo of the woman with the blond chignon and diamond earrings. She jumped up and her fork clattered on the floor.

"I have to go." She glanced at the clock on the wall. "I promised I'd help Brigit dress for the rehearsal dinner."

"We'll go together." Robbie reached into his pocket.

"I can't be late." She walked to the door. "The only reason I'm in Santorini is to make sure Brigit has a wonderful wedding."

"Daisy, wait!" Robbie called.

Daisy climbed the stone steps until the Old Port was far below her. It was only when she reached the top and stopped to catch her breath that she realized she'd left her sketch pad on the table.

Brigit sat on the pastel-colored sofa in the villa's living room and stirred honey into a porcelain cup. She gazed at the grand piano littered with silver Harrods boxes and blue Tiffany squares and her shoulders tightened.

In eight hours their friends and family would gather in Amoudi Bay for the rehearsal dinner. She pictured Blake in a black dinner jacket and her father in a navy Armani suit and her mother wearing her new Chanel gown. She thought about the ivory crepe dress and satin pumps she'd bought in Paris and wondered how to calm the nervous pit in her stomach.

She sipped her tea and wished she could run over to Blake's villa and swim in the infinity pool. Afterward they would sneak up to his bedroom and make love on crisp white sheets.

But Blake was in Athinios picking up the last guests and this afternoon they'd scheduled a tour of the hot springs. She probably wouldn't see him alone until after the reception.

She fiddled with her gold necklace and thought she was behaving like a child who'd received too many birthday presents. The dinner at Kasteli Castle had been spectacular and the cruise to Therasia was heavenly and tonight's rehearsal dinner was going to include lobster and strawberry pavlova.

She glanced at a box tied with a turquoise ribbon and remembered Nathaniel's wedding present. It was all his fault, ever since he'd showed up things hadn't been quite right.

If it weren't for Nathaniel, she wouldn't have known Blake sold the rights to the wedding to *HELLO!* magazine or that Blake and her father had met before the St. Regis gala, or that Blake had invested two million dollars in the foundation. Nathaniel was like the bad fairy at Rapunzel's christening. He wasn't doing anything wrong but bad things kept happening.

"You look like Miss Havisham in *Great Expectations*," a male voice said behind her. "No one should receive so many wedding presents, it creates a fire hazard."

Brigit looked up and saw Nathaniel standing at the entry. His blond hair was freshly washed and he carried a brown paper cup.

"We're lucky to have such generous friends," Brigit said. "The prince and princess of Sweden sent us a silver fondue set and Tom Brady gave us a signed football."

"You'll have an interesting time going through customs." Nathaniel picked up an ostrich egg. "Make sure no one gives you a puppy or kitten."

"Do you remember when you gave me a kitten for Christmas because your mother was allergic to cats?" Brigit asked. "You came over every day to feed it and it got so attached to you, it followed you home. Your mother discovered it in your closet and gave it to your housekeeper."

"Cats are very intelligent, they can sense a good person," Nathaniel replied. "I thought Daisy and your mother would be here and the living room would resemble a scene from *Father of the Bride*. Instead it's as quiet as one of those disaster movies before the tsunami hits."

"Daisy left with her sketch pad and my mother is still asleep."

Brigit placed her cup on the white saucer. "I like being alone. I have to write thank-you notes and prepare my speech for the rehearsal dinner."

"The bride doesn't give a speech at the rehearsal dinner and no one writes thank-yous before the wedding." He paused. "You never know, the ceremony might not happen and then you have to return them."

"Of course we're getting married, I don't know what you're talking about." Her eyes filled with sudden tears. "Blake and I are incredibly happy."

"Then why are you crying?" Nathaniel asked.

"We've only been engaged for six months, it's happening so fast." She bit her lip. "Tomorrow I'll be Mrs. Blake Crawford. I won't be able to walk down the street without cameras flashing in my face and everything will be different."

"You could wait a few months and get adjusted to living in a fishbowl," Nathaniel suggested. "Then have one of those secret weddings where you invite your closest friends to a backyard barbeque and surprise them by exchanging vows."

Brigit glanced at the Regency desk littered with Cartier boxes. She saw a Louis Vuitton travel bag and thought of their honeymoon in Paris and the South of France. She was madly in love with Blake; they just needed some time alone.

"Why on earth would we postpone the wedding? I can't wait to marry Blake." She jumped up and walked to the staircase. "I have a million things to do. What are you doing here anyway?"

"A friend is in love with a girl," Nathaniel began. "He thought she was developing feelings for him too. But he must have done something wrong because now she won't speak to him." He sipped his coffee. "He's smart and compassionate and I want to ask her to give him another chance."

Brigit froze and turned around. She walked back into the living room and perched on a brocade armchair.

"What did you say?" she stammered.

"Robbie is in love with Daisy," Nathaniel continued. "He asked her to go to Mykonos and Crete and she said no. But yesterday I convinced her to change her mind. Something must have happened; she disappeared after the cruise to Therasia and won't talk to him."

"Robbie and Daisy!" Brigit felt the air leave her lungs. "She never said a word."

"She doesn't want to burden you before the wedding," Nathaniel explained. "I've known Robbie for a while and he loves traveling and music and books. Not to mention he's going to inherit a country estate that makes cottages in East Hampton look like oversized tree houses."

"I'll talk to her." Brigit nodded. "It would be wonderful if Daisy fell in love."

"Good. I have to go." Nathaniel stood up. "I promised Winston a background piece on how the Crawford/Palmer wedding is affecting the local economy."

"You hate matchmaking, why are you getting involved?" Bridget frowned. "Whenever I set up our friends you said anyone who graduated from Dartmouth or Yale and runs a hedge fund or stockbrokerage is capable of deciding who to marry."

Nathaniel shrugged and walked to the entry. "This is different, Daisy is family."

Brigit poured another cup of tea and added lemon and honey. She suddenly remembered Nathaniel saying Daisy was family and a pit formed in her stomach. That's what was bothering her. Her father had said that Blake wanted to write him a check at the summit in Jackson Hole. But when she'd asked why he would accept donations from an outsider, he'd protested Blake was practically family.

Did Blake write Francis a check before or after they were engaged? Suddenly it seemed like the most important question in the world and she knew just how to find the answer.

Sydney smoothed the floral sheets and fluffed turquoise pillows. She felt silly making the bed when the villa's maid would arrive soon, but somehow she didn't want her to see the lipstick on the pillowcase or find her panties under the lace bedspread.

She arranged the paperback books on the bedside table and thought she and Francis were in their fifties, it wasn't unusual that they still made love. Then she remembered his mouth on her breasts and his fingers deep inside her and her cheeks flushed.

She had been determined to tell Francis about Oliver last night, but he'd spent an hour with Brigit in the living room. When he finally appeared at the bedroom door, his eyes gleamed and he clutched a cognac snifter.

He loosened his tie and told her he and Brigit had sipped Rémy Martin and talked about everything. It was wonderful to spend time alone with his daughter and he was the luckiest father in the world.

Then he leaned forward and kissed Sydney softly on the lips. He ran his fingers over her nipples and nuzzled her neck. He unzipped his slacks and led her to the bed.

Sydney opened her thighs and pulled him inside her. She wrapped her arms around his back and urged him to go faster. He uttered a low moan and whispered he loved her more than anything in the world. She inhaled his cologne and promised herself she'd tell him in the morning.

Now she thought of the cruise from Therasia and was certain Robbie had looked at her a little too long. She would tell Francis as soon as he returned from buying cigarettes. The last thing she needed was for Robbie to announce at the rehearsal dinner that they'd met ten years ago in Provence.

"You're still here." Francis entered the bedroom. "I thought you'd be downstairs with Brigit organizing the rehearsal dinner as if you were planning the Battle of the Bulge."

"I was straightening up." Sydney smoothed her hair. "And I wanted to talk to you about something."

"You'll never guess who I ran into at the newsagent." He placed a folded-up *New York Times* on the desk. "Harley Adams. I play squash with him at the club. Do you remember you stayed in the villa in Provence they were renting ten years ago?"

Sydney's cheeks were pale and she clutched the upholstered chair. "You saw Harley Adams in Santorini?"

"You'd be surprised how many members of the Colony Club I

run into in London or Hong Kong," Francis mused. "He and Margot are on a cruise of the Greek islands. I told him Brigit is getting married and he made the most tremendous offer.

"The owner of the villa in Gordes died last year and Harley bought it from his son. He suggested we stay there for a couple of weeks after the wedding. Brigit and Blake and Daisy could join us. We could have a proper vacation without worrying if we had enough bottles of Moët & Chandon for the rehearsal dinner."

"But Brigit and Blake are leaving on their honeymoon," Sydney stammered.

"I'm sure they could fit in a few days between Paris and the South of France. And Daisy doesn't have a job, she's in no hurry to go back to New York." He put his arm around her waist. "We can fly into Nice and spend a few days at Hôtel Hermitage in Monte Carlo. We haven't been there since our honeymoon and you loved the elegant boutiques and views of the harbor."

Sydney pictured Hôtel Hermitage with its crystal chandeliers and creamy stone exterior. She remembered the sweeping lobby filled with white orchids and pastel-colored sofas. She'd worn a floral Givenchy dress and carried her new Dior purse and thought she was the luckiest bride in the world.

"You're on the phone all day and you spent the whole cruise in the communications room sending urgent e-mails," Sydney replied. "How could you spend more time away from the foundation?"

"Last night Brigit and I talked about books and art and movies," Francis said. "I realized the most important things are right in front of me. I want to bicycle through vineyards and sample French cheeses and not think about anything except whether to eat fondue or soufflé for dinner."

"It sounds wonderful," Sydney said slowly. "I'll talk to Brigit."

"It really is the most generous offer." Francis gathered his newspaper and walked to the door. "We'll have to take Harley and Margot to the Four Seasons to say thank you."

Sydney sat at the dressing table and picked up her hairbrush. It was one thing to tell Francis about an indiscretion ten years ago with a complete stranger.

What if Oliver was still in Gordes and they bumped into him at the outdoor market? They mustn't go to Provence. But until she found a way to stop it, she couldn't tell Francis about Oliver.

She would say Brigit couldn't change their hotel reservations in Antibes. Daisy was anxious to get back to her designs and Francis really shouldn't neglect the foundation. They could take Harley up on his offer next summer.

But Brigit was the most honest person she knew and she couldn't ask her to lie. She rubbed her lips with red lipstick and remembered when Brigit appeared in the Park Avenue town house a month before the wedding. She wore a crepe dress and clutched a Bloomingdale's brown bag.

"Darling, it's lovely to see you." Sydney looked up. "I was making a list of dresses to take to Santorini. The weather in June is supposed to be quite hot with a cool breeze in the evening."

"I saw Nathaniel's mother in the gift registry at Bloomingdale's." Brigit entered the living room.

"How is Elizabeth?" Sydney asked. "I haven't seen her since the St. Luke's gala."

"I told her I was buying a gift for John and Rachael's wedding this weekend," Brigit continued. "I did buy them a silver toaster but I was also checking on our registry." She paused. "I didn't tell her Blake and I are getting married."

"Why not? Elizabeth has always been fond of you," Sydney replied. "She'd be delighted that you are happy."

"I didn't want her to tell Nathaniel," she explained. "I know it's silly, I haven't spoken to him in years. He wouldn't care if I ran off with a Spanish polo player or joined a monastery in Tibet."

"Then why don't you want him to know?" Sydney asked.

"That's the thing, I have no idea." Brigit fiddled with her diamond ring. "I paid for the toaster and said it was nice to see her."

Sydney gazed at a family photograph taken on the lawn at Summerhill. Brigit and Daisy wore striped bathing suits and carried yellow plastic buckets.

"I'm sure you did the right thing," Sydney said. "When you are young you think everything is straightforward. But people are complicated and sometimes you have to trust your instincts about what to keep to yourself." She paused and her eyes dimmed. "If you don't, you could do a lot of damage."

Sydney stood at the living room window of the Park Avenue town house and gazed at the green trees in Central Park and yellow taxis on Fifth Avenue. Usually she loved September in New York. The summer tourists were gone and the department store windows were filled with winter coats and pastel-colored cashmere sweaters.

She straightened magazines on the glass coffee table and wondered why she felt so empty. She had plenty to do: pick up Francis's tuxedo from the dry cleaner and try on the new fall boots at Bloomingdale's.

But she didn't feel like fixing her hair and braving the lunchtime crowds in Midtown. She glanced at the tuna sandwich the housekeeper had left on the dining room table and realized she wasn't hungry.

She arranged a bunch of purple orchids and suddenly realized she was acting like a neglected wife whose children had their own lives and whose husband spent most of his time at the office.

Francis had started the foundation two years ago, and the first year had been glorious. He'd implored her to travel with him in the beginning but she admitted she was terrified of flying in tiny planes or sleeping in tents with spiders.

She attended charity balls and went to lunch with Brigit and Daisy. But lately Brigit worked straight through dinner and Daisy was busy at Cafe Lalo.

Sydney nibbled a green grape and knew the real reason she was unhappy. Francis had been coming home later every night and closing the door of his study. She'd bring him a turkey sandwich on a silver tray but he'd mumble he'd eaten at the club. She read paperback books until her head ached and she climbed the stairs to bed.

At least they spent weekends together at Summerhill. But by the time they arrived on Friday evening, they were too tired to do anything but eat a grilled cheese sandwich in bed. On Saturday nights she had to cajole him to put on a sport coat and go to dinner at the Palm.

She studied the vase of pink roses and suddenly had an idea. She would go out to Summerhill and pick up prime rib and smoked salmon. When Francis arrived the dining room table would be set with flickering candles and a bottle of Stag's Leap cabernet.

She left a message with Francis's secretary that she was going to Summerhill and he should drive out this evening. She threw her silk Dior nightie into a bag and added a bottle of Chanel No 5. She gathered her purse and took the elevator to the garage. She slid into the driver's seat of the Mercedes coupe and felt like a college coed blowing off a history final.

Sydney pulled into the driveway and adjusted her sunglasses. It was early afternoon and sprinklers played on the lawn. She inhaled the fresh ocean air and thought it had been a good idea to come to Summerhill.

She looked up and saw Francis's silver Audi parked next to the garage. Perhaps his secretary had gotten the message wrong. But when did he leave Manhattan at noon on a Friday?

She stepped out of the car and saw the front door open. Francis stood on the porch with a young woman with long, dark hair. Her eyelashes were coated with thick mascara and she wore a navy dress and beige stilettos.

Sydney froze and gripped the door handle. Perhaps it was a friend of Brigit's or someone Francis worked with. But she knew every employee at the foundation and why would a family friend be with Francis at Summerhill?

She climbed into the car and put the key in the ignition. She wasn't going to question Francis in front of a complete stranger. She backed down the driveway and drove until she reached the shore.

She sat in the Mercedes and gazed at the Long Island Sound. Francis wasn't the kind of husband who paid attention to other wives at dinner or brushed too close to women at a party. He didn't flirt with the hostess at Tavern on the Green or make conversation with the female bartender at King Cole Bar.

She suddenly pictured Oliver with his wavy blond hair and green eyes and felt like she couldn't breathe. But that was different. She had been miserable and it would never happen again.

Now Sydney stood in Summerhill's kitchen and rinsed butter lettuce. She gazed at the marble counter littered with purple asparagus and heirloom tomatoes and thought that whatever she'd seen this afternoon must be completely innocent.

She checked on the roast and waited for Francis to arrive. He would explain he'd come out to Summerhill to catch up on some paperwork and ran into the wife of a member of the club. He'd shown her around the house and then drove her back to the train station.

She heard the front door open and smoothed her hair. She rubbed her lips with red lipstick and took a deep breath.

"Darling, what perfect timing." She looked up. "I asked Fred to give me the best cut of prime rib. There's an avocado salad and cream of asparagus soup."

"I wanted to be here earlier but I was on a conference call with

Singapore." Francis loosened his tie. "And Friday evening traffic was a mess, it took me half an hour to get on the Long Island Expressway."

"You just left Manhattan now?" Sydney asked.

"Myrna gave me your message." He nodded. "This is a wonderful idea. When was the last time we sat down to a bottle of a cabernet and a steak dinner?"

Sydney walked into the living room and poured a glass of scotch. She swallowed it in one gulp and tried to stop her heart from racing. Why would Francis say he was at the office all day unless he was hiding something?

She heard footsteps and saw Francis standing in the hallway.

"Why don't you sit on the porch and I'll fix us two martinis." He tucked her blond hair behind her ear. "Every hardworking chef deserves a dry martini with Bombay Sapphire gin and vermouth and orange-flavored liqueur."

Sydney sat on the stone bench and gazed at the pond filled with goldfish. She suddenly pictured the villa in Provence with its tennis court and swimming pool and vineyards. She remembered the terrible guilt over losing the baby and thinking she would never be happy again.

She pictured the moment of pleasure with Oliver and then the fear she'd lost everything. She remembered the night after the company Christmas party when she and Francis finally made love.

They had come home tipsy and climbed the staircase to their bedroom. Her Chopard watch caught in her zipper and she asked Francis for help. He touched her skin and then suddenly turned her around and kissed her softly on the mouth.

She remembered the scent of his cologne and her sudden intake of breath. Her body shattered in the most exquisite release and she knew she would never do anything to risk their marriage again.

She thought of the slow years of rebuilding: spring at the Ritz in Paris and impromptu dinner parties with friends. She pictured Francis's surprise fiftieth birthday party in a private room at the Pierre. His cheeks glowed and his eyes sparkled and he was like a schoolboy accepting a prize on awards day.

She thought of all the wonderful times: celebrating Daisy's graduation from Swarthmore and Brigit and Nathaniel's engagement and their wedding on the lawn at Summerhill. What if she asked Francis who the woman was and couldn't bear the answer?

But could she sit across from him at the dining room table without knowing the truth? She remembered when she'd arrived home from Provence and thought she couldn't go on without telling Francis about Oliver. Sometimes you had to box things up and put them away like a wedding present you couldn't use.

Francis appeared on the porch and handed her a martini.

"You look very thoughtful," he mused.

Sydney tasted the bitter gin and strong vermouth and sweet orange liqueur.

"I was thinking I should take the roast out of the oven." She smiled. "I don't want it to be overcooked."

Sydney placed her hairbrush on the dressing table and thought she was behaving like a melodramatic schoolgirl. Brigit probably had no desire to spend part of her honeymoon with her parents and Daisy was desperate to get an appointment with a buyer at Saks.

She snapped her Chopard watch around her wrist and thought a marriage shouldn't have secrets. Once you started hiding things it became as convoluted as a thousand-piece jigsaw puzzle.

But she couldn't dwell on the past; she had to move forward. She slipped on her sandals and hurried down the circular staircase.

Chapter Seventeen

BRIGIT STIRRED SUGAR into black coffee and gazed around the main square of Fira. It was almost noon and the outdoor cafés were filled with couples sharing vegetable risotto. The hot sun touched her shoulders and she thought she really should be getting ready for the rehearsal dinner. If she drank too much coffee her eyes hurt and her skin felt like paper.

But she had to find out when Blake had sent her father the check, and she couldn't log onto her iPad in the villa's living room. She'd received the account passwords when she joined the foundation, but so far she had only glanced at the annual report and future projections.

She flipped through the check entries and saw Blake's check for two million dollars. She read the date and noticed it was a week before the St. Regis gala.

She leaned back in her chair and her shoulders relaxed. Blake's donation had nothing to with her and they hadn't even met when he'd sent the check.

She would order a Greek salad and a bowl of fava beans. Then she would stroll up to Blake's villa. She didn't care if it was full of groomsmen drinking Metaxa and playing backgammon. It was their wedding weekend and she wanted to be with her fiancé.

She was about to close the iPad when she saw Blake's name in the check registry. She looked more closely and saw he'd sent another check for three million dollars. She glanced at the date and gasped.

She pictured the weekend in Crete when Blake proposed. She remembered the tiny church in Plaka and the picnic of stuffed grape leaves and feta cheese tapas. Blake had gotten down on one knee and presented her with the Neil Lane diamond ring. He'd whispered that he'd waited all his life to meet the right woman and she had to say yes.

Brigit snapped the iPad shut and shivered. Why did Blake send another three-million-dollar check to the foundation the day after he proposed, and why hadn't her father mentioned it?

"There you are, I came back to the villa but you'd left," a male voice said. "It's the day before your wedding, you should be sequestered in your bedroom like Marie Antoinette."

"I was thirsty." Brigit looked up and saw Nathaniel. He carried a newspaper in one hand and his backpack was slung over his shoulder.

"If you drink too much coffee during the day you'll fall asleep." Nathaniel pulled out a chair. "Do you remember when you drank four cups of black coffee and passed out in your history exam? I told the professor you'd just returned from visiting your dying grandmother in London and needed a few hours' rest."

"He let me go back to my dorm and retake it in the morning." Brigit smiled.

"It helped that you were an A-plus student and never missed a class," he replied. "Sydney was worried about you, you disappeared without telling anyone."

"I had to look up something." Brigit hesitated.

"That's funny, so did I." He handed her the newspaper.

"What is it?" she asked.

"I was doing research for background pieces on Blake," Nathaniel explained. "This was in the *Los Angeles Times* four years ago."

"'Standing on the balcony of his Hollywood Hills home and dressed in an understated Tom Ford blazer, actor Blake Crawford is living the American Dream. With a string of box office hits and a contact list filled with the hottest models, Crawford's meteoric rise to fame is the classic fable of small-town-boy-makes good,'" Brigit read out loud.

"'He arrived in Hollywood by Greyhound bus seven years ago, with no acting experience but fierce determination.

"'"I've never been afraid to work hard," Crawford says, sipping a pale ale from a local microbrewery. "In high school my buddy and I started a car wash business and soon washed all the cars in the neighborhood. I fell in love with cinema when I saw Francis Ford Coppola's *Apocalypse Now*. Coppola overcame budget issues, on-set drama, and a typhoon to shoot the movie. He never gave up and it is arguably the greatest film ever made.

"'Crawford was named *People*'s Most Beautiful Person last month, but he's not resting on his laurels. He's not even sure he wants to stay in Hollywood.

" "'I'm grateful for everything the industry has given me, especially a certain brunette," he says mischievously. "But, let's face it, an actor is always judged by his last movie or the new gray in his hair.

" "'One of my favorite films is Martin Scorsese's *The Age of Innocence*. He captured the undercurrents of power in old New York drawing rooms like no other director. I've always had a fascination with New York society. You never see their photos in newspapers but they rule the world." He fiddles with his new Patek Philippe watch and flashes the irresistible Crawford smile. "If I could be anywhere it would be at the Plaza in New York, drinking old-fashioneds with Rockefellers and Vanderbilts. But it wouldn't be a scene from a movie, it would be my real life." ' "

Brigit's cheeks turned pale and she felt like she couldn't breathe. She dropped the newspaper onto the table and looked at Nathaniel.

"Why did you give me this?"

"I thought you should see it." He shrugged.

"You're just jealous of Blake's success." Brigit's eyes flashed. "You were a rising literary star but you couldn't do the work to finish your novel." She fiddled with her gold necklace. "You should know better than anyone it's probably all lies. The reporter took one quote and twisted it to say something else. Even if Blake wanted to marry into New York society, why would he choose me unless he was in love? There are plenty of New York It girls with better pedigrees and longer legs."

"Maybe Blake is enamored by New York society, but that's not a bad thing." Nathaniel's voice was tight. "You're the one who needs everyone in your life to be as perfect as the cashmere twinsets you wear to work."

"What do you mean?" Brigit demanded.

"Authors can be blocked for months or even years," he continued. "Just because I didn't produce a novel in your time frame didn't mean I wasn't a writer. Nathaniel Hawthorne's wife waited ten years for him to write *The Scarlet Letter*."

"You're the one who quit writing," Brigit whispered.

"Because you stood over my shoulder like a foreman on an assembly line," Nathaniel snapped. "You have to decide if you can accept Blake if he's not quite Cary Grant or Gregory Peck."

Brigit thought of the last months of their marriage when they'd fought over how she opened the cereal box. She remembered going into their bedroom and hearing the front door slam. She pictured lying in bed and waiting for Nathaniel to return.

"You made it perfectly clear you couldn't stand being around me. I'm glad you left and I wish you hadn't shown up in Santorini." She jumped up. "If you spoil the only chance I have of being happy, I'll never forgive you."

"Brigit, wait," Nathaniel implored.

"What is it?" Brigit asked.

"You're too stubborn to see things the way they are. It's not that I couldn't stand being around you, I couldn't stand myself." He shielded his eyes from the sun. "And you're wrong about Blake finding other It girls in New York." He paused. "There's only one Brigit Palmer."

Brigit strode up the steep path and stopped to catch her breath. The farther she got from Nathaniel, the more nervous she became. She flashed on the guest list filled with Forbeses and Whitneys and thought, what if Blake only wanted to marry her to become part of New York's inner circle?

She was being ridiculous. Blake was a movie star; every door was open to him. He had sipped tea with Prince Harry and shared boiled rice with the Dalai Lama. If he wanted to be invited to cocktails at the governor's mansion, all he had to do was ask.

But she thought of her mother's position on the Guggenheim board and her father's membership at the Colony Club and a pit formed in her stomach. Many New York organizations didn't want their charitable endeavors spread over the pages of *People*. And a former secretary of state would rather starve than eat lunch next to someone who dated a *Sports Illustrated* model.

She had to ask Blake why he'd invested in the foundation without telling her. And she had to show him the article and ask if any of it was true. She was an attorney, if she didn't address the facts now, it would be too late.

She would change into a Kate Spade dress and gold sandals. She would fix her makeup and spritz her wrists with Estee Lauder, Beautiful. Then she would go to Blake's villa and demand some answers.

She glanced at the mosaic roofs and pink hibiscus and shimmering ocean. She hoped she was wrong about everything. She was madly in love and couldn't wait to get married.

Daisy gazed at the floral skirts and gauze blouses littering the bed and thought she really should hang them in her closet. But she had been so flustered when she'd returned from Old Port; she'd climbed straight into the shower.

She knotted her hair in a ponytail and tied it with a purple ribbon. She opened her laptop and thought she'd check her e-mails while she waited for Brigit to return. The first e-mail was from an old college roommate who was assistant buyer at Neiman Marcus in San Francisco.

Daisy had sent photos of her designs before she'd left for Santorini. She clicked on the e-mail and read it quickly.

Dear Daisy,

I hope you are having a fabulous time in Santorini, it's freezing cold in San Francisco. Most people hate summer fog, but I think it makes the fall fashions more exciting.

I showed your designs to the head buyer and wish I had better news. Alice said they were "not quite," which in fashion language means they are not quite original enough or elegant enough or bold enough to work at Neiman's.

I so wanted it to be a "yes," I believe in supporting old friends. But I'm just an assistant buyer and I'm not allowed to buy a range of stockings without approval.

I still think they're gorgeous, I'm sure you will have better luck elsewhere.

Daisy closed the laptop and walked to the balcony. If Neiman's wasn't interested, how did she expect to get Daisies into the finest department stores on Fifth Avenue?

She glanced down and saw Robbie enter the gate. He carried a white sketch book and his cheeks glistened with aftershave. She wished he'd stay away. He was like a doctor dispensing medicine that caused nothing but pain.

But she had to go downstairs. If he gave the sketches to her mother, she might ask how he'd ended up with them. She pictured the woman with the blond chignon and soft British accent and didn't want Sydney getting the wrong idea.

She gazed at the turquoise chiffon dress for the rehearsal dinner and her chest tightened. She was thrilled Brigit was getting married, it would just be easier to be happy for her sitting in her own apartment, where no one asked if she'd had any luck with her designs or hoped to catch the bridal bouquet.

She slipped on leather espadrilles and thought in a few days she'd be back in Manhattan. Maybe she'd buy Edgar one of those crochet dog sweaters she'd seen at the duty free store at the airport.

"What are you doing here?" she asked, stepping onto the porch.

"I'm returning your sketch book," Robbie replied. "You left it at the café."

"Thank you, but it could have waited until the rehearsal dinner."

"Blake is taking the groomsmen to swim in the Nea Kameni Hot Springs," Robbie continued. "The water is incredibly warm and the sulfur is good for you. I'm shooting photographs and wondered if you'd like to join me."

Daisy opened her mouth to say she knew Robbie was taking another woman to Mykonos and Crete, so he should really leave her alone. But suddenly she saw Brigit walk up the path. Her cheeks were pale and she looked like she'd been crying.

She wondered if something had happened with Nathaniel. He was always doing something to upset Brigit. Even when he was completely innocent, he often drove her crazy.

Daisy remembered during the first year of their marriage, when

Brigit appeared at her apartment. Her cheeks were flushed and her mouth was set in a firm line.

"We're having our first dinner party and Nathaniel ate a slice of the banana cream pie I bought at Magnolia Bakery," Brigit fumed. "How am I going to serve a pie that has a piece missing?"

"Why would he do that?" Daisy stood at the counter of her galley kitchen, peeling an orange.

"I met our neighbors in the lobby and invited them to come over this evening. I didn't mention it to Nathaniel because he was so intent on his writing," Brigit admitted. "But I set the table with our Lenox wedding china and Baccarat wineglasses. Did he think I opened a bottle of Pegasus Bay pinot noir to go with takeout Thai food?"

Daisy thought of all the times Brigit and Nathaniel fought like children or completely ignored each other and wondered how their marriage lasted. But then she remembered thinking their love was like a searchlight that never faltered.

She was glad Robbie was taking another woman to Mykonos and Crete. Being in love seemed like the hardest job in the world.

She saw Brigit reach the gate and shuddered. What if Robbie took her photo and it appeared in *HELLO!* with the caption: "Brigit Palmer Has Emotional Breakdown the Day Before Her Fairytale Wedding"?

"I'd love to go to the hot springs," Daisy said suddenly.

"You would?" Robbie asked.

"We have to leave right now." She took his arm and led him to the side gate. "I have to be back to get ready for the rehearsal dinner."

"But you're not wearing a bathing suit," he spluttered.

"Don't worry," she insisted. "I'll figure out something."

She strolled down the steep path and thought it would be lovely to splash in the warm water with Robbie. But she was only going so he didn't run into Brigit and she hadn't had time to grab a swimsuit. She would have to stand on the shore and watch everyone else having fun.

Brigit climbed the stone steps of Blake's villa and caught her breath. The villa was perched on a cliff with an infinity pool and wide glass terrace. There were floor-to-ceiling windows and beds of purple lavender.

She opened the front door and entered the living room. The white marble floor was scattered with low silk sofas and crystal vases were filled with yellow orchids.

"This is a pleasant surprise." Blake crossed the room. "Are you going to join us at the hot springs? I promise we'll be back in time to dress for the rehearsal dinner." He circled his arm around her waist. "Though you might be overdressed. We'll have to find you a bathing suit, or you can wear one of my T-shirts."

"I don't have time to visit the hot springs," she said. "I wanted to show you something."

"That sounds serious." Blake grinned. "Don't tell me the

caterer forgot to order pistachio gelato or there's not enough calamari."

"Nathaniel was doing research for a background piece and found this." She handed him the newspaper. "Of course, I'm furious that he showed it to me. But you should read it."

Blake scanned the page and looked at Brigit.

"This was just after I bought my house in the Hollywood Hills." He shrugged. "It's ancient history."

"Is any of it true?" she demanded. "Are you marrying me to become part of New York society?"

"Do you remember when I gave my speech at the St. Regis gala and you assumed my publicist wrote it?" Blake asked. "I'm grateful to be a movie star, if I wasn't I wouldn't have any of this." He waved at the abstract paintings and marble statues. "But it's hard to be taken seriously when everyone thinks you spend your time jumping off trains or saving women from speeding cars.

"When I arrive at Jinnah Airport there's already a swarm of reporters wanting to know why Blake Crawford is building schools in Pakistan. Eventually some magazine will print that it's part of a publicity stunt to make my public persona more endearing.

"If I stop making movies, the tabloids will spend the next five years running 'What Happened to Blake Crawford' stories until I have to appear on the *Today* show to convince Matt Lauer I didn't end up in rehab."

"Of course I envy men who sit in paneled offices on the sixtieth floor of the Chrysler Building or drink Hennessey at the Harvard Club," he finished. "They can change the world without anyone knowing their name."

"So you are marrying me to break into New York's inner circle?" Brigit blinked back sudden tears.

"Do you remember when we stayed at the Hotel Grande Bretagne in Athens and those journalists accosted us in the lobby?" Blake continued. "They asked if you were the woman who was going to drag me to the altar. I said I was lucky you let me buy you a cup of coffee, and if I weren't careful I'd end up in the doghouse.

"From the moment I saw you, I knew you were out of my league. When you enter a room everyone stops, but it's not because of your smooth blond hair and clear blue eyes." He paused. "It's because they can tell at a glance you're the best person they'll ever meet.

"I've been a bachelor for thirty-four years, and the only reason I would ever marry is for love." He grabbed her hand. "I told those reporters I was the luckiest guy in the world and I was right. I fell in love with the girl of my dreams and by some crazy coincidence, she loved me back."

Blake put his arm around her waist and kissed her softly on the mouth. Brigit inhaled his citrus cologne and her shoulders relaxed. Of course they were in love, she hadn't been wrong. Then she suddenly remembered the check registry and her heart pounded in her chest.

"There's something else." She pulled away. "I met Peter Martin, your banker, on the cruise to Therasia. He mentioned you donated two million dollars to the Palmer Foundation. I asked my father and he admitted you sent him a check.

"I was afraid it had something to do with us so I looked through the foundation's accounts," she continued. "I was relieved when I discovered you sent the check a week before we met." She took a deep breath. "Then I noticed another check for three million dollars. It was dated the day after you proposed."

Blake sat on a silk sofa and put his head in his hands.

"Francis flew out to Los Angeles a couple of months after we started dating. We had lunch at the Polo Lounge and talked about slush in New York and the price of gasoline in California.

"He mentioned Sydney had said you and I had been seeing a lot of each other, and I told him we watched the polo matches in Palm Beach and visited friends on Martha's Vineyard.

"Then he put down his turkey club sandwich and asked what my intentions were," Blake continued. "I was so stunned, I almost dropped my blueberry sidecar.

"He explained you had been hurt by your ex-husband and he didn't want it to happen again." He paused. "I told him you were the most amazing girl I'd ever met and I was madly in love."

"He said he had something to tell me and made me promise not to breathe a word. He'd made some bad investments and the foundation was on tenuous footing. With my international appeal and his connections he was confident he could turn it around." He fiddled with his TAG Heuer watch. "But he wanted to make sure the foundation stayed in the family."

Brigit felt suddenly chilled. "He said that?"

"He loves you more than anything in the world," Blake insisted. "He was only being a good father."

"So you waited until I accepted your proposal and then sent him another check?" Brigit's voice shook.

"It wasn't like that. The minute he asked me what my intentions were, I knew I wanted to marry you." He jumped up. "It was such an incredible feeling, I wanted to buy drinks for everyone at the bar.

"For years I'd seen friends settling down and wondered if I was like the robot Hymie in old *Get Smart* episodes," he mused. "I looked good in a suit but didn't have a heart.

"Then I met you and for the first time I understood what is really important. My life wasn't about my next role or a write-up in Vanity Fair, it was about being with the person who made me feel alive. I couldn't get enough of your laugh and smile and whenever we were together I was completely happy." He took her hand. "I was so in love I wanted to rush into your office with two dozen red roses and a ten-carat diamond ring. But I didn't want to scare you away. I designed the ring with Neil Lane and planned the trip to Crete." He looked at Brigit. "When you whispered 'yes' in the church in Plaka it was the best moment of my life."

"I don't understand any of this," Brigit said. "Why would my father tell a stranger about financial troubles instead of his own family?"

"He knew how important Summerhill is to your mother." Blake sighed. "He was afraid he would have to sell it and I was his last resort. But I wouldn't have invested a penny unless it was what I wanted."

Brigit felt something hard press against her chest. She looked at Blake and her eyes were wide.

"What does Summerhill have to do with this?"

"He had already taken out a second mortgage on the Park Avenue town house. Summerhill was all he had left," Blake said.

"He was afraid he was going to lose it and Sydney would never forgive him. But you have to believe me, I didn't do it to help Francis. I did it because I was in love with his daughter."

Brigit pictured Summerhill with its gabled roof and wide porch and views of the Long Island Sound. She saw twinkling lights strung across the lawn on the Fourth of July and the Christmas tree reaching the ceiling on Christmas morning.

She grabbed her purse and ran to the door.

"Where are you going?" Blake asked.

"I have to see my mother." She turned around.

"What about us?"

Brigit gazed at his dark hair and tan cheeks and bright green eyes. "We'll talk about us later."

She raced up the narrow path to the villa. She felt the hot sun on her shoulders and slipped on her sunglasses. She thought of everything she loved: Blake and her parents and Summerhill. She inhaled the fresh sea air and walked faster.

Chapter Eighteen

SYDNEY SAT IN THE VILLA'S living room and flipped through a magazine. Francis was buying cigarettes and Brigit had gone out and even Daisy had disappeared. She remembered how she relished the silence at Summerhill before anyone came downstairs, and thought parents were really the most self-important people in the world. They imagined their children would always be young so they could complain about mud on wood floors and sand on fresh towels and open jars of peanut butter left on the kitchen counter.

She closed the magazine and wished she could enjoy the quiet. Soon everyone would arrive home and there would be the flurry of getting ready for the rehearsal dinner. She imagined Francis not being able to find his tie and Daisy deciding on a pair of earrings and Brigit needing help with the zipper of her Prada dress. She pictured her own silver Carolina Herrera gown and wished she could be more excited.

She thought she had seen Robbie approach the house, but then he'd disappeared. What if he was coming to tell her they'd met ten years ago in Provence?

She had to convince Francis they were all too busy to go to Gordes and then she had to tell him about Oliver. If she confessed privately he might forgive her, but if he heard it at the rehearsal dinner or during the wedding reception, her marriage would be over.

She heard the front door open and looked up. Brigit entered the foyer and placed her purse on the side table. Her hair was tousled and her mascara was smudged.

"Are you alright?" Sydney asked. "You look like you saw a terrible accident."

"I just came from Blake's villa." Brigit bit her lip. "Everything is ruined."

"Nothing can be that horrible," Sydney insisted. "Tell me from the beginning."

"I met Blake's banker on the yacht." Brigit perched on a floral love seat. "He told me Blake invested two million dollars in the Palmer Foundation. I asked Dad and he admitted Blake sent him a check.

"I was worried that it had something to do with us so I looked through the accounts." She paused. "He sent the check even before we met. But there was another check for three million dollars dated the day after Blake proposed."

"I don't understand." Sydney frowned.

"This morning I was having coffee in Fira and Nathaniel showed me an old article in the *Los Angeles Times*. He discovered it while he was researching a background piece on Blake."

"Nathaniel!" Sydney interrupted. "I didn't know you were seeing him."

"I wish Nathaniel had never shown up in Santorini. All he's

done is cause trouble and I never want to talk to him again." Brigit sighed. "But that doesn't change the facts. The article was about Blake's rise to fame and how he wasn't happy being a movie star." She fiddled with her gold earrings. "What he really wanted was to be part of New York society."

"Every college kid who reads F. Scott Fitzgerald wants to be Jay Gatsby." Sydney shrugged. "That doesn't mean anything."

"I asked Blake and he said he envied men who controlled the world from their private clubs, but it had nothing to do with our falling in love," Brigit replied. "I'm the most amazing woman and he is the luckiest guy in the world."

"Of course he is! Newspapers make up stories every day. Nathaniel shouldn't have shown it to you." She hesitated. "Perhaps he doesn't want you to marry Blake."

"I thought so when he arrived, but I don't anymore." Brigit shook her head. "All he wants is for me to be happy and I believe him."

"I wouldn't give it another thought." Sydney smiled. "You and Blake are going to be incredibly happy. I can't wait to spend summers at Summerhill with our grandchildren."

"I haven't told you the worst part." Brigit took a deep breath. "Dad accepted Blake's donation because he made some bad investments and the foundation is in trouble. If he doesn't turn things around he'll lose Summerhill."

"What did you say?" Sydney gasped.

"He's already taken out a second mortgage on the Park Avenue town house. Summerhill is all he has left," she explained. "He's afraid he'll have to sell it and you'd never forgive him."

"He can't sell Summerhill, it's been in my family for a hundred years." Sydney stood up. "There must be a simple explanation. Your father would tell me if there was anything wrong."

"What if it's all true?" Brigit twisted her hands. "What if Blake agreed to marry me so that Dad could save the foundation and Blake would get his entrée into New York society?"

"You sound like a character in an Edith Wharton novel," Sydney scoffed. "It's the day before your wedding. The only thing you should worry about is whether you want to wear peonies in your hair and if you chose the right shade of lipstick. I'll talk to Francis and clear everything up." She walked to the door. "He could never sell Summerhill, it's part of the family."

Sydney hurried down the narrow path towards Fira. She couldn't let Brigit see how upset she was; it was the day before her wedding.

She suddenly remembered Francis standing on the porch of Summerhill with the young woman with long dark hair and thick mascara. Perhaps there were other things she didn't know about Francis. He had a whole secret life she knew nothing about.

She slipped on her sunglasses and gazed at white sailboats bobbing in the harbor. The sun glinted on mosaic roofs and there were beds of pink and purple anemones.

Whatever Francis had done, she couldn't let it spoil their time in Santorini. Their daughter was getting married tomorrow and it was going to be the happiest day of their lives.

She pictured Summerhill with its white stone porch and thick green ivy. Brigit had to be wrong about everything, or she really couldn't bear it.

Daisy opened the front door of the villa and slipped off her espadrilles. The hot springs had been spectacular but now she desperately wanted a cool glass of lemonade. She entered the kitchen and saw Brigit nibbling a peanut butter and jelly sandwich.

"What are you doing here?" Daisy walked to the fridge. "I thought you would be soaking in lavender bubbles and getting ready for the rehearsal dinner."

"I found a jar of peanut butter in the pantry and realized I was starving. Do you remember when we were children and begged to eat with the grown-ups at a dinner party?" Brigit asked. "Mom finally said yes and we were determined not to eat all afternoon so we'd be hungry. By five o'clock we were hungry and made peanut butter and jelly sandwiches. Then we sat at the dining room table and gazed at prime rib and roasted potatoes and couldn't eat a bite."

"Mom was furious." Daisy giggled, pouring a glass of lemonade.

Brigit put the sandwich on her plate and looked at Daisy.

"Remember last winter when we had brunch at Sarabeth's and I told you Blake and I were engaged? You asked if we were rushing and I said he was charming and handsome and we wanted the same things." She paused. "What if I was wrong, what if we're getting married too soon?"

"Every bride thinks she's getting married too soon the day before her wedding. She spends so much time choosing the perfect dress; she doesn't want it be over," Daisy said. "But you're going to honeymoon in Paris and Aix-en-Provence and have the life every woman dreams of."

"It all happened so quickly." Brigit hesitated. "What if Blake isn't in love with me?"

"How could he not be in love with you?" Daisy asked. "You're Brigit Palmer."

"That's the thing." Brigit's eyes were bright. "What if he loves me for my name instead of who I really am?"

"You don't understand, you're not Brigit Palmer because of our Park Avenue address," Daisy said. "You're Brigit Palmer because you make everyone feel special. Ever since I was a child, I've watched you charm guests on the lawn at Summerhill. There's something about the way you listen that makes people feel important. Everyone falls in love with you, it's impossible to resist."

"Blake is a movie star." Brigit sighed. "He doesn't need me."

"He may be one on the red carpet or at Spago," Daisy mused. "You make him feel like a star when he's standing at the fridge wearing striped boxer shorts."

"Blake would never wear striped boxers." Brigit giggled. "Even his underwear is monogrammed Ralph Lauren."

"You're going to be the most glamorous couple I know." Daisy smiled. "I can't wait to be an aunt and buy up Dylan's Candy Store."

"I've been so busy with the wedding, there are so many things I want to tell you." Brigit dusted crumbs from her skirt. "I saw your sketches on the dining room table. I think they're gorgeous."

"You do?" Daisy asked.

"They're stunning, the colors remind me of Santorini." Brigit nodded. "And Nathaniel came over yesterday. He thinks Robbie is in love with you."

"He told you that?" Daisy gasped.

"He said Robbie asked you to go to Mykonos and Crete," Brigit continued. "Something must have happened because you won't talk to him."

"He's wrong, Robbie and I are just friends." Daisy flushed. "I should go up and shower, I smell like sulfur from the hot springs."

Brigit gave Daisy a small hug. "The best part of getting married in Santorini is the family being together. I'm so glad you're here."

"I am too," Daisy agreed.

"You better catch the bouquet." Brigit grinned. "Or Gwen Hastings will catch it and her boyfriend will be furious."

Daisy tossed her orange skirt onto the bedspread and slipped on a cotton robe. She had wanted to ask Brigit what she had been crying about earlier, but she didn't want to upset her.

She remembered what Nathaniel had said about Robbie and knew he was wrong. Robbie couldn't be in love with her, he had invited another woman to Mykonos and Crete.

She gazed out the window at white stone churches and beds of purple lavender. It didn't matter anyway. In two days the wedding would be over and she wouldn't have to think about Robbie anymore.

Chapter Nineteen

BRIGIT SLIPPED ON HER SUNGLASSES and ran down the stone steps of the villa. She remembered when she first saw Nathaniel and Robbie in the garden and shuddered.

Instead of hiding in the rosebushes she should have confronted him and sent him away. She should have told Blake she didn't care if they had to pay *HELLO!* two million dollars, Nathaniel wasn't going to spoil their wedding weekend.

She smoothed her skirt and knew she was being silly. Nathaniel wasn't the reason Blake had invested in the foundation without telling her. He had nothing to do with her father getting into financial trouble and having to sell Summerhill.

But if Nathaniel hadn't shown up with his short blond hair and backpack she wouldn't have known anything was wrong. She would be sitting at her dressing table deciding which diamond earrings to wear.

She had made a peanut butter and jelly sandwich to calm her nerves. But then Daisy had appeared and she wasn't ready to tell her they might lose Summerhill. She remembered Daisy's expression when she said Robbie was in love with her and smiled. Maybe the one good thing that came out of Nathaniel's arrival was the young British photographer.

She opened the gate and walked up the narrow path to Imerovigli. She just needed to sit by herself and think about everything Blake had said.

She suddenly remembered when she was at Dartmouth and had a Shakespeare exam. Nathaniel insisted they study together, even though it was impossible to concentrate when he kept asking for a bite of her Subway sandwich.

She'd crept back to the library after Nathaniel went to bed. She reread the whole textbook until she memorized the names and dates of Shakespeare's tragedies. She remembered Nathaniel pouting when she got a hundred on the exam and he managed a B-plus.

Now she perched on a stone bench and gazed at silver cruise ships. It was late afternoon and in a couple of hours their friends and family would gather at the restaurant on Amoudi Bay. She imagined platters of grilled octopus and tomato keftedes. There would be strings of yellow lights and a harpsichord.

She thought about the article in the *Los Angeles Times* and knew her mother was right. Journalists had to create a story. What could be better than a small-town boy from Ohio craving to be accepted into the elite drawing rooms of New York?

But then she thought of the guests he'd invited to the wedding and his donation to the foundation and her shoulders tensed. Why did Blake keep secrets unless he wasn't sure of his intentions?

Maybe he did see her as the key to memberships into private clubs and friendships with the most important families in America.

She remembered all the wonderful moments of the last few months: being caught in a spring rain shower and running back to her apartment. Undressing in the living room and ending up in bed. Gazing at Blake's wide shoulders after they made love and wondering how she could be so happy.

They attended cocktail parties and movie premieres but they also ate at cafés on the Upper East Side. She remembered Blake stepping into the kitchen of an Italian bistro and donning a checkered apron. He'd ladled spaghetti onto wide plates and served them to the patrons. The owner kissed Blake on the cheek and exclaimed he was the greatest movie star.

She pictured the check dated the day after he proposed and felt like a pawn in a nineteenth-century marriage contract. How could her father accept Blake's donation without telling her? Then she imagined Summerhill's vast kitchen and sloping lawn and knew he would do anything to protect it.

She heard footsteps and turned around.

"I've had more exercise in the last few days than when I was preparing for the sequel to *The Hunt for Red October*." Blake appeared beside her. He wore leather loafers and his sunglasses were propped on his forehead.

"What are you doing here?" Brigit asked. "I thought you were visiting the hot springs."

"I told my groomsmen to go without me." Blake shrugged. "I stopped by the villa and Daisy said you went out. I need to talk to you."

"It's not a good time." Brigit hesitated.

"Ever since I was in my early twenties and arrived in Hollywood everything was simple. I bought shiny cars and dated pretty girls and won bigger roles," he began. "But I realized I wanted to do more than entertain teenagers eating buttered popcorn. Then I met you and it all made sense. You are beautiful and intelligent and want to change the world.

"But I went about it all wrong. I don't need the CFO of Sotheby's or the curator at the Guggenheim to see us recite our vows. Let's elope and not tell anyone we're married. Or run off to Portugal and live on a sailboat. I don't care where we are, as long as I wake up beside you."

"We can't elope, all our friends flew to Santorini." Brigit gulped.

"I want to show you something." Blake pulled her up.

"I don't need any more jewelry and you already bought a catamaran." Brigit tried to smile.

"Come with me," Blake insisted. "It will only take a minute."

He led her to a yellow taxi and opened the doors. He handed the driver a wad of euros and climbed into the backseat.

"Where are we going?" Brigit asked, sliding in beside him.

"You'll see." Blake grinned, clutching the vinyl headrest.

Brigit sat on the hard seat and watched the harbor fade into the distance. The car bumped along the gravel until they reached the village of Oia.

Brigit stepped into the main square and felt the warm sun on her shoulders. There was a white stone church with gold inlaid doors and stained-glass windows. Elegant restaurants had striped awnings and window boxes full of purple hibiscus.

"Oia is the highest village in Santorini," Blake explained. "It isn't as central as Fira but it has some of the loveliest architecture on the island."

"I feel like Sophia Loren in *Boy on a Dolphin*." Brigit smiled. "A waiter in a white dinner jacket will appear carrying frothy blue cocktails with sliced pineapple."

Blake pulled her close and kissed her softly on the mouth. He tucked her hair behind her ear and grabbed her hand. "Follow me."

They crossed the cobblestones and entered a whitewashed building perched on the cliff. The wide salon had gold-and-white marble floors and gold silk sofas. Crystal chandeliers dangled from the ceiling and ceramic vases were filled with white hibiscus.

"The hotel Katikies is the most exclusive hotel in Santorini," Blake explained. "It has a rooftop swimming pool and a spa and a Michelin restaurant."

"Why are we here?" Brigit gazed at the abstract paintings and marble statues.

"This weekend isn't about cruising to Therasia or exploring the ruins at Akrotiri. I don't care about the hot springs or the Pyrgos castle," Blake began. "The most important thing is that we are in Santorini to begin our life together. Every night I lie in the king-sized bed and wish I was beside you."

"You do?" Brigit looked up.

"I thought it would be wonderful to rent separate villas so you could enjoy your family and I could be with my groomsmen," Blake continued. "I don't care if we're not supposed to see each other the day of the wedding. I have to sleep with you tonight." His face broke into a smile. "So I rented out the whole hotel."

"You did what?" Brigit gasped.

"I didn't want to bump into families with screaming children or couples on their honeymoon the night before our wedding," Blake continued. "We have our own masseuse and a choice of three restaurants. If you want to get ready at the villa, you can leave your dress there." He took her hand. "Will you stay with me here tonight?"

Brigit flashed on the *Los Angeles Times* article and the foundation and flinched. But it could all be worked out if they spent time together. She pictured their legs entangled in cotton sheets and a shiver ran down her spine.

"Yes," she whispered.

He took her hand and led her down a narrow hallway.

"Where are we going?" she asked.

He turned and grinned. "We have to decide if we want to sleep in the Captain's Suite or the Katikies Suite."

They explored the Captain's Suite with its round white bed and blue-tiled bathroom. They peeked in the Master Suite and saw an orange wool rug and pastel-colored furniture.

Finally they climbed a flight of stairs and opened a lacquered blue door. The suite had a living room with turquoise silk sofas and a marble bar. The ceiling was mosaic tile and the walls were thick white plaster.

Brigit stepped onto the balcony and caught her breath. The sun was a yellow ball and the clouds were ribbons of beige satin. The Aegean glittered like a magic carpet and she could see the whole caldera.

"I like this one." She turned to Blake.

"You can't decide yet." He took her hand. "You haven't seen the bedroom."

Blake led her up a few stairs and opened a wooden door. The bedroom had peach-colored walls and a white marble floor. A canopied bed was covered with a lace bedspread and littered with silk pillows.

Blake pulled her close and kissed her softly on the lips. She inhaled his scent of aftershave and cologne and felt almost dizzy.

He unbuttoned his shirt and slipped off his loafers. He leaned forward and slipped his hand under her dress.

"Come here," he whispered. "God, you feel good, I want to stay like this forever."

"I do too." She felt his fingers against her skin and gasped.

His fingers slid in deeper and she pressed herself against his chest. The warmth became a hot wetness and she clasped his shoulders. Her body tipped and she cried out and shuddered.

She unzipped her dress and pulled him onto the bed. She opened her legs and drew him on top of her. Blake kissed her mouth and her breasts and her hair. He lowered himself into her and she felt the exquisite heat and sheer pleasure.

"I love you," he murmured. "I never want to be apart."

"I love you too," she said, inhaling his cologne.

He moved faster and she wrapped her arms around his back. He paused and studied her blue eyes and slender cheekbones. Then he picked up speed until the ripples became endless waves and her whole body cracked open.

Brigit listened to Blake's even breathing and tucked herself against his chest. She glanced out the window at the pale blue sky and turquoise ocean. In twenty-four hours they were getting married. She closed her eyes and thought she couldn't wait.

Chapter Twenty

SYDNEY PACED AROUND the living room and wondered where Francis could be. She had checked every tobacco store and newsagent in Fira. She debated sitting at a café and waiting for him to appear but she could hardly accuse her husband of seeing another woman and selling her grandfather's estate in front of tourists carrying plastic buckets and ice cream cones.

She walked back to the villa and entered the foyer. Daisy was upstairs getting ready and Brigit had gone out. She patted her hair and wished she could go upstairs and take a bath. But she glanced at her watch and knew she had to speak to Francis first.

Now she poured a double scotch and thought she really should be drinking soda water. But if she was going to lose her husband and her family home, she needed a cocktail before she welcomed their closest friends to the rehearsal dinner.

She heard the front door open and turned around.

"I was afraid I'd be late, I had to stand on a cliff to get phone reception." Francis entered the living room. "The Greek afternoon sun is hotter than when we visited the pyramids in Egypt." He loosened his collar. "A stone farmhouse in Provence sounds very inviting."

Sydney pictured the villa in Gordes and flinched. She poured another scotch and handed it to Francis. "I have to talk to you about something."

"An ice-cold scotch and a cool shower and I'll feel almost human." Francis glanced at Sydney. "I thought you'd be getting dressed."

"I saw Brigit earlier, she was very upset," Sydney began. "Blake donated two million dollars to the foundation without telling her."

"Brigit came to me and I explained the whole story." Francis nodded. "It will be good to have Blake involved. He's young and energetic and we share the same vision."

"You didn't tell her he invested another three million dollars the day after he proposed." Sydney's voice shook. "And you didn't tell her you're in financial trouble and might have to sell Summerhill."

Francis's face clouded over and he sank onto the sofa.

"I didn't want to worry you," he said. "I thought I could handle it."

"You didn't want to worry me about selling the cottage that has been in my family for a hundred years?" Sydney demanded. "Do you remember the first time we drove to East Hampton? We had been dating for two months and I said I couldn't be involved with anybody who didn't love Summerhill.

"We pulled up the driveway in your Jaguar. You jumped out and I thought you were going to say you imagined it would be much grander or it was too quiet without the noise and excitement of Manhattan.

"You plucked a pink rose from the garden and said it was the most beautiful place you've ever seen. If I'd let you, you'd make sure the pond was always full of goldfish and the vegetable garden had baby carrots and sweet peas. All you wanted was to spend your life with me at Summerhill.

"We've celebrated every Christmas and Fourth of July there since we were married. Daisy kept her pony in the stables and Brigit and Nathaniel got married on the lawn." She stopped and her eyes were bright. "I still don't understand how you could do such a thing. What other secrets are there? I want to know everything."

"I made some bad investments with our capital after I started the foundation. I took a second mortgage on the town house and thought that would be enough." Francis downed his scotch. "But then the school we are building in Haiti flooded and we had to start from scratch.

"I've landed on airstrips no wider than a Band-Aid but I've never been as frightened as when I brought an appraiser to Summerhill," he mused. "She walked around examining Daisy's drawings in the nursery and Brigit's tennis trophies in the den and I wanted to call and tell you everything." He paused. "But I knew you'd never forgive me and I couldn't risk it. I promised myself I'd do whatever it takes to save Summerhill."

"You brought an appraiser to Summerhill?" she exclaimed, her heart pounding in her chest.

Sydney remembered the young woman on the porch wearing a navy suit and beige stilettos.

"It was on a Friday afternoon when I thought you were in the city," he continued. "But then Myrna left a message saying you went to East Hampton early and I panicked.

"You asked if I'd just left Manhattan and I said I'd been at the office all day. That's the only time I lied to you except for the cotillion where we met."

"What happened at the cotillion?" Sydney asked.

"You thought your date had food poisoning but I paid him to leave." Francis's face broke into a smile. "I saw the most beautiful girl wearing a white satin gown and silk gloves and had to ask her to dance."

Sydney walked to the french doors and gazed at the garden. She turned around and her eyes glistened.

"I pulled into the driveway and saw you on the porch with a young woman with long dark hair and thick mascara," she admitted. "I got terribly flustered and drove away. When I returned you were gone."

"Why didn't you ever say anything?" Francis asked.

"The last ten months you've been so distant." She hesitated. "I was afraid if I asked questions, I couldn't bear the answers."

"I was so ashamed." Francis clutched his shot glass. "I wanted to provide children in Africa with computers but didn't put aside enough to fix Summerhill's roof after a wet winter." He paused and his eyes were dark. "I couldn't look at myself in the mirror when I shaved. What kind of a man puts his family's well-being in jeopardy to help strangers?"

"You're hardly putting your family in jeopardy." Sydney twisted her hands. "Brigit earns an impressive salary and Daisy has more talent than she knows. We have rooms full of important artwork, we're not going to go hungry."

"Summerhill is part of you," Francis replied. "I see you when we're out there. Your smile is wider and your step is lighter. You're like a flower in full bloom."

"I love Summerhill, but you should have told me. We could have solved it together." Sydney paused. "In the end all I need is you and Brigit and Daisy. We could move to a fifth floor walk-up in the East Village and be perfectly happy."

"I don't think anything drastic will happen. With Blake's involvement things are turning around." Francis gazed at Sydney's slender cheekbones and small waist. "Though I would like to see those gorgeous legs climb five flights of stairs."

Sydney felt the tension and fear of the last eight months dissolve. Suddenly she pictured Oliver and the château in Gordes and thought if she didn't tell Francis now, she never could. She fiddled with her scotch glass and took a deep breath.

"There's something else we have to talk about," she began. "I've been wanting to tell you for years, but I haven't known how."

"Whatever it is, maybe it can wait until after the rehearsal dinner." He grinned. "I thought we could take advantage of a quiet villa and sneak upstairs."

"It can't wait." She jumped up and walked to the bar. "We have to talk about it now."

"That sounds serious," Francis said.

Sydney looked at the man she had loved for thirty years and her courage disappeared. But then she thought of all the years they had ahead of them and her shoulders tightened.

"When I went to Provence after I lost the baby, I'd never been so miserable," she began. "No matter how I tried, the pain wouldn't go away. I'd see people sipping espresso in the village square and wondered if I would ever be happy. And I didn't just feel bad for myself; I couldn't be the wife I wanted to be for you or a good mother to Brigit and Daisy.

"I met a young man, the son of the owner of the château. It was perfectly innocent, he helped me get in the house when I locked myself out and brought me groceries during the mistral.

"The last night I was there, he asked me to dinner. I don't know why I said yes, but he was barely twenty-two, it was like dining with one of Brigit's or Daisy's friends. He drove me home and came into the château." She stopped and bit her lip. "Somehow we ended up in bed."

"I see." Francis's cheeks were pale and he looked like he'd seen a ghost.

"The minute it was over I knew it was a terrible mistake," she said. "I've wanted to tell you a hundred times, but I was terrified you would never forgive me."

"I never would have thought . . ." Francis stumbled.

"It made me realize that even though losing the baby was heartbreaking, there was something much worse." Sydney looked at Francis and her lips trembled. "Losing the man I love most in the world. "

Francis clenched his hands and paced around the room. He poured another glass of scotch and took a long gulp.

"I have to admit this is terribly hard, but life is full of twists and turns. Sometimes you are on top of the world and things happen that you can't imagine. But as long as you have the most important thing, you can get through the rest." He walked over to Sydney. "You are beautiful and gracious and the best wife and mother I could ask for." He paused and a small smile lit up his face. "We have two daughters to marry off and grandchildren to look forward to, and I couldn't do any of it without you."

"Neither could I." Sydney felt the air leave her lungs.

"We still have time before the rehearsal dinner." He touched her arm. "Why don't we go upstairs and try to forget about my bad knee and the new gray in our hair?"

"And be late to Amoudi Bay?" Sydney asked.

"We won't be late," he whispered. "I'll take a very quick shower."

Sydney sat at the dressing table and brushed her cheeks with powder. She rubbed her lips with red lipstick and dabbed her wrists with Chanel No. 5 perfume.

She gazed at the rumpled bed and towels strewn on the wood floor and shivered. It had been wonderful to climb into bed with Francis. It had been glorious to feel his thighs between her legs and not wonder about the young woman in the navy dress.

But as soon as Francis got up to put on his dinner jacket, Sydney remembered Robbie and Oliver and the villa in Provence. Even if Francis knew the truth, what about Brigit and Daisy? Their trust in Sydney would be ruined if they discovered she'd had an affair.

She'd told Francis she couldn't find her favorite earrings and to go ahead to the rehearsal dinner without her. Now she straightened the bedspread and wondered if she should confront Robbie and beg him to keep her secret.

She walked down the circular staircase and heard a knock at the door.

"Robbie!" She opened the door. "This is a surprise, Nathaniel isn't here. Everyone is at Amoudi Bay."

"I wasn't looking for Nathaniel," Robbie said.

He wore a white dinner jacket and tan slacks. His hair was neatly brushed and his silver camera was slung over his shoulder.

"You weren't?" Sydney stammered. She walked into the living room and began straightening magazines and arranging flowers.

"I was looking for Daisy," Robbie explained, following her into the living room.

"Daisy!" Sydney exclaimed. "I didn't know you were friends."

"She showed me her sketches." He nodded. "She's quite talented."

"Do you think so?" Sydney asked. "I think they're gorgeous, she has a wonderful eye for color."

"Daisy is very special," Robbie said. "She's beautiful and intelligent and self-effacing."

Sydney looked at Robbie and her heart raced. Could Robbie be attracted to Daisy? What if he told Daisy he'd met Sydney ten years ago and she'd had an affair with his roommate?

"Have you and Daisy become close?" Sydney asked.

"She's focused on the wedding." Robbie shrugged. "I took some photos of her at the hot springs and thought she might like to see them."

"It must be wonderful to travel to different places and take photographs for a living." Sydney twisted her hands.

"I studied history at Oxford. I love to read but I have a terrible memory," Robbie explained. "I memorized the names of Henry VIII's wives for hours and couldn't remember them when I took the test."

"Is that so?" Sydney looked up.

"I've always been that way." Robbie grinned. "But with photography all your memories are stored in the camera. I hope I help people remember important moments with my photographs."

"It's getting late." Sydney glanced at her watch. "If we don't leave for the rehearsal dinner, the fried tomato balls will be gone."

"Would you like to walk together?" Robbie asked.

"I still have things to do." She held out her hand. "It was lovely talking to you. I'll tell Daisy to find you at the rehearsal dinner."

Sydney waited until Robbie had walked through the gate and then gathered her purse.

If Robbie had a bad memory, would he remember a woman he'd met in a French bistro a decade ago? He had been twenty years old and in a foreign country. He must have met a dozen new people a day. It was all in the past and she had nothing to worry about.

She ran down the steps and opened the gate of the villa. The sky was a liquid orange and the ocean was turquoise and she thought the colors had never been brighter. She hurried down the gravel path and couldn't wait to join Francis and Daisy at Brigit and Blake's rehearsal dinner.

Chapter Twenty-one

BRIGIT GLANCED UP at the red cliffs and white windmills and lacquered window boxes. She saw the circular inlet and chipped fishing boats and thought they couldn't have picked a more romantic spot for the rehearsal dinner.

Taverna Katina had sliding glass doors facing the ocean. A long wooden table was set with a peach linen tablecloth and white bone china. Chairs were covered with green damask and twinkling lights hung from the ceiling.

Brigit admired the gleaming silverware and flickering candles and thought the room looked stunning. She had wanted to talk to Blake about everything but they had to make sure the French champagne was chilled and there was enough caviar.

She fiddled with her pink and white diamond bracelet and thought there would be plenty of time to talk to Blake after dinner.

"You have outdone yourself," a male voice said. "The baklava is sweet as honey and melts in your mouth."

Brigit turned around and saw Nathaniel wearing a black dinner jacket and white bow tie. His blond hair was freshly washed and his cheeks glistened with aftershave.

"I hope you haven't gone into the kitchen and eaten all the dessert," Brigit said.

"I was making sure the chef did a good job," Nathaniel explained. "I don't want your guests complaining the baklava is sticky or the fava beans are lumpy."

"I chose the menu," Brigit said hotly. "The tavern is owned by an old lady named Katina. She does all the cooking."

"I met her in the kitchen." Nathaniel nodded. "I said I was worried the bride was too thin and she promised to serve you an extra portion of shrimp risotto." He gazed at Brigit's pink Prada dress and beige pumps. "I was wrong, you don't look thin at all. You're positively glowing."

"I had a restful afternoon." Brigit blushed.

"Getting married agrees with you, you should do it more often." Nathaniel popped a cherry tomato in his mouth. "Next time try Capri, the pizza is the best in Italy."

"There won't be a next time," Brigit snapped. "Blake and I are working everything out."

"I'm glad." Nathaniel fiddled with his cuff links. "Dressing for weddings can be tedious, it took me half an hour to fasten my cuff links."

"You didn't have to get dressed up," Brigit said.

"People trust you more as a journalist if you blend in," he explained. "Do you remember two hours before our rehearsal dinner, I discovered I'd left my gold cuff links at the apartment in Manhattan? You said you didn't mind, but I knew you'd never look at the photos if my shirt cuffs were undone."

"You hired a messenger and had them delivered to Summerhill," Brigit said. "The cuff links arrived at the same time as the photographer."

"I wanted everything about our wedding weekend to be perfect," Nathaniel mused. "The rehearsal dinner in my parents' gazebo and the ceremony and reception on the lawn at Summerhill.

"An hour before the ceremony it started raining and the wedding planner panicked. But then the sky cleared and the grass was bright green. It was like a scene in a Monet painting."

"It was lovely," Brigit agreed.

"We did our best. We can't cry over spilled milk." Nathaniel shrugged. "Do you remember when we were five years old and you had a wooden puzzle with triangles and rectangles and squares? I kept trying to fit the circular block into the square and it didn't work.

"You took it out of my hand and placed it where it belonged." He paused. "You're all grown up and have figured out how to solve your own puzzle."

"I have to go." Brigit's eyes were bright. "My father is making a speech."

Nathaniel reached into his pocket and brought out a piece of paper. "I wrote a toast."

"A toast?" she repeated.

"I am a writer." He shrugged. "But then I realized your ex-husband shouldn't give a toast at your wedding. Keep it and read it later." He glanced at a passing waiter. "If you'll excuse me, I'm going to get a glass of Dom Pérignon."

"You promised you wouldn't get drunk and cause trouble," Brigit fumed.

"I'm not fifteen, I'm hardly going to get smashed from a couple of glasses of French champagne." He paused. "It is the rehearsal dinner. It's only polite to toast the bride and groom."

Brigit gazed around the restaurant and saw Daisy wearing a patterned chiffon dress and gold sandals. Her eyelashes were coated with thick mascara and she wore diamond teardrop earrings. She noticed her father in a white dinner jacket and black slacks. His cheeks glistened with aftershave and he looked like Gregory Peck. She glanced at the door and saw her mother enter wearing a silver Carolina Herrera gown. Her blond hair bounced at her shoulders and she wore a sapphire pendant.

Suddenly she remembered when Blake had stepped onto the podium at the St. Regis gala. She pictured his green eyes and wide smile and how she knew he was only looking at her.

Who would have imagined six months later they would be getting married on a Greek island? She tucked the piece of paper into her purse and thought she wasn't going to worry about Nathaniel getting drunk and ruining the rehearsal dinner. She smoothed her skirt and crossed the room to join Blake.

Daisy opened the sliding glass doors of the taverna and stood on the balcony. The sky was black velvet and tall sailboats bobbed in the harbor.

The stuffed artichoke had been delicious and the red snapper was the best she'd ever tasted. She'd nibbled purple asparagus and listened to her father's speech and felt light and happy. But then someone had asked her to make a toast and she'd pushed her chair back from the table.

"I thought I'd find you out here." Robbie appeared beside her. "It's too warm to stay indoors."

"The dinner was wonderful," Daisy said. "I just needed some air."

"Amoudi Bay is one of the best swimming spots in Santorini." Robbie rested his elbows on the railing. "The weekend is almost over and there are so many things to do: take the cable car to Oia and visit wineries and fava bean farms."

"I didn't come to Santorini to go sightseeing," Daisy said tightly.

"It's a shame not to see as much as possible before you go back to New York," he insisted. "I'm going to hike to Megalochori tomorrow night to watch the sunrise and wondered if you'd join me. We'd be back in plenty of time for the ceremony."

"I don't want to go on a hike with you." Her cheeks flushed.

"You came to the hot springs," Robbie stammered. "I thought . . ."

"I was trying to give Brigit time alone." Daisy's eyes flashed. "In two days I'm going home and you're taking another woman to Mykonos and Crete. You've been very kind but I don't need new friends." She walked to the entrance. "If you don't mind, I'd rather you leave me alone."

Daisy strode to the bar and grabbed a champagne flute. She hadn't meant to be rude but she couldn't bear being around Robbie knowing he was leaving with another woman.

She turned and saw the woman with the blond chignon and British accent. She wore a red silk dress and emerald earrings.

"You're the bride's sister, we met on the yacht." The woman held out her hand. "We weren't officially introduced. I'm Geraldine."

"It's nice to meet you." Daisy clutched her champagne flute. "I hope you're enjoying the dinner."

"Robbie told me all about you," Geraldine continued. "You are a dress designer and your sketches are fabulous. Send me a note when you stage your first fashion show, I'd love to come."

"I'll try to remember," Daisy murmured.

"Here's my card, I adore fashion." She reached into her purse. "Whenever I travel, my husband is terrified I'll come home with a whole new wardrobe. The last time we visited Milan I had to buy two new suitcases."

Daisy froze and could hardly swallow.

"Your husband?"

"He broke his leg playing polo and his doctor won't let him fly," she explained. "At least that's what he said, Scott hates to travel. He's one of those Englishmen who can't stand foreign airports. He'd be perfectly happy if we took all our holidays in Brighton or at his parents' castle in Scotland."

"But you're going to Mykonos and Crete with Robbie," Daisy stammered.

"Robbie and Scott are cousins," she explained. "Scott is relieved I'm traveling with Robbie, he'll make sure I don't bring home a priceless Greek artifact." She frowned. "Though I don't see the point in visiting exotic destinations if you can't buy a souvenir."

Daisy sipped the champagne and felt almost giddy. She hurried to the terrace and saw Robbie walking along the beach.

"You didn't take my card," Geraldine called.

"Don't worry." Daisy's face lit up in a smile. "Robbie will tell me how to find you."

She gathered her skirt and slipped off her sandals. She ran along the sand and called Robbie's name.

"What are you doing here?" He turned around.

Daisy suddenly thought, what if she was wrong and he only liked her as a friend? Then she remembered Nathaniel saying Robbie was in love with her and took a deep breath.

"You asked me to go to Mykonos and Crete and I said no because I have to go back to New York," she began. "I'm twenty-six and I've never done anything except bake banana cream pies. If I don't meet with buyers, I'll never get my designs in department stores.

"But then Nathaniel said you were falling in love with me, so I was going to tell you I'd love to go." She paused. "On the yacht to Therasia I met a gorgeous woman with a British accent. She said she knew you years ago and you'd invited her to Mykonos and Crete." Daisy's eyes were huge. "I didn't want to be around you if you were seeing another woman."

"Geraldine is married to my cousin." Robbie grinned. "Scott asked me to take her. He was afraid she'd fly to Paris and buy up Chanel and Dior."

"She just introduced herself." Daisy sighed. "She told me the whole story."

"Does this mean . . ." he asked.

"I'd love to go to Mykonos and Crete." She nodded. "How could I leave Greece now? I'm just getting used to riding donkeys."

Robbie drew her close and kissed her softly on the lips. Daisy tasted honey and vanilla and kissed him harder.

"We live in different countries and you're always traveling taking photographs." She pulled away. "Maybe this is silly, we should just be friends."

"I've seen tsunamis wipe out villages and people lose everything in a minute. When you're on a Greek island and you meet a girl with auburn hair and brown eyes you don't let her get away." He took her hand. "We'll figure it out."

Daisy gazed at the sky full of stars and the moon glinting on the ocean and her shoulders relaxed.

"In that case, we should go back and have dessert." She smiled. "I saw a crème brûlée that looked delicious."

Sydney gazed around the taverna and thought everything had been perfect. The grilled trout melted in your mouth and the eggplant moussaka was light and fluffy.

She saw Brigit standing with Blake and smiled. They really were a lovely couple. Blake was charming and sophisticated and Brigit was elegant and glowing.

Whatever had happened with Blake it seemed they were sorting things out. She was so relieved. It was difficult to find someone who made you happy; once you did it was important to make it work.

She glanced at Daisy talking to Robbie and her heart lifted. Wouldn't it be wonderful if Daisy fell in love? She had so much to offer.

"I just saw Harley." Francis approached her. "He asked if we were going to take the villa in Provence."

"Do you remember when your parents offered us their estate

in Bermuda for our honeymoon? It was right on Elbow Beach with a personal chef and swimming pool," Sydney said. "We considered going until we discovered they were staying there the same week." She paused. "It might not be the best time to vacation with Blake and Brigit. Newlyweds need time to find their own footing."

"Daisy could join us," Francis suggested.

"Daisy is serious about her designs, and she wants to get back to Manhattan." She pointed to Robbie and Daisy. "And it seems she's found her own distractions."

"We could go by ourselves, it would be a pity for it to go to waste."

"Provence is quite humid in June, it even rained while I was there." She hesitated. "Why don't we try somewhere new?"

"Where?" he asked.

"I've never been to Switzerland." Her eyes sparkled. "We could go to Montreux and listen to jazz and boat on the lake."

"There is a banker I'd like to see in Geneva," he mused. "And the Alps are glorious in the summer."

"I remember reading about the Montreux Palace when I was a girl." Sydney clapped her hands. "It was built in 1906 and the guests were Venetian counts and maharajas and Russian princes."

"I'll make the reservation." He beamed. "I can't think of anything I'd rather do than drink German beer and nibble Swiss chocolates."

"There's something I'd rather do." Sydney laughed.

Francis put his hand on the small of her back and whispered, "I promise we'll do that too."

Chapter Twenty-two

BRIGIT SAT AT AN OUTDOOR café in Fira and stirred honey into a porcelain cup. It was almost midnight and the square was filled with people laughing and drinking shots of ouzo. She saw couples dancing and thought no wonder Europeans drank espresso at night. They couldn't eat dinner at ten p.m. and dance all night without endless cups of black coffee.

Blake had taken some guests on a night cruise after the rehearsal dinner and had begged her to come. But she had to stop by the villa and then take a taxi to the Hotel Katikies. He offered to skip the cruise and join her, but she said she'd be fine.

Now the euphoria of the rehearsal dinner wore off and she wished she'd taken him up on his offer. She thought of the article in the *Los Angeles Times* and his donations to the foundation and tried to stop the queasy feeling in her stomach.

She looked up and saw a man wearing a white dinner jacket and beige slacks. His silver camera was slung over his shoulder and he carried a brown paper sack.

"Robbie!" she exclaimed. "What are you doing here?"

"I took Daisy home and stopped at the newsagent for a packet of Maltesers." He offered her one. "Whenever I can't sleep, I crave English candy."

"You took Daisy home?" She raised her eyebrow.

"We had a terrible misunderstanding," Robbie explained. "I asked her to go to Mykonos and Crete and she said no because she had to return to New York. She later discovered I was taking someone else and thought I was involved with another woman. Geraldine is my cousin's wife, we're just friends." He paused. "Tonight we sorted everything out."

"I'm glad." Brigit sipped her tea. "Daisy deserves to be happy."

"Your sister is beautiful and talented, she just has to believe in herself," Robbie continued. "Her designs are going to be a huge success."

"Do you think so?" Brigit asked.

"I'm sure of it." He grinned. "Geraldine spends more time at Stella McCartney's studio than in her own flat. She thought the sketches were fabulous."

"That's wonderful." Brigit smiled. "Sometimes it's hard to know where we belong."

"I wanted to thank Nathaniel. He told Daisy I was falling in love with her and she should give me another chance," he said. "But he left the rehearsal dinner early and disappeared."

"Nathaniel disappeared?" Brigit looked up.

"He took a bottle of whiskey and walked out." He shrugged. "I checked our hostel but he wasn't there."

"I'm sure he got what he needed for *HELLO!*" She fiddled with her diamond ring. "He's probably writing the article in a café."

"I'm going to the village of Pyrgos to take some photos." Robbie popped a Maltesers in his mouth. "The windmills are spectacular at night."

Brigit finished her tea and wondered where Nathaniel had gone. It was fine for him to drink a couple of glasses of champagne but whiskey made him crazy. She opened her purse and thought Nathaniel wasn't her problem. She had to make sure her wedding dress was pressed and Blake's boutonniere didn't wilt.

She took out a five-euro note and saw a crumpled piece of paper. She realized it was Nathaniel's toast and read out loud:

For any of you who don't know me, I'm Nathaniel Cabot. You might wonder what the bride's ex-husband is doing at Blake and Brigit's wedding. But when you receive an invitation to the wedding of the year, you don't turn it down.

I've known Brigit since we were five years old and I climbed under the fence and crashed her dolls' tea party. She taught me many things: how to tie my shoelaces and tell time and read Hemingway without judging the author as a person.

One of the most important things she taught me is to be honest in a relationship. And to be perfectly honest, I wasn't good enough for Brigit.

Blake is all the things Brigit deserves: he's intelligent and hardworking and has high ideals. And we can all agree; no one looks better in a Hugo Boss tuxedo.

I couldn't be happier that Brigit ended up where she belongs, on a Greek island about to marry the man she loves.

After tomorrow we will go back to our lives and I will try to remember everything Brigit taught me. When you are lucky enough to have someone instruct you on the etiquette of eating grapefruit with the correct spoon, you want to live up to her expectations.

Brigit crumpled the paper in her hand and her heart raced. What if Nathaniel did something silly?

She remembered when he got the terrible review in the *New York Times* and drank half a bottle of whiskey. He threatened to toss his laptop out the window because he had been foolish enough to think he had written something important. He was no better than the kids at Dartmouth who believed they deserved millions of dollars because they developed an app to sort laundry.

She pictured Robbie saying Daisy was so talented and flinched. Maybe it was her fault Nathaniel didn't finish his novel.

All he had needed was someone to say he was going to be a success and then leave him alone. She should have come home from the law firm each day and suggest they jog in Central Park or drink cappuccinos at Joe Coffee instead of asking how many pages he'd written.

She placed five euros on the table and gathered her purse. She would leave a note in his hostel saying he was too talented to waste his time writing for trashy magazines. Surely his parents would give him a loan to complete his novel.

She turned into a narrow alley and climbed the stone steps to the hostel. She knocked on the door and waited. She knocked again and opened the door.

The room had a narrow bed and wooden desk and white plaster walls. Nathaniel's backpack hung on a chair and a selection of paperback books rested on the bedside table. She glanced at the worn covers and thought Nathaniel was the only person she knew who traveled with James Joyce's *Finnegans Wake* instead of the latest Grisham thriller.

She searched the desk for a pen and noticed a thick stack of papers. She glanced at CHAPTER ONE written on the first page and started. Nathaniel had never mentioned he was writing a new novel.

She remembered the first year of their marriage when Nathaniel was so excited about his writing. He finished the first chapter of his novel and insisted he print it out. It was the middle of the night and their printer wasn't working and the closest Kinko's was on East Seventy-Second Street. Brigit mumbled she'd print it at the law firm in the morning but Nathaniel insisted he needed it right now.

He collected dollar bills from the kitchen counter and ran out the door. He returned an hour later with twenty pages and a bag of David's Bagels. He turned on the bedroom light and propped up the pillows and read her every word.

She pictured the months before he left when Nathaniel slept on the sofa in the living room. She remembered being late for work because she couldn't leave without clearing up packets of potato chips and empty scotch glasses. She remembered returning home in the evening to find Nathaniel staring at a blank computer screen.

Now she flipped through the stack of papers and suddenly froze. The last page was numbered three hundred and said THE END. She glanced at the door and thought the last thing she wanted was for Nathaniel to discover her at his hostel. But she had to know what he had written. She pulled out a chair and turned the page. She read four chapters and her face lit up in a smile. The characters were beautifully drawn and the prose was exquisite and the plot was riveting.

Nathaniel didn't need her at all. He had written a complete novel on his own. She breathed a small sigh of relief, as if an additional weight was lifted from her shoulders.

She hurried down the stairs and walked through the square. It was past midnight and a few couples lingered on the cobblestones. She climbed the narrow path to the villa and opened the gate. Suddenly her feet ached and her head throbbed and all she wanted to do was to climb into the canopied bed.

She entered the living room and slipped off her sandals. If only she hadn't taken the time to read Nathaniel's novel. Now she was too exhausted to gather her things and hire a taxi to Oia.

She walked up the circular staircase and opened the bedroom door. She could call Blake and say she would drive to the Hotel Katikies in the morning, but he had rented out the whole hotel just for her.

The thought of sitting in a bumpy taxi and navigating the mountain road to Oia made her feel as if she was getting a fever. Finally she dialed his number and left a message saying she was sorry, she had a terrible headache and was going to bed. She would take a taxi to the hotel first thing in the morning and they would eat fresh melon and scrambled eggs and go for an early swim.

She gazed out the window and took a deep breath. The moon shimmered on the dark ocean and the air smelled like hibiscus. She unzipped her Prada dress and suddenly felt a shiver of excitement. Tomorrow she would be a married woman.

Chapter Twenty-three

BRIGIT STOOD ON THE BALCONY of her bedroom and gazed at the whitewashed houses and beds of purple bougainvillea. It was midmorning and the sea was a sheet of glass. She saw silver cruise ships in the harbor and donkeys lumbering up the path and thought how much she'd miss Santorini.

She walked inside and glanced at her Oscar de la Renta dress laid out on the floral bedspread. It had an ivory bodice and pleated skirt and pink satin bow.

She remembered the final fitting at Metal Flaque in Paris. She had studied her reflection in the dressing room mirror and gasped. She was marrying the man of her dreams wearing the most exquisite dress she'd ever seen.

She walked out of the department store and made her way onto the Champs-Élysée. She wanted to hug the doorman and the taxi driver. She stood on the balcony of her suite at the Hôtel de Crillon and thought she would be this happy for the rest of her life.

Now she smoothed her hair and saw Nathaniel's crumpled-up toast on the bedside table. She picked it up and a shiver ran down her spine.

How could she marry Blake while she still had feelings for Nathaniel? All night she'd tossed and turned, thinking she was being ridiculous. She and Nathaniel had been divorced for two years; there was nothing between them.

Just because he had written a wonderful novel, that didn't mean they belonged together. Nathaniel had moved on: he had a flat in London and steady work and probably a dozen different girlfriends.

She pictured Blake's dark hair and green eyes and her shoulders tightened. He was charming and ambitious and they shared the same goals. She thought of dinners at Per Se and weekend trips to Palm Beach and her office filled with yellow roses. She remembered him standing in the lobby of the Hotel Grande Bretagne in Athens and telling reporters to leave them alone or he'd be sleeping in the doghouse.

But she would be the one who was dishonest if she agreed to marry him without being sure she was in love. She thought of everything she'd learned in the last few days: that Blake knew her before the St. Regis gala, that he craved to be part of New York society, that he'd donated to the foundation without telling her.

She gazed at the diamond tiara and wondered if his dishonesty was giving her doubts or if it was something else. It didn't matter the reason, she couldn't walk down the aisle unless she was certain she couldn't be anywhere else.

She suddenly pictured the day Nathaniel walked out of their apartment. She removed his toothpaste from the bathroom and stuffed his white T-shirts in the drawer and was relieved he'd left. Then she sank onto the king-sized bed and wondered if she would ever be happy again.

Now she glanced out the window and thought about the welcome dinner at Kasteli Castle and the cruise to Therasia and the rehearsal dinner at Amoudi Bay. Fifty of their closest friends had flown across the world to celebrate with them in Santorini. How could she tell them that there wasn't going to be a wedding?

She remembered when she was sixteen and came down with a horrible flu. Her mother had planned a sweet sixteen party on the lawn at Summerhill. There was a dance floor and a band and her favorite chocolate fondant cake.

Nathaniel had appeared with a bowl of chicken soup and ordered her to stay in bed. Brigit insisted she should go down and greet her guests, but he'd said everyone was here because they loved her. If attending her own party made her fever rise, she wasn't being fair to anyone.

Their friends had come to Santorini because they wanted the best for Blake and Brigit. They would understand if the wedding was called off for the right reasons.

She bit her lip and wondered if they should postpone the wedding. They'd take a year to really get to know each other. They could have a quiet ceremony at city hall followed by lunch at Tavern on the Green. But she glanced at Nathaniel's crumpled-up toast and thought that wouldn't change anything.

She descended the circular staircase and saw a man standing in the living room. Blake wore a white shirt and navy slacks. His dark hair was slicked back and he wore leather loafers.

"I'm sorry, I'm late. I overslept," she stammered. "I was going to take a taxi to the hotel."

"I came home from the night cruise and fell right asleep." He ran his hands through his hair. "Should I go upstairs and get your wedding dress?"

"It's too delicate to cart around. I thought we'd have breakfast and I'd get dressed at the villa later." She fiddled with her pink and white diamond bracelet. "I'm starving. I'd love some muesli and tzatziki with walnuts."

He took her hand and sat on the pastel-colored sofa.

"I listened to your message four times," he said slowly. "Your voice was different, it was as if you were talking to a stranger."

"I was exhausted, I couldn't bear the thought of packing my things and sitting in a bumpy taxi." She tried to smile. "But we still have hours before the ceremony. We can take a swim and sit in the Jacuzzi." She took a deep breath. "And there's something I want to talk about."

"I watched you at the rehearsal dinner," he continued. "It's as though part of you wasn't there. All weekend I feel like you've been moving away when we should be drawing closer together. I thought it was my fault. I shouldn't have invited so many grooms-men or planned all the excursions or rented separate villas." He paused. "But now I think it's something else."

Brigit opened her mouth and then closed it. She stood up and paced around the room.

"I could say that it's too soon and we hardly know each other but that would be a lie." She looked up and her eyes glistened. "I've had the most wonderful time. But I don't think we should get married."

"What do you mean?" Blake demanded.

"You're handsome and generous and charming." She fiddled with her earrings. "But I don't think we are quite right for each other. I could never be with someone who isn't completely honest."

"I may have not told you everything but there was always a good reason," he protested. "I would never do anything to hurt you."

"The first few months of marriage are wonderful," Brigit mused. "All you want to do is discuss the day over thick steaks and glasses of cabernet. You like all the same movies and agree on the temperature in the bedroom. You think you'll never tire of making love and you can't stop giggling in the elevator.

"But then someone says something at a party and you hurt each other's feelings. You can't understand why I work long hours and I think you've attended too many red carpet galas." She paused. "Marriage can be difficult but as long as you are honest you can make it work. If you don't have that, you don't have anything."

"I've been a bachelor all my life. I'm not used to considering how my actions affect someone else. If I know I'm doing the right thing, that's always been enough." Blake rubbed his forehead. "But I can change, I'm in love with you."

Brigit took a deep breath. All she had to do was say yes and there would be a wedding. She pictured running upstairs and slipping on her Oscar de la Renta gown. She imagined the white stone church with its stained-glass windows and view of the whole caldera.

Then she saw Nathaniel's wedding present on the grand piano and her chest tightened.

"I don't think so," she said quietly.

"Are you sure?" Blake whispered.

Brigit glanced at his dark hair and bright green eyes and white smile.

"I'm sure."

"If you don't mind, I think we should make up a story," he said. "I came down with food poisoning at the rehearsal dinner and had to be airlifted to Athens. I'll make a complete recovery but we have to call off the wedding."

"Whatever you want." Brigit nodded.

"Why don't we take the sailboat and cruise around the Greek islands?" he suddenly suggested. "We'll be alone on the blue Aegean instead of surrounded by actors and senators and Robbie with his silver camera. I'm sure we can figure this out," he continued, his eyes sparkling. "We don't have to get married as long as we're together. We can take months or a year to see if we're right for each other."

"You have to report to a movie set in a few weeks and I have to get back to New York," she replied, her heart beating a little faster. "I think it's better if we make a clean break."

He stuffed his hands in his pockets and walked to the entry. He turned around and his green eyes flickered.

"Can I ask a question?"

"What?" Brigit asked.

"Are you sure you aren't still in love with Nathaniel?"

She suddenly pictured Nathaniel appearing in the garden. She saw his short blond hair and navy backpack. Her lips trembled and something shifted inside her.

"He's given me a few things to think about." She shook her head. "But I have to sort out things with my father and the foundation. This isn't the right time to think about love, I just need to be on my own."

Brigit smoothed her hair and straightened her skirt. She had insisted on giving Blake back the diamond-and-ruby ring and paying half their expenses. She gave him a small hug and watched him walk out the gate.

Now she had to tell her parents the news. She entered the kitchen and saw the round table set with platters of whole wheat toast and poached eggs and bacon. There was a bowl of cut berries and a pitcher of orange juice.

"Darling, there you are." Sydney looked up. "Daisy made eggs and your father fried some bacon. It's going to be a long day, you can't exist on a piece of fruit and a cup of coffee."

"It all looks delicious," Brigit said weakly.

"I saw Blake come up the steps, you should ask him to join us." Sydney buttered a slice of toast.

"Blake left," Brigit replied, sitting next to her father.

"That's probably better. It is bad luck for the bride and groom to see each other before the wedding." Sydney smiled. "It seems like such a silly superstition. It's the most exciting day of your life, you want to spend every moment together."

Brigit took a deep breath and looked at her mother.

"There's not going to be a wedding."

"What did you say?" Sydney gasped.

"Blake and I decided not to get married." Brigit's voice wavered. "I'm sorry I dragged you all to Santorini."

"I don't understand," Francis interrupted. "Blake gave a wonderful speech at the rehearsal dinner."

"Why don't you postpone the wedding?" her mother asked. "Maybe it's all been too much: starting a new job and getting an apartment and moving part-time to Los Angeles. You need to take things slower."

Brigit stood up and walked to the marble counter. She poured a cup of coffee and tried to stop her hands from shaking.

"It was the best thing to do," she replied. "I'll pay you for the dress and flowers and caterers."

"Don't be silly, money has nothing to do with it," Sydney scoffed. She looked at Brigit and her lips trembled. "If you're quite sure."

"Very sure." Brigit nodded.

"Then we've had a wonderful vacation in Santorini." Sydney dusted crumbs from her skirt. "Your father and I were going to spend a few days in Switzerland. We'll change our plans and fly back together."

"You don't need to do that," Brigit protested. "Daisy and I will fly back to New York."

"Actually I'm not going to New York," Daisy interrupted.

"You're not?" Sydney raised her eyebrow.

"Robbie sent photos of my sketches to a friend who works at Stella McCartney in London," Daisy continued. "I have an interview next week."

"Stella McCartney! That's wonderful news." Her mother beamed. "Your sketches are stunning, they'd be lucky to have you."

"I don't mind going back alone, I have a lot to do." Brigit paused. "I've decided not to join the foundation."

"What do you mean?" Francis asked.

"I need to accomplish some things closer to home before I help people in Asia and Africa," she explained. "I'm going to go back to Bingham and Stoll if they'll have me. Blake said he still wants to be involved in the foundation and you should get other investors." She looked at her father. "You could achieve great things without having all the financial obligation."

"I can't say I'm not relieved." Sydney smiled. "I won't have to worry about you catching a rare disease. And I'll have someone to have lunch with while your father is visiting some remote village in Ghana."

"I'm not really hungry." Brigit pushed back her chair. "I'm going to go pack."

"What does Nathaniel say about this?" Sydney asked.

Brigit turned around and bit her lip. "I haven't told him."

Brigit moved around the villa's living room folding wrapping paper and collecting ribbons. It was midafternoon and she'd spent the last few hours canceling caterers and alerting guests.

Her parents were upstairs packing and Daisy had gone to Fira to see Robbie. In a couple of hours they would board the ferry to Athens. She pictured the scene around the kitchen table this morning and smiled. She really did have the most supportive parents and Daisy was going to London! It was wonderful to see her happy and excited.

She heard the front door open and looked up. Nathaniel wore a short-sleeved shirt and carried a blue backpack.

"What are you doing down here?" he asked. "I thought you'd be sequestered in your bedroom with an army of makeup artists and hairdressers. I remember when I wanted to give you a message the morning of our wedding. I was shooed away by a woman holding an electric curling iron."

"Haven't you read the tabloids or checked online?" Brigit asked.

"I don't read the tabloids." Nathaniel shrugged. "None of it is true."

"There's not going to be a wedding," she said.

"What did you say?" Nathaniel gasped.

"The wedding is called off," she repeated.

"How could Blake do that?" Nathaniel exclaimed. "Are you feeling alright, would you like a vodka or an aspirin? You must be in shock, why don't you sit down and I'll fix you a drink."

"I'm quite alright," Brigit said, sitting on a brocade love seat.

"You shouldn't take it too hard." He rubbed his forehead. "Blake has been a bachelor for thirty-four years. I'm sure it has nothing to do with Olga, the Swedish model he was secretly engaged to five years ago."

"What do you mean?" Brigit looked up.

"They never made it official." He shrugged. "The article said they were engaged to be engaged. You are the only woman he ever agreed to meet at the altar."

"Why are you here anyway?" Brigit asked suddenly. "Everyone was supposed to meet at the church."

"There's something I wanted to show you, but you look a little peaked. I don't want to be responsible if you faint." He walked to the kitchen. "Why don't I make a chicken sandwich and a pitcher of lemonade and we'll sit in the garden." He paused. "We may as well enjoy the view if this is your last day in Santorini."

"Alright." Brigit nodded. "That sounds lovely."

They sat on the stone steps and ate whole wheat bread and Santorini tomatoes and thick hunks of feta cheese. They talked about Daisy's job interview in London and Robbie's upcoming photography spread in *National Geographic*.

Brigit felt the sun on her shoulders and sighed. The sky was pale blue and purple flowers cascaded down the cliff and she was sorry to leave.

"I wanted to give you this." Nathaniel reached into his backpack and took out a thick stack of paper. "It's my new novel. I've been working on it for two years and for a while I thought it would stay in my desk drawer. But being around you gave me the confidence to finish it." He paused. "You're all grown up and know right where you are going. I didn't want to be left behind."

"I read some of it," Brigit admitted. "It's fantastic."

"When did you do that?" He frowned.

"I stopped by your hostel after the rehearsal dinner," she said. "I was worried because you'd left in a hurry. I only meant to read a few pages, but I couldn't stop."

"My publisher loved it." Nathaniel wiped his mouth with a napkin. "They're releasing it next Christmas."

"That's wonderful news." She beamed. "I'm so happy for you."

Nathaniel stood up and brushed the crumbs from his slacks. "I never told you why I walked out of the apartment. It wasn't because you looked over my shoulder or got angry when I put my socks in the wrong drawer." He paused. "It's because I couldn't stand disappointing you. When I saw myself through your eyes, I couldn't bear it."

"It's my fault." Brigit shook her head. "You are a great writer, you just needed someone to believe in you."

"That wasn't your job," Nathaniel insisted. "I had to learn to trust myself."

Brigit blotted her lips and looked at Nathaniel.

"I broke it off with Blake."

"You did what?"

"I told Blake I couldn't marry him."

"You called off the wedding to *People* magazine's Most Beautiful Person?" Nathaniel spluttered. "Are you sure you aren't being hasty? You get nervous when you have to do something new.

"Do you remember when we were nine and I wanted you to try my mother's cheesecake? You said cheese couldn't possibly taste good in a cake; cake was about sugar and flour and cinnamon. I finally pretended it was vanilla cake and cut you a slice. You said it was the best thing you'd ever tasted."

"I'm quite sure," Brigit said tightly.

"It's probably just pre-wedding jitters," Nathaniel continued. "Blake will appear at the gate and you'll throw yourself into his arms and kiss him. Then you'll race to the church and all the guests will cheer."

"He already left." She flushed. "We made up a story that he got food poisoning and was airlifted to Athens." She paused. "I'm terribly sorry, I hope you get paid for your article."

"Winston will plaster Blake's face on the cover of *HELLO!* and sell a million copies. Hollywood's most eligible bachelor is back on the market." He looked at Brigit. "Why did you break it off?"

"As much as I tried to ignore everything you said, you were right," she explained. "I couldn't be with someone who lied. He had a good reason for everything he did, but there's never a reason not to tell the truth." She twisted her hands. "I couldn't go through with it."

"You did the right thing." Nathaniel nodded. "It's much easier to undo the damage without a ring on your finger."

"I have to go." She stood up. "I still have to pack and we're taking the ferry to Athens in a few hours."

She took the plates into the kitchen and put the lemonade pitcher back in the fridge. She entered the living room and saw Nathaniel standing by the fireplace.

"Thank you for the sandwich and lemonade. I feel much better." She smiled. "I don't need any help, I can manage the rest myself."

"I actually forgot one thing." He reached into his backpack and pulled out a box wrapped in gold paper. "I didn't give you your wedding present."

"But you already gave us a wedding present." Brigit pointed to the silver box on the piano.

"I forgot part of it." He handed her the box. "Why don't you open it?"

She tore open the gold tissue paper and discovered a yellow bucket and two plastic shovels. She opened the bucket and saw a sapphire ring surrounded by small diamonds. She glanced at Nathaniel and gasped.

"It's my grandmother's ring, you gave it back." He stopped and looked at Brigit. "Unless you already have one."

"I returned Blake's ring," Brigit murmured.

"I've been carrying it around all weekend," he explained. "If I had seen you and Blake were perfectly happy I would have thrown confetti on the church steps and clapped when you left for your honeymoon. But if I suspected you had a shadow of a doubt, I wanted to see if I had a chance." He looked at Brigit. "Do I?"

"So much has happened." Brigit hesitated.

"Do you remember the morning of our rehearsal dinner, I came up to your bedroom," he continued. "I convinced Daisy to go into Montauk and give us some time alone. I gave you a yellow bucket with a diamond-and-ruby pendant. I said I wanted to keep our marriage fun, but you were a beautiful woman and deserved the most exquisite jewels.

"I failed at all of it, but I think I've grown. I learned I'd rather be sitting in our living room on East Eighty-Second Street bickering over semantics in the *New York Times* than anyplace in the world.

"I may not be perfect, but I promise I will never walk out that door without a clear path home." He got down on one knee and took Brigit's hand. "Brigit Emily Palmer, will you marry me?"

Brigit gazed at the sapphire-and-diamond ring and took a

deep breath. She pictured Nathaniel shooting an apple off her head with his plastic arrow when they were ten years old. She saw them building sand castles at the beach and eating peanut butter and jelly sandwiches in Summerhill's vast kitchen. She remembered walking down the carpet of pink roses at their wedding and knowing she was right where she belonged.

"Yes," she whispered.

Nathaniel pulled her up and kissed her softly on the lips. Brigit kissed him back and wrapped her arms around his back. She inhaled his familiar scent of citrus aftershave and shampoo and felt she would die of happiness.

"God, I missed that." Nathaniel groaned. "We could run up to your bedroom."

"Certainly not." Brigit smoothed her hair. "We're not doing anything until we're married."

"We could get married right now," he exclaimed.

"What do you mean?" she asked.

"You have the church and flowers and cake." He jumped up. "I met a lovely old priest at the Corner restaurant, I'm sure he'd perform the ceremony. Think how much time we'd save planning our honeymoon. We can charter a boat and sail around the Greek islands."

"But all the guests left." Brigit hesitated.

"Your parents and Daisy and Robbie are here," he insisted. "We'll have a big reception when we get home and I'll promise my mother she can choose the menu." He paused. "I've waited months for this, why should we wait any longer?"

"You have?" Brigit asked.

"I needed to grow up first," Nathaniel said slowly. "I was

determined this time you were going to marry a man; not some kid who pictured himself his generation's Tom Wolfe."

"Why not?" She felt suddenly lighter, like a balloon sailing up to the sky. "We'll get married today."

"Are you sure?" His face broke into a smile.

"I'll tell my parents and you find Robbie." She walked to the circular staircase. "I haven't packed my wedding gown and I still have my bridal bouquet. I'll get dressed and meet you at the church."

"Brigit," he called. "We can't get married yet, we have to wait."

"We do?" She felt a lump in her throat.

"I only brought a black dinner jacket." He glanced at his watch. "I can't wear black tie until six o'clock."

Brigit felt the air leave her lungs and her eyes sparkled.

"I think we can let it slide."

"Brigit Palmer breaking the rules of etiquette?" He grinned.

Brigit gazed out the french doors at the pale blue sky and glittering Aegean. She saw the blue domed roofs and whitewashed buildings.

She turned to Nathaniel and smiled. "If something is important, anything is possible."

Chapter Twenty-four

SYDNEY STOOD IN FRONT of the Church of Panagia Episkopi and thought Brigit had picked the most picturesque setting. The church had a blue domed roof and white plaster walls and stained-glass windows. Green trellises connected stone walkways and there was an altar with a gold cross.

She peered out the double brass doors and gazed at the sharp cliffs and the Kamari coastline far below. It was late afternoon and a soft breeze blew up from the Aegean. After everything that had happened, she couldn't quite believe that Brigit was in the ante-room, waiting to walk down the aisle.

When Brigit burst into their room and said she and Nathaniel were getting married, Sydney wondered if she regretted not being able to put on her satin wedding dress and gold sandals. But Brigit explained how Nathaniel had finished his novel, and that they both finally had grown up. She realized you didn't have be perfect, you just had to be in love.

Now the priest arrived in his embroidered gown and pointed hat and Sydney stifled a laugh. Trust Nathaniel to find a traditional Greek priest, an hour before the wedding. She thought about Nathaniel and her heart warmed. Ever since he snuck under the fence and sauntered into the kitchen when he was five years old, he belonged in the family.

Voices drifted up the path and she saw Francis talking to another couple. She looked closely and realized it was Harley Adams and his wife Margot.

"Look who I found in the square in Fira." Francis climbed the stone steps. "I invited them to the wedding. I thought we should fill some pews."

Sydney's cheeks turned pale and she wondered if Harley would mention the château in Gordes. Then she looked at Francis and her shoulders relaxed. It didn't matter if they talked about Gordes; she had nothing to hide.

"I'm thrilled you came." She turned to Harley and Margot. "We need more people to drink all of this Veuve Clicquot and toast good health to the happy couple."

"I told them we are going to Montreux after the wedding," Francis said. "Harley suggested we visit the Grand Hotel du Lac in Vevey."

"Margot and I stayed there last year." Harley nodded. "It's on Lake Geneva and the restaurant has a Le Cordon Bleu chef. It was like a second honeymoon."

"We'll have to try it." Francis squeezed Sydney's hand. "Visiting these exotic destinations is exhilarating, I feel like I'm twenty-five again."

"I completely agree," Sydney said and a tingle ran down her spine. "I can't wait to go to Switzerland. The mountains and lake sound so romantic."

Daisy smoothed her yellow chiffon dress and clutched her bouquet. Topaz earrings glittered in her ears and she wore silver sandals. She inhaled the scent of jasmine and roses and thought the floral decorations looked breathtaking.

She had been hesitant when Brigit appeared at the café in Fira and said she and Nathaniel were getting married. But Brigit was calm and confident, like an astronaut who had just returned to earth. She begged Daisy to be the maid of honor and asked Robbie to take photographs.

It wasn't just that Brigit looked so in love, it was more she looked like herself. She was right where she belonged and this time nothing would stop her and Nathaniel from being happy.

Daisy had sipped her lemonade and suddenly panicked. What had she been thinking, saying she would go to London with Robbie? She had to return to New York and take care of Edgar.

But the house sitter called and said she was delighted to stay in the apartment and watch Edgar until she returned. Daisy had her whole future ahead of her and nothing to worry about.

————

"Brigit picked a spectacular church." Robbie appeared beside her. "It was built in 1767 in the foothills of the highest mountain in Santorini. Previously a Christian basilica stood on this land and some of the frescos date back to 1100."

"I never thought I'd fall in love with a place as much as Santorini." Daisy sighed. "Everywhere you turn there are gorgeous views and spectacular sunsets."

"Most people don't think they should enjoy life, they just wait for the next thing." Robbie touched her arm. "But there is nothing better than exploring interesting locations, and being with the person who makes you happy."

"I saw Brigit in the anteroom." Daisy blushed. "She's the most beautiful bride."

"I'm sure she's lovely." He kissed her softly. "But the most beautiful woman in Santorini is standing in front of me."

Daisy kissed him back and wondered if she would catch the bouquet. She grinned and thought she didn't want to get ahead of herself. But there was nowhere she would rather be than sitting in the pew with Robbie, waiting for Brigit and Nathaniel to say "I do."

Brigit rubbed her lips with red lipstick and brushed her cheeks with powder. She paced around the tiny room and felt like a ballerina waiting to go on stage.

Her mother and Daisy had helped her button her Oscar de la Renta gown but then she asked them to leave. She wanted a few minutes to savor the intricate mosaic ceiling and vases of hyacinths and the knowledge that in a few minutes she would be married.

She glanced at the clock and wondered where her father was. He was supposed to arrive fifteen minutes ago to walk her down the aisle. She heard footsteps and smoothed her skirt.

"God, you look more radiant than the first time we did this," Nathaniel said. He wore a black tuxedo and yellow tie. His hair was slicked back and his cheeks glistened with aftershave.

"What are you doing here?" Brigit gasped. "You're not supposed to see me until my father walks me down the aisle."

"I told him I wanted to do it," Nathaniel explained.

"You can't walk me down the aisle." She flushed. "You have to wait at the altar."

"Technically your father already gave you away," he said. "I thought this time we could do it together."

"You want to walk down the aisle at the same time?" Brigit asked.

Nathaniel studied her high cheekbones and slender neck. She wore sapphire earrings and a pink coral necklace.

"We wasted two years, I don't want to miss another minute." He took her hand and opened the doors. "Everyone is waiting for us. Will you join me?"

Brigit saw the afternoon sun streaming through the stained-glass windows and thought everything looked so beautiful. She clasped his hand and smiled. "I wouldn't miss it."

Acknowledgments

I am so lucky to work with such gracious, talented people. First and always, thank you to my wonderful agent, Melissa Flashman, and my amazing editor, Lauren Jablonski. Thank you to my incredible team at St. Martin's Press: my publicist, Staci Burt; Karen Masnica in marketing; and Elsie Lyons for her gorgeous covers. Thank you also to Laura Clark, Jennifer Weis, and always to Jennifer Enderlin.

And thank you to my family who love and support me: my husband, Thomas, and my children: Alex, Andrew, Heather, Madeleine, Thomas, and daughter-in-law, Lisa.

1. Brigit is in Santorini to celebrate her wedding to Blake and discovers her ex-husband, Nathaniel, hiding in the bushes. Have you ever attended an important event where an "ex" was present? How did it make you feel?

2. Blake has been less than honest with Brigit, though he has never done anything to hurt her. Do you think it is important to be completely honest in a relationship, or is it all right to tell a few little white lies?

3. How do you feel about Brigit's sister, Daisy? Do you admire her for trying to find her passion or should she stick to one job?

4. Daisy often feels like she is trying to live up to Brigit. If you have a sibling, do you experience that dynamic in your relationship and how do you handle it?

5. Do you think Brigit should let Nathaniel back in her life? Why or why not?

6. Blake showers Brigit with presents, but do you believe he really loves her? Give examples to support your opinion.

7. Sydney is hiding something terrible that happened in her past. Given the circumstances, should Francis forgive her for what she did?

8. How do you feel about the ending and why?

9. Santorini is such a gorgeous and romantic setting. Do you think being in Santorini affects the characters' actions and in what ways?

10. If you could plan a destination wedding or family reunion, what would be your dream location?

St. Martin's
Griffin